Folk
of the
Loch

Written and illustrated by
Irene F. Brandt

Matador
9 Priory Business Park,
Wistow Road, Kibworth Beauchamp,
Leicestershire. LE8 0RX
Tel: 0116 279 2299
Email: books@troubador.co.uk
Web: www.troubador.co.uk/matador
Twitter: @matadorbooks

ISBN 978 1838592 493

British Library Cataloguing in Publication Data.
A catalogue record for this book is available from the British Library.

Printed and bound by CPI Group (UK) Ltd, Croydon, CR0 4YY
Typeset in 11pt Minion Pro by Troubador Publishing Ltd, Leicester, UK

Matador is an imprint of Troubador Publishing Ltd

North-west Highlands of Scotland

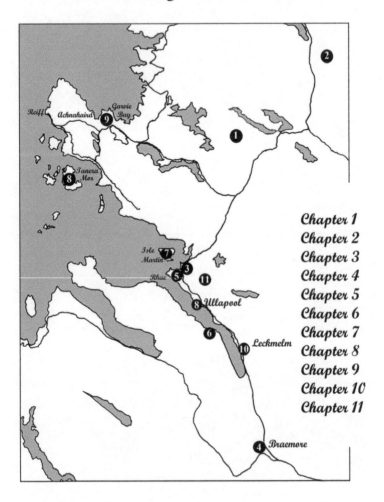

Contents

Introduction

The North West Highlands of Scotland are unique. The scenery boasts spectacular mountains and remote areas of wilderness, inland lochans and pounding seas at the coast. The land breathes great age but great endurance. No doubt it will be here long after the human race has gone.

Its geology is world renowned, featuring some of the oldest rocks and earliest life in Europe. In the nineteenth century, the strange anomaly of older rocks overlying younger ones sparked a heated geological controversy which was finally explained by the theory that mountain building in the south had thrust huge areas of land over the younger rocks. Much later on, successive Ice Ages scoured out valleys and deep-sea lochs, giving the landscape its unique form and character. This part of Scotland is still a Mecca for geologists and new discoveries are still being made.

The archaeology of the North West Highlands is similarly celebrated. Although the last ice age destroyed much of the earlier evidence of life here, in previous warmer periods, animals and perhaps humans may have visited. Although often ephemeral, the evidence shows the presence of Mesolithic, Neolithic, Bronze- and Iron Age people, right up to the coming of Christianity.

Later historical periods were dominated by turbulence, caused by the incursions of the Vikings, battles between warring clans, and social upheaval as modern ideas of 'improvement' forced the people to move to the towns or foreign lands. These events have left the land virtually empty of its indigenous people. But the land here is rich with natural resources and untapped potential. Perhaps, in the future, a new wave of immigrants will bring innovative ideas, tempered by a respect for the past, to revive the old country.

Although these stories are works of fiction, they are based on places, events or artefacts found in the north-west. Likewise, though the main characters are fictional, some of those mentioned are real historical people.

Chapter One

Rock

deep time

An area of land owes much of its character and human interaction to its rock formations and geological processes. This is nowhere more apparent than in the NorthWest Highlands of Scotland. The ancient gneiss bedrock forms the knolls and water-filled hollows of the Assynt coastline, while the jagged outlines of Stac Pollaidh, Suilven, Quinag, An Teallach and the other Torridonian peaks are all that is left of a seven-kilometre-thick layer of sandstone laid down in primeval eras. In the nineteenth century, geologists, most notably Benjamin Peach and John Horne, were able to use their discoveries here to uncover some of the secrets of Earth's history. So it is fitting that the story of this land should begin with its rock.

Rock

The lifespan of man is insignificant relative to geological time. The Earth has her own timescale and rocks are her children. They are born, and breathe, and move at an aeonic pace, and they, too, will eventually die. Who knows what lumbering thoughts fill their crystalline matrices; what ponderous urges impel their movements?

Gneiss

The world turns, ages roll. There is only movement in an endless fiery ocean. We are conceived in the eternal deep, in the infernal womb of the Earth. There is fluidity and current and heat; we seethe and boil, turn with the lazy motion of the planet, and wait for birth. We are aware only of a cooling. And with that cooling we lose an essential part of our nature – our elasticity, our liquidity, our coalescence. We become distinct and hard, growing apart. But in this change there is no regret for our loss of warmth and completeness, as within us begins a strange incarnation, giving us identity. Crystals grow: dark and greasy feldspars, blue opalescent quartz, hornblende and biotite, pyroxene and olivine. Energy flows through our crystal veins, but slowly, so we are only lightly aware of growth. At last the moment of birth comes near. We strive towards the sun.

Cataclysm. Our mother is young and she plays with her embryonic children without concern for our welfare. The land crust, of which we are a part, is crushed and mangled, and powerful forces drive us back into the depths of the Earth again. It is not the warmth of Mother's womb that we remember – it is torture and deformation, intense heat and pressure, shattering our structure, mixing and blending, changing our nature – until we are new beings. Out of adversity comes complexity. For now our veins glitter with new treasures: pyroxenite, needles of anthophyllite, peridotite, dunite, garnet, orthorhombic pyroxene, spinel, talc, hypersthene, hypersthene-augite, augite feldspar, epidote. For 1,500 million years, give or take a few hundred million, Earth's processes uplift and erode and fold, so that we gather ancient sediments, newborn lavas, all heated and compressed and changed. Augmented with our new wealth, we turn towards the surface again.

Strangely enough, 1,200 million years ago the land surface, which was formed by the ancient metamorphosed Lewisian gneiss, would have had much the same configuration as it does today: rough, twisted bumps of rock and small hollows. But there would have been one major difference. Whereas now the chaotic appearance of the landscape is softened by grasses, heathers and small hardy trees, in those days there was no life worth talking about to cover the harsh rock.

This land, which was to become the NorthWest Highlands of Scotland, lay north of the equator at the south-east edge of Laurentia, a continent which included Canada, Greenland and Scandinavia. Although life had appeared by then, it was still very primitive in nature and probably only thrived as yet in the seas. So the land was a lifeless, desolate desert, in which the only movement came from the swirl of dusty whirlwinds or the stately progress of huge rivers over its mighty expanse. As the earlier period had been marked by tumultuous upheavals and burials (the eras of igneous and metamorphic rock formations), this was a time of erosion, as wind and water gnawed away the higher continental interior. The great rivers carried this material, at first as large chunks of rocky debris, sand and clay, to the low-lying gneiss foreland and buried it in a continually changing pattern of alluvial fans and ephemeral lakes. From time to time, volcanic episodes testified to the still youthful nature of the Earth. Later, russet-brown to purple-coloured sands and rougher conglomerates accumulated so that the bedrock was completely buried in a thick layer of sand. Already a new process was influencing the geological record. Our earliest ancestors, the stromatolites, slimy prokaryotic bacteria, left undistinguished thin, brittle layers, like filo pastry, in the rocks at Stoer, Clachtoll and Achnahaird.

Movements in the Earth's crust brought further continents together. Laurentia, Baltica and Siberia collided with Gondwana to form a vast supercontinent subsequently named Rodinia by geologists, and causing a mountain-building episode called the Grenvillian Orogeny. Lying at the centre of these turbulent events, the ancient gneiss was further troubled and sediments laid down to the east were metamorphosed by pressure into the Moine schists. Now, subterranean pressures were forcing Rodinia to break apart.

To the east, Baltica was cumbrously splitting away, leaving Scotland at the south-east corner of Laurentia again. For 200 million years heat and cold cracked rocks; rain and wind tore away at the continental mountains; rivers flowed lazily or burst and flooded. All the processes of erosion combined to transform and transfer the rocks of the interior to the eastern coastline and its shallow sea. Following the geological principles of transformation and recycling, the red desert sands which had hardened into the Torridonian mountains were in turn eroded and leached of their rust to form dazzling white quartz beaches and deltas on the coast. By this time, the slimy bacteria had evolved sufficiently to leave their marks forever in the hardened quartz sands and muds.

Life

Underneath the sea where it is warm and calm, there is little to disturb the march of millennia. The moon pulls the tides, river currents swirl and, from time to time, upheavals in the seabed send shock waves round the planet. Curious combinations have been growing, and experimenting with different forms of reproduction. Most are obliterated by time, but some survive. There is no reason or design in these ventures. It is all just random chance and mutation and, if there is a law in operation at all, it is most likely to be the certainty of failure. For each new successful adaptation, a thousand others wither away. Chance disaster takes out the fittest as much as the weakest. But through thousands of millions of years, life has been developing complexity. Succeeding generations build on the success and failure of others. Then, ever and anon, Earth arches her back and sloughs off these irritating parasites.

The warm, shallow waters now are home to sea worms, waving arms to catch minuscule prey, retreating into burrows in the sand. The sea is rich in food. Life forms of all manner of type and size proliferate, but, since all their bodies are soft and insubstantial, no trace of them remains after death, except the worm burrows filled up with white quartz sand like organ pipes. In due course these are succeeded by tiny snails in their millions.

In fine, dark silt the strangest ancestors survive: the trilobites; hard-shelled sea slaters with articulated bodies, an armoured head, and perhaps a sting in the tail. A most successful and definitive life form, they spread throughout the oceans of the Earth in many varieties and sizes. Yet these too come to an end. Each wave upon wave of life is swept away. Some leave their imprints on the pages of the book of time; others leave no trace at all. Finally the great book is closed and the pages pressed by the covering seas until all is bound and finished in the story of the rock.

It is strange how the development of Scotland as a country has shadowed its physical formation. Although sometimes at the centre of continents, for much of its history, Scotland, and in particular the north-west corner, has dwelt at the periphery of lands. Similarly, the political boundary between Scotland and England follows a major geological division. England once lay hundreds of miles away to the south on a different continent. The closure of the ocean clashed three continents together, creating a Himalayan-size mountain range in the centre of Scotland and the Moine Thrust over the west. It is only chance which has given us England as our nearest neighbour. Would the history of Scotland have been different if Scandinavia or Italy had gatecrashed the party instead?

The Waltz of Continents

The skin of Mother Earth is fragile and impermanent, continually circulating down into the depths of the mantle and resurfacing in an endless cycle of death and rebirth. So continents split and reform in new combinations. Now the sea is narrowing again, pulling the southern plate northwards to meet the northern continent.

Land meets land mass with a resounding crash so slow it is inaudible. Only the stars hear. Buckling, folding, melting, subducting, pulverising, bending, grinding, giant forces rip through the land. Enormous mountains are pushed up; slabs of ancient rock are squeezed over younger ones; the edges of continents are sutured together with volcanic needles; syenite plugs boil limestone into marble; seeping magma intrusions lace the mountainsides.

Even our oldest gneiss, having resurfaced from the eroded sandstone at a leisurely pace, is unceremoniously heaved up to perch self-consciously over its younger sisters.

Unaware of this titanic upheaval, life has crept out of the seas onto the land and, in a matter of a mere 200 million years, carpeted the Earth with plants and evolved enormous reptiles, ancestors of the dinosaurs.

Our land, however, situated as it is, in the arid heart of the new supercontinent, Pangaea, is hostile to most forms of life. It is a dry, hot highland only capable of supporting tenacious creatures on the edges of great rivers flowing south-east to the Tethys Sea. If ever lumbering monsters patrolled these lands, only their bones remain as the relict outcrops of Torridonian mountains: the ridge-backed stegosaurus of An Teallach; the protruding ribs of Stac Pollaidh; and the supine diplodocus of Quinag. By now most features of our curious landscape are in place ready for the next major round in the dance of continents.

In the life of Earth, none of her features last for very long. Like a young woman on the approach of middle years, she changes her cosmetics to disguise the signs of age. Perhaps when she has finally become old enough to accept herself as she is, she will cease her restless movement and fickle reconfiguration. So Pangaea, after only 100 million years, began to dislocate and drift apart. Adventurous lands initiated a process which has been followed by their children in later years: emigration to the west. The settlers from Lochbroom, who pioneered the voyage to America on the Hector, were unaware that their new lands in Nova Scotia had indeed once been part of the same continent.

The separation of North America, like its political severance millions of years later, was not accomplished peacefully. The whole of Scotland was raised one kilometre and tilted towards the North Sea. Greater uplift, of nearly two kilometres in places, formed the basis of a mountain chain lining the eastern edge of the Minch. In Mull, Ardnamurchan and Skye, the rift in the seabed resulted in violent tectonic activity. Volcanoes erupted and swiftly cooling lavas formed basalt plateaux and the curious columns of Staffa. Life must have been particularly precarious here, with earthquakes, tsunamis, suffocating ash falls, and a blanketing cloud of sulphurous gases blocking the light of the sun.

About the same time, whether wiped out by calamitous planetary events or collision with a meteor, thousands of species disappeared and, after a reign of 215 million years, the dinosaurs bowed out to more lowly creatures. Thus began the Cenozoic Era, the Age of Mammals.

Slowly, the land settled down and life reasserted itself, but the shifting of continents and processes of orbital perturbation had set the scene for an age-old protagonist – ice.

The Age of Winters

In the fourth age of the Earth, the land is at peace. Mother Earth sleeps, dreaming deep dreams of her fiery youth, but, like a sleeper, often her face is troubled by expressions: a crease here, a frown there, and sometimes a gentle smile creeps over her lips. Unbeknownst to her, the shifting continents have altered ancient patterns of circulation and made her climate susceptible to tiny dips in her orbit around the sun. While the continents massed at the South Pole or wandered individually in opposite directions, equatorial currents circled the planet, warming the land and controlling the climate. Now two great land masses block the passage of the currents, ushering in an era of winters which last ten thousand years or more: the Age of Ice.

We rocks have found a troubled rest. Lying exposed to the weather, we feel no touch of the growing cold. Our vast sandstone barrier pacifies the force of the westerlies, and the blanketing snow lulls us into gentle dreamlessness. So deep is our unconsciousness that we cannot feel the weight of ice, the dragging of boulders, the scrape of stones, the polish of sand. In our limestone arteries, silent galleries wait for a thousand years for the occasional quick melt and rush of water carrying newly eroded sediments from the surface. When we wake briefly, although never completely awake, we find the frigid glaciers have cut out valleys, dug troughs and deepened sea lochs. Like hibernating creatures in the brief periods before the return of the ice, we bask in a tepid sun and nurture the strange animals which relish our tundra wastes: mammoth, woolly rhinoceros, deer and bison. But soon the snows return and we fall asleep again.

Each time we wake we find more changes. Each Ice Age deepens our valleys. Each glacier dumps rubbly moraines, moulds kames, terraces and eskers, and exposes the old bones of the Torridonian mountains. Each ice sheet presses us down. Each time the ice melts, the sea erodes high beaches on our shores. Each time the pressure of the ice relieves, we rise slowly up again. As far as we are concerned, it is only a rhythmic rocking to send us to sleep.

In the last of the ice winters, the Late Devensian, which lasted for ten thousand years, the ice sheet lay up to a mile thick, extending from Scandinavia to west of the Hebrides. Some mountaintops, called nunataks, rose like jagged islands in a frozen sea but, otherwise, all of Scotland and most of England lay beneath a featureless plain of ice. Nothing lived here, and the pressure of the ice was so great that it swept away most evidence of previous glaciations. At its last retreat about fourteen thousand years ago, apart from a couple of episodes when the glaciers returned to high mountains and lobes of ice pushed down into Loch Broom, vegetation, animals and finally humans slowly colonised the warming land. The interglacial period of present times had come. Notwithstanding global warming, the end of this summer is due and, perhaps, some day soon, the glaciers will return.

Chapter Two

Reindeer

before the Great Ice

The Bone Caves in Assynt have yielded, amongst a proliferation of other species, the remains of hundreds of reindeer antlers. Carbon dates indicate that they were present during three periods: at forty-three thousand to forty-eight thousand years ago, and between twenty-two thousand and thirty-two thousand years ago before ice smothered the whole area. They returned about twelve thousand years ago after the ice had retreated. The last antler, dated at 8,300 before the present, coincides with the probable arrival of early hunter-gatherers in the north-west of Scotland. Did early man contribute to the reindeers' disappearance here? Whatever we may guess, for forty thousand years the reindeer pursued their endless migration and sought their calving ground on the karst plateau above the valley of the caves. Perhaps some day in the future the reindeer herds will return.

I

Moss came into the world in much the same way she would spend the rest of her life – fighting. Although her mother White Flank was old and experienced in birthing, she was late this season and Moss was one of the last to be born to the herd, which generally synchronised its births to one or two weeks of the year. The calf was clearly large and fully mature, but stubbornly refused to leave the warmth and protection of the womb for an uncertain future in the cold air. It is good for a reindeer calf to be big and strong at birth since it virtually needs to hit the ground running, but it is not good to be born late in the year with little enough time to fatten up on its mother's rich milk before the herd leaves on its return trip to the south.

The birth contractions had started early in the afternoon but by evening, White Flank was still straining, becoming weaker and more exhausted as the day waned into purple twilight. The other mothers paid scant attention, busy as they were with their own young, but Herb, the Sky Watcher, came to offer encouragement and willow bark if necessary to dull the pain. In a world in which death was ever present and accepted, it was not unusual for a mother and calf to die. But this time the medication was not required. The calf's kicking legs finally freed the head and she dropped, squirming and barking indignantly, to the ground. Although White Flank was completely exhausted, she licked and nudged her offspring insistently to persuade her to stand and feed. The young one complied with a healthy appetite and suckled avidly, so that mother and calf could at last curl close in a warm huddle against the freezing breeze. Herb watched approvingly and noted the ancestors prancing in the northern sky. This was a portentous birth.

As the calf grew bigger and stronger in the brief northern summer, Herb's predictions were justified. Inquisitive and fearless even at an early age, Moss displayed the characteristics which would one day make her leader of the herd like her mother. She would stamp her hoof into the lemming hole just to see what the occupants would do; she would snuffle the warm air emanating from Bear's snowy den; she would trample the brittle ice skirting the lochs where the herd came to drink; and, when wolf howls echoed in the mountains, she would lead the other calves in a defiant romp through the herd. At other times Moss showed a more contemplative nature. When ragged lines of geese passed overhead, honking rustily, she would cock her head to the heavens, listening. She would watch the colours of the sky change with the setting sun, from reds and oranges to purples and indigo. Even the cloud shapes, growing large and cumulous or streaky and fragile with high, icy strata, seemed to fascinate her.

Herb noticed all this but said nothing. Sky Watchers were born at the whim of the gods and no amount of wanting would make one. The little calf would fulfil her potential and follow her fate whatever Herb wished. But the signs were favourable and soon Herb realised that she must act soon before the herd set out again on its perpetual migration.

On a day of the dark moon, when the herd was foraging widely for a last mouthful before nightfall, Herb approached White Flank.

"Good eating, sister. The calf grows strong and swift?"

"Very! Of all my offspring, and I have been blessed with many, this is the best, but she is headstrong. If I take her to the loch edge, she will not drink. If I show her how to scrape for lichen, she turns away. When fear stalks on the edge of the herd, she will not run with me. But yet, I think she is already the fastest of the new-born youngsters when she takes it in her mind to race." Moss's mother spoke witheringly but the light of pride and love shone in her eyes.

"Well, White Flank, obstinacy is either a curse or a blessing. She may fall into the jaws of death, or wisdom may temper her opposition into strength. In any case she will need understanding and guidance. Will you let me walk with her awhile?"

White Flank and Herb were born of the same season and had grown together. They had made the journey south and back north again eleven times and seen many of their generation pass to the lands of the ancestors. So White Flank knew why the Sky Watcher would wish to talk to her child but, if she disapproved, she did not say so. She understood how important the Sky Watchers were for the herd: they interpreted the clouds; they forecast the days of departure; they knew the way of the wind and the reindeer. She had many children to pass on her blood to future calves, so one less would not be missed. But why this one? White Flank guessed she had few calving years left and this might be her last child – the youngest, the beloved, the favourite. Yet where the gods chose, she must acquiesce.

"Yes, take her if she will go with you. I have no power to make her start or stay. She follows her own will." A double permission was hidden in the words and Herb acknowledged it with a bow of her head.

On this occasion, Moss accompanied the elder willingly. Perhaps she was overawed, or more likely intrigued and curious.

The sun was setting as they made their way over the plateau of the calving grounds and up the steep quartz flank of the mountain behind. As the shadows fell, a stiff, cold breeze ruffled their coats and picked up flurries of snow from the gullies. The stars were coming out when they reached the snow-covered top of the mountain and turned to face the north. Throughout their climb, Herb had said not a word and Moss had not dared to interrupt her silence. As often happens as night descends, the breeze dropped off but a sparkly energy seemed to emanate from the pale glow growing in the northern sky. A golden ray pierced the heavens and moved slowly from east to west as if directed from a source beyond the horizon. The ancestors were lighting their way to Earth. More rays followed and soon the background glow had swollen across half the sky, and pulsed with a regular heartbeat. The two reindeer stood watching silently. Slowly a rippling sheet spread upwards, with waves of green and red and blue, undulating up and down behind the snowy mountains in the north. Sometimes the colours changed intensity, flaming to dazzling golds and deep reds, or vibrant green. Sometimes the whole array faded into a pale grey. Sometimes the pulses grew faster, and the reindeers' hearts beat faster with the rhythm. The spectacle passed timelessly and Herb glanced occasionally to see what her young protégée made of it. But Moss merely stood quietly, white breath clouding from her muzzle and the moving lights reflected in her eyes. At length the colours faded, the pulses disappeared and the light dispersed to a pale glow again. Both reindeer sighed their living breath to the passing of the ancestors and turned to make their way back down the mountain.

Although there was no moon, at this time of year it never grew completely dark, and starlight reflecting on the snowfields gave sufficient light. At any rate, the reindeer followed their own footprints precisely in the snow. At last Herb spoke.

"What did you see in the sky, little one?"

Moss took a little while to reply. "I saw the ancestors, honoured one."

When nothing else seemed to be forthcoming, Herb pressed eagerly. "But what did they look like? What did they do?"

Again the reply was slow in coming. "I saw colours and lights and movement. My mother has told me that they are the souls of departed reindeer dancing their everlasting dance in the heavens."

"Did you not see more? Could you make out their heads and antlers, their pawing hooves? Could you see any of your own ancestors – your father, your grandmother? Did they speak to you?"

"No, elder one. I saw only the colours and heard only the song of the wind and the stars. I do not think the ancestors wished to speak to me."

If Herb was disappointed she did not show it. A Sky Watcher was born only once or twice in a generation and perhaps the time was not yet right for her to pass on her training and knowledge to another. She had a few years yet and could wait. Patience was a learned virtue and this calf evidently had none of it. Now she clattered down the slope, eager to be with her mother again.

There was no need for words when they reached White Flank at last. Moss's mother knew from the look in Herb's eyes that her calf would not be chosen, and, if she was relieved, she said nothing. Time and the gods would decide her calf's future. Now was the time to set off for the protection of the forests in the south before the hard grip of winter closed over these lands again.

By the end of June, all the surviving calves were fit and strong and ready to move with the herd. On a day which she judged to be propitious, Herb indicated that it was time to begin the summer migration. White Flank set off purposely and, called by an instinct greater than any voice, the rest of the mothers followed with their calves. They were setting out on a trek which would take them 400 miles to the south and into the great forest where they would find protection from weather and wolves during the long winter months.

The first part of their journey was relatively easy: along the coast and then into a deep valley which would lead them into the mountains of the interior. Down at the sea edge, they passed White Bear on an ice floe, but she was too busy showing her two fluffy cubs how to listen and watch for the puff of breath from surfacing seals to pay notice to the herd. She knew by now that the calves were too swift to waste time and energy chasing, and the sea provided riches enough to feed her family. Perhaps in less abundant years, she would follow the herd for a while on the off chance that a calf had strayed or an adult become injured, but she had no intention of moving far from the sea which was her major source of food. Soon the sea would freeze over and she and her cubs would range far away from their home den on the mainland.

Every year calves were lost at the beginning of the trek, when young mothers failed to keep an eye on their youngsters or weaker ones could not keep up. Mothers knew their calves by sight and smell and their distinctive calling, so that the passage of the herd was announced by the plaintive bleats of separated calves and the barks of searching mothers. It was inevitable that some would not be reunited, and the pursuing hunters waited for darkness to take advantage of such opportunities. However, there were not many predators here. This was why the reindeer came to these cold lands to calve – only the odd lone wolf or Arctic fox ventured this far north. There was not enough food during the rest of the winter for non-hibernating creatures to survive.

Soon the confusion of the outset had settled and, by the second day, the herd had left the sea and begun the long walk through the high mountains which lay behind the calving ground. The migration route was not fixed, but it was constrained by land formation and the need to find sufficient food for several hundred reindeer. They had many miles to go before they would reach the lower, more sheltered lands where they would meet the bull herd and luxuriate in a profusion of grass and fodder on the open tundra. This year the snows had melted from the northern lands very late and, indeed, all of the high land was covered in permanent snowfields. The lichen on the calving grounds had been rich enough to fatten up the mothers and calves for their long journey. It was not so certain that there would be enough forage in the colder interior.

Surprisingly, Moss stuck close to her mother at first. She was too busy watching everything around her and keeping up the relentless pace of the march to stray or get into mischief. She observed Eagle soaring above, her splayed fingers feeling for currents in the wind. Eagle was capable of lifting a straying calf, but she too had a family to feed and would not follow far from her sea-cliff eyrie. Lemmings also watched the progress of the eagle, chirping danger signals and scampering to the safety of their green mounds. Golden and sea eagles alike feasted on the ever-growing lemming population, and tundra voles and hares, all so busily engaged in eating and breeding before the winter snows sealed them into their underground tunnels.

The herd followed a high valley which cut through the western mountains. Snow lay here all year round but it was a short transit. Calves grew fat on their mothers' milk and strengthened their muscles with the continual marching. This part of the journey was relatively easy and soon they had crossed the mountain belt and reached the good lowlands around the river estuary on the east coast. Here they met the first of their potential hazards: a broad, swiftly flowing river.

White Flank led a group of the older mothers and calves to the low bank. The river was so deep that all the reindeer had to swim, and it was essential that there were enough experienced animals to surround the calves. Although they could swim well, buoyed by the hollow hairs in their coat, a young one could be easily swept away in the current. Moss and White Flank crossed without mishap. Some of the stragglers were not so lucky. A group of young deer had stopped to snatch a mouthful of the rich grass beside the river and now stood tentatively, unsure of what to do. Herb, habitually watchful at the rear of the herd, encouraged them and, at last, they plunged into the icy waters. All went well for the first part of the crossing until one bull calf, thinking it easier to swim away from the current, turned downriver. His mother followed, bellowing anxiously, and soon others turned too. It was a disaster. The river picked them up and carried them far past the crossing place where trampling hooves had made an easy exit. By the time they had reached the other side of the river, there were only high banks too difficult for the weaker calves. Most of the adults could leap ashore but the young were swept past, scrabbling frantically at the edges and calling piteously. Mothers raced along the shore, trying to encourage their children. Some managed to scramble ashore but several were carried down the river and out into the open sea, where drowning would be the most peaceful death that awaited them.

When Herb saw that nothing could be done, she pulled the grieving mothers away from the river. The herd was already well ahead and no one could afford to be left behind. Losses were inevitable but there was no need to court more by inattention.

Before them lay a massif of huge mountains cut by river gorges, lochs and wide valleys. There were two principal routes, both of which presented different but equally severe hazards. One lay through the middle of the mountain chain. All the land was high and would be covered with deep snow and, lower down, occasional rivers would be swollen with meltwater. The other route followed the coast but was somewhat longer. It might be easier but White Flank knew there would be more predators this way. She consulted Herb and together the two experienced reindeer chose to take the route over the mountains. They had travelled this way on the journey north.

Their choice seemed to be justified as they made good time in the first few days, along a river valley leading into the mountains. Snow lay on the ground but there were enough patches of grass for feed. The little burns which fed the river were not too swollen to cross. Young Moss gambolled along, investigating this and that and worrying her mother by disappearing regularly, only to jump out from behind a rock as if nothing had happened. White Flank soon learned to ignore this behaviour. The calf might be wilful and inquisitive but she had a strong instinct for self-preservation and would always find her mother in the herd.

There was a great deal of interest for a first-year calf. Winters were getting harder and longer, so that there was no time for spring or autumn: just a bare two months of summer in which all creatures had to get through the business of mating and raising young before the hard weather closed in again. Birds swooped and called anxiously around their nests; frogs and toads croaked in the swamps; brilliant dragonflies flitted; even flowers and the stunted trees hurried the business of growing, spreading pollen and dispersing seed. Moss investigated everything with a seemingly scientific interest. Most of all she liked to play with the other calves, butting heads, racing, stotting and playing 'king of the castle' on lemming mounds. They were unwittingly establishing relationships and dominance for the future. It was clear that Moss could make a herd leader. It was she who initiated games and led the others, and she seldom tolerated interference. This was an idyllic time for young deer who had no care for present dangers or difficulties ahead.

White Flank was worried. So far the trek had gone well. Only a few weak or careless calves had been lost. The river valley rose gently but soon they would reach the higher land, and she could already see the snowfields gleaming under the pale sunshine. This would not be a problem for adults but the youngsters would flounder through thick snow and could become weakened through exhaustion and lack of food. The pass through the mountains was long and it would be a race against time to clear the snowy heights before the collective strength of the herd gave out. There was also the possibility of a blizzard. Reindeer were used to that, of course, but it would put more pressure on the calves. White Flank allowed the deer to graze well on the last patches of good grass before they set off into the snowy wastes.

White Flank led the oldest, most experienced deer, cutting a path through the snows. As long as the others kept close together following their tracks, all went well. There was no stopping on this part of the trail. During the day the herd plodded doggedly on, occasionally scraping away the thinner patches of snow in hope of a mouthful of lichen: there was none in this barren land. By night, the deer marched like mournful grey ghosts under the icy gaze of the stars and moon. From time to time an anguished cry testified to the success of the ever-watchful predators but, mostly, the march proceeded in silence, except for the distinctive clicking of the reindeers' ankle tendons. By the second day it was clear that some of the calves were coming to the end of their strength. All depended on how far the snows reached into the southern river valley which was their route out of the mountains.

White Flank saw a few mothers and tiring calves fall back. Herb, at the rear of the herd, would chivvy these along, but some, inevitably, could not keep up. At least these ones would keep the hungry wolves from attacking the stronger animals. Inexorably, nature was weeding out the weaker elements from the herd.

At last they crossed the highest point of the mountains and began the slow descent to the next river valley. With her remarkable distance vision White Flank could already see the river winding out of the snows, and patches of green here and there on its banks. The worst part of the migration was over. But the reindeer had new tribulations to face. They had to cross many streams tumbling down from high glaciers. A deer could break a leg stumbling on the hidden boulders in the foaming current, and whenever they crossed one of the bigger rivers, more would be swept away and drown. The large wolf packs had come north as a dubious reception committee and would select young or old at leisure for dinner. But perhaps the smallest of the afflictions which beset the herd was the most annoying – mosquitoes. In the cold wastes of the north mosquitoes did not breed, but in the warmer swampy lands great clouds of them would rise up and smother the bodies and faces and noses of the deer. The older reindeer were resigned to this sort of vexation but the calves would panic and bolt. For this reason White Flank led the herd through snow patches, and walked into the wind if it was coming from a suitable direction. Their route, however, was still restricted by high mountains on either side, so often it was not possible to avoid the attentions of the little tormentors. Moss evaded them by running circles round her mother. She was growing daily in strength and size. The trials of the trek seemed only to have increased her confidence and bravado.

By the twelfth day of their march, the reindeer had descended into the lowlands where they faced the last of their major obstructions – a mighty river which drained the whole area and meandered slowly for many miles east to the sea. The herd had been walking by now through rich grasslands and many of the deer were foraging widely. White Flank and Herb had to gather them together at the selected crossing place and persuade them into the sleek black coils of the river. Many were reluctant after their experiences of previous river crossings, and this one had a particularly menacing aspect. At length the vanguard followed White Flank into the water and swam vigorously across. Fortunately on this occasion, River was in a magnanimous mood and took no sacrifices. Now it was the task of White Flank to find and reunite with the bull herd which generally made its way north to meet them, but which could be roaming about for many miles in the wide, open tundra grasslands.

The deer were in no hurry, luxuriating in the profusion of grass. Reindeer have a more efficient digestive system for green plants than any other grazing animal, and already their summer coats were growing in dark and sleek. By midsummer, there was plenty of food for everyone. The calves could supplement their diet with buds, willow shoots and leaves, herbaceous plants and sedge, and would eagerly snuffle out delicious fungi, the fat brown 'penny bun' of the boletus being particularly favoured. White Flank was content to lead the herd into the wind away from biting insects.

When the females had left on their arduous trek north to the calving grounds they had been accompanied by a few juvenile males, yearlings, but the bull herd had remained in the more hospitable lands in the south. It was the young males' task to grow strong and fit ready for the rutting in the autumn.

When the two herds met there was hardly a fuss of reunification and renewed acquaintances. Reindeer are not like that. In just one morning the herd doubled in size, bulls grazing contentedly beside mothers and calves. But the herd did not stop moving. During the late summer the collective herd might roam for many hundreds of miles in any direction, but always towards the wind and away from mosquitoes and black flies. The reindeer were now led by a massive bull chief; the prime animal of the herd, but also a wise and experienced leader. Now that the responsibilities of the calving trek were over, White Flank was happy to defer to him. She was more concerned about the behaviour of her calf, who was now proving to be even more of a problem.

Like all intelligent young creatures, Moss thrived on activities and interests. She was much intrigued by the new male animals with their fascinating velvet antlers. Female deer lose their antlers just after calving so Moss had no idea what these strange branched contraptions were for. She would pester the bulls, sniffing their urine, butting them and urging them to play. For the most part the males tolerated her attentions but, from time to time, an angry hoof would strike out and Moss would jump away just in time. She thought it was all part of the game. She also interfered with the other females, nosing in to see what was going on when the calves were suckling. And it was at this time that she learned a trick which was to stand her in good stead in the future. Usually when a female was suckling her calf, all her attention would be on her offspring. So Moss could grab a teat on the other side and earn herself a mouthful of stolen milk. It wasn't that she needed it; she was big and strong and thriving both on her mother's milk and the good herbage. So White Flank was not duly concerned, as long as her daughter did not get into serious trouble.

It was White Flank herself who made a fatal error.

She had been bitten unmercifully by insects during the march and had rubbed the itchy areas on tree trunks and rocks. Now she had open red wounds. These became infected and started to fester. She grew weaker and slower, dropping to the back of the herd where Herb, the Sky Watcher, still kept an eye out for stragglers. Herb did what she could, applying mosses and lichens to the wounds, but nothing could take away the infection. She kept her counsel to herself but privately she guessed that the time had come for her friend to join her ancestors.

As the reindeer roamed across the endless tundra, they moved into new wolf-pack territories. The wolves had new cubs to feed and they would look out for weak or elderly deer in the herd. An injured animal was easy killing. The Scarp Pack had noticed the laggardly mother with calf and waited for an appropriate opportunity to attack the adult and maybe secure a succulent youngster at the same time. The time came when the herd passed through one of the increasingly frequent copses of woodland which occurred in this area. As the herd moved out of the trees, the wolf pack closed in on White Flank and her child. It was a foregone conclusion.

White Flank fought for her young one, she fought for herself, she fought for the memory of all her children and the bright years of mating, birthing and leading her herd in the eternal migration. But most of all she fought to save Moss. If the wolves expected an easy kill they soon found they had to give all of their attention to this whirling animal with her sharp hooves and lethal antlers. There was no need for White Flank to urge Moss to escape. She may have wanted to stay by her mother, but fear drove her away from the terrible grey beasts with pointed fangs and wicked eyes. She ran as she had never run before, catching up with the safety of the rest of the herd and then wondering what to do now.

Instinct took over. The desire to march alongside the others was greater than her need for her mother. But by the time night fell she was hungry and lonely, and sought out Herb for solace.

"Where is my mother?"

Not one for many words, Herb raised her newly growing antlers to the dim glow in the northern sky. "There is a new dancer among the ancestors, little one."

It is very unlikely for a three-month-old calf to survive the death of its mother, but Moss had the tenacity and the quick intelligence which allowed her to take advantage of every opportunity. She followed the leaders of the herd, who always knew the best places and types of feeding. She stole milk from other mothers when she could. She missed the warmth and comfort of her mother's companionship but, as summer waned into autumn, her independent spirit strengthened and developed. There was much to fascinate and intrigue her and the world was far too interesting a place to spend time mourning one who had passed beyond.

The time of rutting was approaching and the bulls were already beginning to strut with their antlers held high, although it would be some weeks before the mating season started in earnest. Moss regarded this with interest and admired the majestic sweep of tines and branches with some envy. Her own antlers were growing but they were covered in a soft, dark velvet and would only reach a short height in her first year. Bulls' antlers could grow to four or five feet with several branches, and they had already shed their velvet covering so that they gleamed hard and vicious in the sunlight. Most of this was for show, although sometimes a full-scale battle would develop. Usually this only occurred when two big bulls of relatively equal strength had failed to establish their dominance in preliminary displays, or when a young bull came forward to challenge an established leader. So the early rut was marked by increasingly fervent activity: males vocalising with short coughs and performing ritualistic skirmishes, establishing a hierarchy of mating rights. By October, when the first cows were coming into season, the lead bulls had gathered a harem and were constantly engaged in protecting these from the attentions of unwelcome suitors, rounding them up and sniffing out who was ready to mate. In a frenzy they dug pits and urinated into them as if to mark their chosen breeding sites. Moss watched all the activity from some distance but she was not interested in mating and soon turned her attentions to other distractions on the edge of the herd.

At this time of year, the boletus mushrooms and other edible fungi were prolific. Animals would scour around dry ridges and forage through scrubby undergrowth, hunting for these tasty morsels. Great excitement would permeate through the herd when a good source of fungi was discovered, and the bulls were driven to frustration trying to keep their harems together. Moss followed Herb and learned where the best spots were, and also which fungi were advisable to avoid. Some were fatally poisonous but others had various degrees of hallucinatory properties, and reindeer often sought these out. There was one toadstool which Herb would gather, very distinctive shiny red with white flecks, but she would not let Moss eat it – it was Dream Maker; only Sky Watchers were allowed to eat it, and only for very specific purposes. Moss observed everything and stored all the knowledge for future reference.

By now winter had closed in on the tundra. The reindeer had roved well to the south where Forest gave them protection from blizzards and biting winds. There were no mosquitoes now to harass them but there were predators, and the continual need to scrape out food from beneath the snow forced them to keep moving. Moss cemented friendships and tried out her small antlers, which were now stripped of velvet, on mock battles to establish dominance with her equally assertive peers. Most of the older bulls had cast their antlers, so she even made playful attacks on them. On the whole they tolerated her impudence but occasionally they would give her a severe butt to remind her of her position in society. Despite her early trials, or perhaps because of them, she was growing into a handsome, wily and resourceful reindeer. The other youngsters followed her lead.

Inevitably winter's grip weeded out the weak and the old and, as the freezing months dragged on, the wolves grew hungrier and more persistent. Although mainly territorial, they would follow the herd for hundreds of miles, looking out for likely prey. When starvation drove them, they could attack even the strongest members of the herd, singling them out from the others. Moss soon learned that keeping a big group of large and active reindeer around her would deter the depredations of the wolves.

And so the winter passed. Although lengthening days marked the turn of the season, food was even more difficult to find. The reindeer had to dig through two or three feet of snow to find the lichen which would sustain them. Their thick winter coats kept them warm even in the wildest blizzard but they all grew thinner, using up the reserves of fat which they had built up in the summer plenty. At last the first signs heralded spring. On warming days, snow melted in large drips from the tree branches; the cracking and creaking of ice on the lakes predicted the thaw. Of course, the weather would close in again and, for a time, the deer had to hunker down amongst the trees and wait out the worst of the snowstorms.

For Moss her first spring was like a fiery young deer bounding, a-sparkle with life and energy, out of the deep forest of winter. It set fire to her blood and made her want to run and jump in the glint of sunbeams and glitter of ice crystals. Snow melted and patches of tired green appeared here and there. Streams tumbled and gurgled. You could almost hear sap rising in the birch trees. Suddenly life, which had slept all winter long underneath the protective blanket of snow, poked its nose into the golden air and made a few tentative steps out of its cosy den. Buds swelling on the trees made luscious, protein-rich morsels; early flowers and blossoms made honey-sweet feeding. When spring came in earnest it was very fast. Within a few weeks leaves were sprouting and grass was growing. The reindeer herd was beginning to split, with the bulls tending to steer clear of the females, who still retained their antlers and could be fiercely aggressive in the competition for good food.

Soon the round of the reindeer season led the cow herd back on its long trek to the northern calving grounds. Moss, as a non-pregnant yearling, accompanied them, staying close to Herb as a substitute for her mother. Herb understood the youngster's need but she often wondered if the ancestors had been wrong and missed the opportunity to select a new Sky Watcher. In any case, she was glad to impart her knowledge to another. This one would make a leader even if she was not one of the Chosen.

If the trek north was more difficult, the mountain passes deeper in snow and the fodder less abundant, Moss did not notice. It was glorious to be marching into the high mountains in the footsteps of thousands of generations of reindeer. She sensed her mother beside her, and sometimes, when the night was lit by the dancing of the ancestors, she felt their spirits breathing warmly on her muzzle and whispering in her ear.

The trek was arduous and, as always, some reindeer did not complete it, but at last they dropped down to the sea on the western shore and made their way to the higher plateau of the calving grounds. Returning to the place of her birth brought memories flooding back to Moss; she cherished rather than mourned them.

While the other females proceeded with the business of calving and rearing, Moss and a few other yearlings were left to their own devices. Herb kept an eye on them. Although she made the trek to the north every year, mating and calving were not for her. Sky Watchers must keep their minds fully alert to their instincts and messages from the spirits. They must never be distracted by the trials of parturition and the vagaries of calves. Increasingly, however, she took Moss with her in her climbs to the mountaintops, and the two animals would observe in silence the dancing lights and weaving curtains and the majestic progress of the stars across the dome of the sky.

II

In due time Moss herself mated and produced with ease a fine bull calf. Life fell into a pattern: the circuit of the reindeer year; always on the move, north, south; rutting in the autumn, calving in the spring; growing antlers bigger every year and casting them. By her fourth year Moss had inherited her mother's leadership of the cow herd and stalwartly broke the snow crust on their mountain passages. But every year it became harder. The snowfields were growing larger and there was less and less fodder for the

36

migrating animals. The rich feeding on the calving grounds had dwindled and fewer and fewer calves were surviving the rigours of the trek. Life in the winter forest was much the same as ever but each year the reindeer ranged further south to find the safety and protection of the trees.

The third year of Moss's leadership was a disaster.

Even the tundra lands that spring had remained covered in snow till very late, so the reindeer were thin and weak before they began the mountain crossing. Moss had chosen the route to the west which, although longer, might afford more pasturage. But there was very little, and more and more exhausted animals fell to the starving wolves. When the depleted herd at last reached the site of its collective birthplace, it was still deep in powdery snow. There was enough lichen to be scraped out and the process of calving went on much the same as usual. But this year fewer calves were born alive, and those that did were weak and undernourished. Moss had given birth to her fourth calf, a fine female named Sedge. But she was very dispirited about the dead and dying calves, and anxious about the future. Rather than increasing its size, the herd was smaller than it had been before leaving the south. Moss sought out Herb for advice.

"Herb, we must talk. I fear there will be no herd for me to lead before long. You walk with the spirits. What do they say?"

Herb recognised the concern in her voice. She herself had consulted the spirits but had received no clear answer from them. All was confusion: many images, strange and distorted, but no message within to tell her what to do. Even the ancestors had not given directions. "Come with me, then. We must go on a journey to the land between lands, where the spirits will talk to us."

Leaving the calf to amuse herself with the other youngsters, the two adults made their way down the valley from the high plateau. Herb was now very elderly for reindeer, who normally do not live past seventeen summers, but she was sprightly enough for her advanced years. Moss wondered where they were going; usually Herb led her to the high mountains.

Presently they left the valley bottom and made their way to the edge of a steep limestone cliff which bordered the valley to the south. Moss had never been this way before and soon she saw a number of dark openings in the base of the cliff. They looked gloomy and oppressive.

Herb stopped at the entrance to the largest cave. "These are the sacred places of our ancestors. No one but Sky Watchers may enter here, but today you may come with me."

Moss followed obediently. The cave entrance was small and overhung, but at the back, a passage opened out into what must be a larger cavern. The light was very dim but Moss could vaguely make out shapes of pillars and walls, and could hear faint echoes of their movements resounding in the dark void above. She felt a growing sense of unease, as if the huge weight of the mountain above were pressing down and forcing all the breath out of her chest. Her eyes gleamed with white flashes of fear.

Herb stopped here and, after scrabbling about on the dusty floor of the cave, produced some dull grey cakes which Moss recognised as dried portions of fungus.

"Moss, are you afraid? You must risk your life to find the answers you seek. Never before has anyone but a Sky Watcher undertaken the journey to the spirit world. You are strong and determined but I do not know if you can survive such a trek."

Moss thought a little before answering. "I do not think any of us will survive. We have lost the love of the snow spirit and the mountain spirits and we must find out what to do to propitiate them. If they need my life as a sacrifice, then let it be so."

"Then you must eat these." Herb indicated the small pieces of dried mushroom. "Too much will kill you, but a little will open your mind to the gods."

Tentatively, Moss nibbled a little: it was slightly peppery but nothing more. Herb nodded and she took a little more. Herb ate a little herself.

"That will be enough. Now we must wait for the spirits."

For a long time the two reindeer stood side by side in the dimness of the cavern. Herb scratched patterns in the earth with her hoof but nothing seemed to change, nothing seemed to be happening. It grew very still. By now Moss's eyes had become accustomed to the darkness and she could see the walls of the chamber leaping up into what appeared to be a vast emptiness, expanding into a space greater than the sky itself. The huge expanse daunted Moss and she dropped her eyes to Herb's hoof patterns on the floor. They seemed to be moving, changing shape, giving transitory glimpses of vague images: a mountain here; a running calf there; a great, black river twining its way along the cavern floor. She drooped her head closer. The images were pulling her in.

Time has no meaning in the spirit world. Perhaps the two reindeer stood for hours or even days, but at last, when Herb was beginning to fear for the life of her friend, Moss showed signs of returning: a twitch of the skin, the blink of an eyelid. Soon – indeed, like a traveller slightly dazed and weary after a long journey – she shook her head and stretched her legs.

Herb was relieved. "What did you see?" she asked.

"At first I saw only images; images in the sand. But then it was as if my spirit flew and I could look down on our two bodies here in the cave. But there was no cave, just space and stars. I felt you with me somehow but could not talk to you. Then in the darkness I began to see a huge herd, greater than any I have ever seen, stretching back into the far distance and forward, on and ever on. They were all marching on the great migration, young and old, weak and lame, strong and bold. There was no end to that long line of reindeer. I think I could make out some I knew. I saw my mother and called but she did not hear me. And I saw my own calves – Sedge was there, walking behind her grandmother, and there were many others I recognised and others I did not know but who seemed familiar. Was that not strange?

"And then I was floating, soaring like Eagle, far above these birth lands but they had changed utterly. There was nothing to be seen in any direction but a white sea of ice and snow. Only some mountaintops stuck up like islands. I flew higher and higher to see if there was an end to the ice. And at last, well to the south, I saw a glimmer of blue mist where the glaciers ended and the tundra began.

"It was as if ages passed and then, from my viewpoint in the clouds, I could see the ice melting very slowly, grass growing in uneven patches, and at last, the reindeer returning here for their birthing.

"But then I saw strange things, creatures I could not understand. They were pale animals walking on their hind legs, naked, so they wore the skins of other animals to protect them from the cold. And when I looked closer, I could see the worst horror: those were the skins of reindeer. Do they dress in our skins to *be* reindeer? But they were not like us at all. They built themselves shelters of sticks every night and conjured fire from the earth to warm themselves. Are they spirits? If so they are evil because I saw them cutting the life from reindeer with flashing stones at the throat. And they killed so many, Herb, that in the end there were no reindeer left to come to our ancestral home. They had all disappeared and left these wicked beings as masters of this land.

"They killed all the fish in the sea, and no birds flew. I cried to see the desolation, but, when my eyes cleared, the evil spirits had gone; the land was green and full of life again. And I saw a few reindeer making their way north once more, and, during the last of my vision, I joined the great herd walking forward into the vast distance. Then slowly I came back to my body again and the vision was gone."

Herb sighed a long sigh of satisfaction and sorrow. "You have seen very clearly, Moss. I too have seen some of these stories but I did not understand them until now. I think the ancestors have given you a message and a glimpse of the future. I have seen the evil beings too, and wondered at them. They will come, but they will pass away. You saw the reindeer herd on its great migration through the tundra of time; you saw the ancestors of the past; you saw the calves yet to be born in the future. And it is clear that, after the evil ones have left this land, the reindeer will return to bear their calves in this place and consult with their ancestors in these caves as they have always done. But before that, a long winter will come. It will lie over these lands for many seasons and no life will be possible here. That message is for you, Moss. This time you must lead the herd far south, where there is still grass and forest, and then you must find a new calving ground in the north, perhaps under the rising sun. You will not return here again."

"I understand," said Moss sadly. "But how will I find a new land? You are wise and very old. Can't you lead us there?"

Herb bowed her head. "I'll not be coming with you. I'm too old for another journey. I must stay here to guard the caves of the ancestors until the reindeer return at the end of the long winter. You must ask other deer about new lands. Ask the birds who know no boundaries; ask the whales who rove the seas. They will know where reindeer may go to calve in safety from the ice and the coming years of evil. I know you will succeed; the ancestors have said so."

Herb scraped her hoof to obliterate the marks she had made in the sand. "But what I do not understand is why the ancestors did not choose you at the first for a Sky Watcher. No other reindeer before you has survived the spirit journey without hurt, and you saw the images clearer even than I. Why did the spirits not tell me that when you were young? You should have become the Sky Watcher for the herd and let me travel on my own journey long ago."

Moss turned her head away from the troubled gaze of the old one. "It was my fault, Herb. When you took me to the ancestors so long ago, I saw them, they spoke to me. But I did not like what they had to say. They told me that I must undergo sad trials in life and undertake a great task for the sake of the herd. I did not want that, and I did not want to suffer childlessness just to be a Sky Watcher. So I did not tell you the truth then. I pretended I saw nothing. Do you forgive me? I was young and headstrong."

Herb shook her head a few times as if understanding something at last made clear. "Of course I forgive you. No one becomes a Sky Watcher eagerly. But you did not understand the messages of the ancestors. They tell you what must come, and you cannot change your destiny. You have met those trials, and you must face the great task. Perhaps it is better that you never became a Sky Watcher, but leader of the herd instead. You will need strength, experience and resilience to lead the herd to new lands. Come now. We have been away a while and your calf will be anxious."

The two reindeer made their way out of the cave and back to the herd, where a delighted Sedge pranced excitedly around her mother in welcome.

The summer, which was hardly a summer, waned. Moss saw that they must leave as early as possible even if some of the calves were still too weak for the journey. They must grow strong on the way. The herd was much depleted, only a few hundred animals, but at least that might make it easier to keep track of them on the march.

On a calm day which presaged a period of good weather, she gathered the herd together and led them off into the icy mountains. Many would die on the way, but the strongest would survive and join Moss in her search for new calving grounds.

It is not written whether they succeeded or not, but lands in the north and east, and very far to the west, still see the passage of reindeer on their seasonal migration. Perhaps they are descended from Moss and her children. At any rate, when Moss led her herd away this time, no reindeer would return for thousands of years. The land would become the province of ice.

Only one reindeer remains to watch the departure of the herd. She stands above the cliff of the caves, solitary and still, a small patch of pale fur and proud antlers in a stark wilderness. She will watch forever until she sees the forerunners of the herd making their way back to their ancestral calving grounds.

Chapter Three

The Shelter

seafaring hunters

Some miles north of Ullapool, in a rough rock shelter overlooking the beach, is a possible Mesolithic shell midden. It has never been excavated or dated but, along with similar sites on the shores of the mainland and nearby islands, it testifies to the fleeting presence of human beings shortly after the end of the last glacial period.

Malele scanned the shore. Nothing moved, neither beast nor man, but the thick brush which skirted the back of the beach could hide many dangers. She signalled to Tepak and Kalem to stop paddling.

A hawk screeched as it hovered on the wind, a bird piped in the bushes – all was as it should be. Malele nodded her thanks to the faithful guardians and signalled for the boats to go forward. While the men dragged the boats above the high-water mark, Malele placed her hands on the sand and spoke to the local spirits. It had been many seasons since they had last visited this place and the spirits would likely have forgotten them. But she could feel a welcome in the warm sand and could sense no threat or opposition.

Everyone, even old Mother Grimal, helped to carry their belongings – the skins and baskets, weapons and food stores – up to the rock shelter. Malele was glad to see that the protective wall they had built on their previous visit still stood. An animal had used the shelter at some time but the droppings were hard and the place smelled fresh. It was not as comfortable as their usual skin tents

47

but it afforded better protection. This land was as close to Tepe, the fixed star, as the people ever travelled. It was a place where the spirits ruled and humans must pay homage and respect.

The women cleaned out the shelter, spread sleeping skins inside for themselves and the children and erected a tent for the men on the level plateau outside. Tepak was organising a scouting party to check for hunting and fishing opportunities at the edge of the wide estuary which fed into a substantial river leading into the interior. As usual Pele was hanging around, hoping that he would be included. Malele called him inside but he refused to listen.

Tepak grabbed his arm and propelled him into the shelter, whining and squirming. "When you are old enough to behave like a man, you will be allowed to take part in manly activities. For now you will stay where you belong: with the women."

The dismissive rebuke silenced Pele's protests but he humped about the shelter, dropping things in the wrong places and generally getting in everybody's way. Malele sighed. This, the youngest of her surviving children, was the biggest handful of them all – obstinate, self-willed and impulsive. She hoped that these traits would prove an asset as he matured, but at present they were annoying everyone. Perhaps he could be distracted by foraging on the shore.

All the women and the other children were delighted to be ranging along the beach, poking in tidal pools for crabs and hammering limpets off the rocks, but Pele wandered about, kicking over stones and scowling. He would reach manhood this season but it wasn't soon enough for him. He no longer played with the other children, preferring to be on his own chipping flakes off flint cores or pestering the men to teach him hunting skills. Mostly they tolerated his behaviour. They too scorned women's work, and expected him to prepare for his proper place in the group.

"Pele!" Malele called. "Go fetch a spear and look for flatfish in the shallows. The tide is going out and you might find some sea urchins or oysters too."

Pele was very fond of oysters, as were all the people, and this occupation might suit him better. He grumbled quietly but there was a lightness in his step as he went back to the shelter. Soon he was whooping and splashing in the water, his black mood forgotten. He wouldn't catch many fish that way but at least he was happier.

The people soon settled into their respective routines: the women collecting and preparing shellfish, crabs and edible seaweeds, and the men fishing from the boats close to the shore or hunting for wildfowl in the estuary and reed beds. Pele could go with the men, carrying their bows and spears, and was occasionally allowed to practise shooting ducks. He was showing some skill but still had to learn to curb his enthusiasm. There was no point in hollering when he pinned a bird if it scared all the others away. Malele was pleased with this in one way but unhappy in another. Pele had to learn reverence for the animals he killed; if he didn't, one day the spirits might retaliate.

Everyone, even the younger children, was employed in stringing nets across the narrower inlets. As the tide retreated, fish became trapped and could be easily speared in the shallow water. The fish were dried on racks or preserved by smoking on fires at the back of the beach. This was a good time of year: food was in abundance, the weather was calm and the days were stretching out.

As the time of Pele's manhood approached, he became increasingly excited and wearisome. He was the only child of his age in the group and would have to go through the ceremony on his own. This only made him more intolerable, boasting to the younger children and sneering at the women. His older brother, Kalem, who had long since passed into manhood, cuffed him about a bit to teach him his place but it only seemed to encourage his arrogance. It wasn't only Malele who was relieved when the day of the highest sun arrived and the men could take him away on his first hunt.

Before they left, Malele drew Pele aside. He was unusually subdued; perhaps he at last understood the gravity of the situation.

"You are leaving as a child for the last time. You will come back a man. But you will still be my son and I will always be here for you. Your new position brings responsibility – you must protect everyone and perform your duties with compassion and understanding. And always – *always*, my son – remember that the spirits are watching and judging your actions. They will not tolerate thoughtless actions or deliberate cruelty."

"I'll remember, Mother. I will never do anything to make you ashamed or displease the spirits. You will be proud of me."

Malele placed her hand on her son's heart to give her blessing. She still feared his bravado would lead to trouble.

She watched with some misgiving as the men left the camp: Tepak, Degan and Jot, Kalem having elected to stay behind and guard the women. Malele suspected that he wanted to take advantage of the men's absence to be alone with Fela. That was good – it was time that her oldest son took on some responsibility and had children of his own. Even her daughter, Ele, who had attained her bleeding this season, was beginning to cast her eyes appealingly at the menfolk. It wouldn't be long. Malele smiled, remembering her own young times. She had her pick of the men then but had chosen Tepak to be her primary mate. It had been a good decision: he had never questioned her authority on important matters and often sought her advice about the right times to hunt and the prospects for the weather.

The hunting party left the beach and made its way inland following the banks of the river. There were plenty of seabirds and ducks but they did not stop to shoot them. There was more important prey further in to the mountains.

Pele was unnaturally subdued as they forged deeper into the interior. He had never left the safety of camp at the seashore before. The wild lands held all sorts of dangers, both known and unknown. There were bears, wolves, wild boar and all kinds of malevolent beings on the prowl in these woods. Even the louring trees seemed to press in on all sides and whisper maliciously between themselves.

They were making their way out of the lowlands, and soon the trees began to thin out into more isolated patches of woodland. Tepak led them through these, passing quickly through the open ground, until they came to a deep gorge below the highest mountain in the area. They dropped down into it, sometimes having to wade through the icy water when the banks became too steep. Tepak gave the sign for 'very quiet'; they were hidden from any animals but a careless splash would alert them. By now Pele's apprehension had settled into a calm anticipation; at last he was taking part in a real hunt. Today, if he did well, he would become a man.

The top of the gorge opened out into a high pass which led over the mountains. As they approached it, the men slowed and crouched, wanting to betray their presence by neither sight nor sound. The wind was funnelling down towards them from the mountain, so their scent would be carried away. Pele saw Tepak raise his head and sniff the breeze; he must have detected the smell of prey. He made the sign for 'deer', and everyone dropped to the ground. They wriggled on their stomachs and Pele had to suppress a giggle as he followed his father's squirming bottom through the heather tussocks.

The deer herd was grazing calmly in the plateau in the middle of the pass. It was not an ideal situation as there was very little cover to allow the hunters to approach near enough to shoot off an arrow or hurl a spear. Tepak pondered what they should do. This was Pele's hunt. He should have the chance to make his kill and show that he could provide for his family – that was how he would become a man.

Tepak indicated that Degan and Jot should follow him up the side of the mountain until they were concealed from the animals below. Pele was to wait in hiding until they had driven the herd towards him. Then he could pick out his kill. Everyone nodded in agreement and crept off, leaving Pele on his own behind a large nubbly boulder.

Pele waited impatiently but soon the enormity of the occasion settled him. He heard the stream bubbling through the rocks, the wind whurrying over the mountaintops and even the gentle chomping of the deer. It seemed to be taking forever for the men to reach their ambush position.

Then, suddenly, something alerted the deer and every head turned towards some threat behind them. As one, they panicked and pounded towards the gorge. The men must be attacking. Pele ducked behind the boulder – nothing must prevent the herd from running in his direction. He could hear the thunder of many hooves, and raised his spear in readiness. He must judge exactly the right time to step out from his hiding place: too soon and the deer would scatter; too late and they might run over him. He decided the latter was the best option. He would be bound to strike one as it came past him. He waited till he could hear the animals nearing. He waited until the fleetest deer had sped by. He waited until the main body of the herd rounded the rock. Then he stepped out from behind it and lowered his spear.

It was only then that he realised his mistake. He was looking right into the face of a huge lynx. Neither of them had time to change tactics; only instinct remained. The lynx sprang at Pele, pinning him to the ground. It mauled his face and sank its teeth into his neck. Strangely, Pele felt no fear or pain. He felt himself slipping away – so this was what it was like to die. But then the pressure on his throat released and the weight on his chest fell away. The cat had impaled itself on his spear and its lifeblood was soaking into the earth.

When the men came upon the scene, Pele was spreadeagled under the cat's body, at first seemingly lifeless but his heart was beating and his breath was warm. When they pulled him out, his face was mangled, his nose chewed and his eyes pools of blood.

They took it in turns to carry Pele back to camp. They brought the body of the lynx as well; it was a trophy and, although it would not compensate for his injuries, its blood would be a symbol of his attained manhood.

Malele was devastated when she saw Pele's condition. "How did this happen?" she berated Tepak. "You were introducing Pele to the hunt, not putting him in a position of danger."

"There was nothing we could do," Tepak pleaded. "The lynx was stalking the deer as well as us but we didn't see it. We were trying to keep hidden and make as little noise as possible. The first we knew was when the deer stampeded. We didn't even know why; we thought they'd picked up our scent. We didn't know until we found him with that cat on top of him. But he had killed it himself. No one has ever killed a lynx on his first hunt – it is a great feat," he finished lamely.

"What good is a great feat if the hero is dead? It will be a legend told round the campfire to amuse children," Malele scolded. "Bring him into the shelter and I'll see what I can do for him."

Malele washed and tended Pele's wounds. His nose was ruined and his cheeks deeply scarred but she was most worried about his eyes. The lids were torn and scratched and swollen shut. She carefully prised them open and peered into his pupils. Both were badly damaged. Now she would have to summon up all her skills to heal her son. She consulted with old Grimal.

Grimal had been leader of the tribe until her weakening body and failing health led her to pass on her duties to her daughter Malele. But she still possessed arcane knowledge and was nearer to the spirit world, which she expected to enter very soon. She prodded Pele's wounds, listened to his chest for his heartbeat and breathing, and inspected his eyes.

"His heart is strong. I can find nothing wrong with his body. But his soul is weak – I can hear it crying and screaming in pain. The wounds on his face will heal in time but I do not think he will ever see again."

Malele bowed her head in sorrow. "Tell me what to do for him, Mother. What herbs will help? How will we propitiate the spirits? How can we call his soul back to the land? I think it is my fault – I knew he was too arrogant, and the spirits have punished him."

Grimal placed her hand on her daughter's shoulder. "No, it is not your fault. There is another reason. Yes, perhaps Pele was too bold and tempted the Gods, but see it this way. The lynx's spirit chose to give its life for him. He killed it and now it will be his protector and guide forever. If he survives now, I believe he will be very great."

"I hope you're right, Mother. But that makes it more important for me to cure him. What must I do?"

Grimal collected her wits for a long moment. "Very well; I can tell you what herbs will heal and what magic we must perform. But Pele must himself want to return; if he has decided to die, there is nothing we can do," she warned.

"So, first you must find some yellow celandine. It is much like a poppy, but smaller. There are usually four petals in a cross. It is not very common here so you must get everyone to search in woods, amongst rocks. It will heal his eyes and a very little of the juice will speak to his spirit."

Malele knew the weed. It was very powerful but also dangerous – too much could kill.

"Then," Grimal went on, "you must wait for the time of the full moon and collect some catchweed. It grows everywhere but is ruled by the moon and can only be plucked in her waxing or fullness. We will use that for his skin wounds. As for his soul, leave him in my care and I will summon the spirit helpers."

Malele was glad to have some positive activities to organise. She set all the women and children to explore the meadows near the beach, looking for the yellow poppy. She sent the men into the woods and rocky outcrops. Most of them returned with nothing, but enough was found for her to be able to prepare a medicine. Following Grimal's instructions, she pounded the herb to extract its orange juice and then diluted it with fresh spring water. With some soft cotton grass, she bathed Pele's eyelids, brushing gently towards the corners. He moaned and twisted away but did not wake. His sleep was not peaceful. Wherever he walked in the dreamworld, foul beasts and ghosts tormented him.

"He is in much pain," judged Grimal. "I think you must let him drink some of the juice – just a few drops, though. It will settle the pain and bring a natural sleep."

Malele did as she was instructed and it seemed to calm the boy a little. Grimal watched over him day and night, burning aromatic herbs in the fire and chanting incantations to the spirits.

As the days passed, Malele tended the wounds on Pele's throat and face with the catchweed. They began to heal but he would carry the scars forever. She smoothed a little of the celandine juice on his eyes. They were open but he showed no sign of sight or consciousness. Grimal instructed the men to cut the skin from the lynx, scrape the flesh from it and rub it with as much salt as they could gather from the edges of the rock pools. When she judged it sufficiently preserved, she wrapped Pele's body in it so that it could imbue his spirit with its animal strength. Then they waited.

At length even Grimal admitted that it seemed hopeless. "It is the boy himself – he doesn't want to live. Everything he wanted has been taken from him and I think there is only one thing we can do. I will have to go into the spirit world and bring him back. You must collect more celandine," she told Malele, "and prepare a stronger mixture this time. I will tell you just how much of the juice to add and no more."

Malele realised it was the only way to save her son.

When the plant had been collected and prepared, Grimal instructed all the people to build a big fire at the mouth of the shelter and leave her alone with Pele. She lifted his head and poured a little of the extract into his mouth. Then she took a similar dose herself and lay down beside his body.

The fire is bright and warm but there is a darkness outside. Shadows, animals are gathering, summoned by the magic. I hear their soft breathing and the padding of their paws.

"Go away – I do not want your help now. It is not his time to meet you yet."

I see his body, broken, sightless and bleeding, but I cannot feel his spirit. It is very far away. "Come, Pele. You must come to me for I am afraid to follow you."

I reach into the darkness within him. There is still nothing there.

Then I see a little spark, a tiny light wavering and dimming. "Pele, you must come back. Your people need you. You have a purpose, and the lynx spirit has chosen you for its own."

I reach out to the padding shadows and call the restless one. I know his name and he must obey me. He comes slinking, his eyes fearful of me. He doesn't understand, but knows what he must do. His shadow glows with a blue-red flame and sinks into the boy's body.

Pele's light flickers but then grows a little brighter. "Let me rest – let me run with the spirits. I will never be a man now. Let me go." His voice is petulant. This is better.

I try different tactics. "Are you so afraid that you cannot face the truth of life? A true man would face up to death like a warrior, not whimper like a coward."

The light sparks very brightly for a moment. "I am no coward, but what use will I be? How can I be a man without strength to fight and without eyes to see?" The light flickers again and I think it will go out.

I am angry now too. "Do you think being a man is all that's important? What about us women? We toil and provide. We carry you in our bodies and bring you into the world. We nurture you throughout your lives and protect you. Do you not understand that we are the warriors who fight an eternal war against the evil spirits? I have battled all my life, and Malele, your mother, carries on as my strength fails."

The light is constant now. He is listening to me.

"I believe that what has happened is not an accident – indeed, nothing is. You have taken the lynx spirit into your body. It will give you strength and it will give you wisdom. I believe that you have been chosen to be more than a man. Will you accept the fate that the Gods offer?"

He says nothing, but the light does not fade. I hope he understands.

Many suns passed and Pele began to recover but, as he did so, Grimal seemed to fade. He was drawing on her soul's strength. At last one morning, he called for Malele and asked for something to eat. It was the first sign that he had returned to the living. She fed him a nourishing broth but she had to hold the bowl to his mouth. He could see nothing at all.

That night Grimal passed quietly into the light. In the morning, Malele found her withered body curled against Pele's and did not doubt that she had given some of her magic to him. On the same day, the children came running up from the beach with news that the body of a seal had been washed up, and everyone hurried down to strip the skin and cut up the blubber. It would provide a feast to celebrate Grimal's passing. Malele also understood that the seal sister had come to accompany Grimal on her journey.

It would soon be time for the family to return to the south for the winter. Malele needed to make preparations as quickly as possible. Grimal's body was laid on a platform so that the sky spirits could take her flesh. Malele watched in satisfaction as buzzards and eagles swooped and then the kind ravens came to pick what was left. Grimal was slowly giving her life back to the earth. On a day which Malele judged propitious, they collected what remained from the platform. The large bones would travel with them, but they placed the smaller ones, mostly from Grimal's hands and feet, in a shallow grave on the shelf below their shelter. Grimal would protect it until their return. Malele also laid the bones from the seal sister beside Grimal's. The rest of the seal, which hadn't been eaten in the feast, had been preserved for their winter stores.

Throughout all this activity, Pele sat gloomily in the shelter. Tepak gave him cores to chip and he soon learned to feel the right shapes for points and barbs and scrapers. It even seemed that lack of sight made him more sensitive to the properties of the stone. Malele was glad that he had found something useful to do but she knew it wasn't enough. When she felt he was ready, she led him up to a small knoll behind the beach. The sun was setting in the west and he could feel the last warmth from its rays on his face. Malele collected some brushwood and lit a fire, putting on some aromatic herbs. She warmed some nettle tea on the fire and gave him some to drink, adding a drop of what remained of the celandine extract. She did not want him to sleep but she wanted his mind to be open.

As night fell, Malele began to talk. "You were brought up to become a man and perform the duties of a man. That is right, and it is also right that men think they are more important than women. But there is a greater truth and a deeper magic. Who do you think keeps the sun on its course, the sea in its place, and brings the animals close for men to hunt? We women control all the daily aspects of life, but some of us must do more and stand as guardians and intercessors between the underworld and the world of the living. Grimal was one such, and I have taken her place now. I will lead our little family and will join the other wise women of our tribe in choosing the times and the seasons for all our journeys and activities." She let Pele ponder this for a minute.

"You think that your blindness has made you worthless – all you can do now is sit beside the fire and chip away at rocks. I tell you that lack of sight can bring greater vision. Grimal knew this. That is why she gave her spirit to help you live."

Pele thought for a moment. "I… I didn't realise that. She was just an old woman. It was her time to pass away."

"No, Pele." Malele was a little angry. "You don't know what she did for you. She had to go into the spirit world and call you back. That was very dangerous and she did it willingly. You would not have lived otherwise. She summoned the lynx and together they brought you back. But it was too much for her."

Pele felt a strange memory – a voice calling, a warm breath on his cheek, a mighty strength flowing into his body. Yes, he knew now, and the knowledge filled him with both joy and sorrow. "I understand but I don't know why. Grimal was more important than me. Why not just let me die? What have I to offer?"

Malele was angry at his self-pity, but she heard the plea in his voice. "You cannot know why you have been chosen. I don't fully understand myself. Maybe Grimal did. But I know that you have a long and bright future ahead of you. Perhaps you will have some very important function which will serve all the peoples of all the tribes."

She let him absorb her words. "If you agree to it, I can instruct you in the secrets of our knowledge – women's wisdom – and, if you prove worthy, you could one day become the shaman of our people. You could tell them the legends of our clan and the stories of how the animals made the Earth and the sun and the moon. You could learn the great magic which keeps everything turning and in its proper place. It will be a gift, but it will also be very hard. You will have to give up much but will gain a great deal."

Pele's head was bowed so she could not read his feelings. At length he looked up, and she could see that there were tears in his clouded eyes. "I don't think I *have* a choice. It seems that the spirits have chosen my future for me."

During the last few days of their sojourn in the north lands, Malele instructed Pele in the simple magics of plant, animal and water. A little of his sight returned in one eye, although he was never able to see more than vague shadows, light and dark. It helped him to move about and, along with touch and smell, identify the plants for healing. In the evenings, with the family gathered around the campfire, she told the stories of her tribe, the legends of how the world was made. He listened carefully and she knew he was committing it to memory. She left the greater magic for their return to winter camp when she would have the assistance of the other women. This was not a task for herself alone and she had to ask their advice about giving the teaching to a man. This had never been done before. Perhaps it was a mistake but she felt that something great would come of it – it would change life for the tribes forever, though for good or bad she did not know.

On the evening before their departure, Malele led Pele up the little hill again. It was too dark for him to see anything. Again she lit a fire and together they took some of the celandine potion. Pele understood its properties now but he was not afraid. He had changed a great deal in the last moons – and not just physically as his body adapted to the loss of his sight. He was no longer arrogant and impatient, but she could also sense a great strength as his lynx nature grew within him.

As the stars whirled above their heads, she took his hand and together they soared into the sky. The winds whispered their secrets, the night birds welcomed them with song, and soon the Moon Goddess rose above the eastern hills and smiled upon them. Pele felt the fear of small animals scampering in the grass, the chill of the sea where the fishes swam; tasted the tang of blood when the eagle swooped; even heard the creaking of the rocks as they cooled. His body tingled as all life flowed through it. At last the sensations drifted away and he was aware only of a vast, endless peace, a rhythm which pulsed through the sky and beat with his heart.

By morning the fire had died down and Malele and Pele returned to this world. As the sun rose, they joined the others in packing up their belongings and launched the boats into the waves. Malele took a last look at the shelter above the beach. She fancied she could see a dim figure with a smaller animal shape by its side. She nodded in satisfaction and turned to face the ocean's waves.

Pele's sight never returned but in time he did become a great shaman of his tribe. They called him Lynx after the cat skin which he habitually wore and the story of how he had earned it. He was famed throughout the lands where people voyaged, and many men chose to learn the secrets of women's magic.

Chapter Four

Sky Magic
religions of the
sun and moon

In May 2008 an intriguing site was excavated at Braemore on the long strath at the head of Loch Broom. What was originally thought to be a hut circle revealed a paved area of flooring and, in the centre, a small deposit of burnt charcoal and several white quartz stones. A possible interpretation is that this is an offering placed carefully at the base of a ritual cairn.

Atol was the first. He created everything: Heaven above with the smaller gods, the land beneath where the tribes dwell, and the underworld. He gives light and warmth to the Earth. He bestows life and sustains every living thing. He makes the crops grow and ensures fecundity in the animals. Without him there would be no tribes on the land, and all people worship him.

When Atol had finished making everything, he felt alone. So he made Alui to shine in the night and be his mate. But Alui is fickle. She is pale and inconstant and sometimes hides her face, leaving the land in darkness.

The story I am about to tell explains why our tribe chose to worship Alui over Atol, and why we celebrate her seasons over his. Now listen carefully and learn.

In the far-off early days when the tribe first came to this land, Gol was the priest of Atol and Serin was the priestess of Alui. As befits the priests of the greatest gods, Gol and Serin mated in the seasonal rites, but they loved each other well all year round. Gol was a strong and handsome man. Serin was clever but wise enough to keep this hidden.

Now it happened that for several years the crops had failed and the animals had not prospered. Rain had not fallen in the spring and Atol had parched the earth with his heavy beams. Even the hunters could not bring back enough food to nourish the tribe. Old ones died and mothers had not enough milk for their babies. The tribe elders came to Gol and asked him to consult the Gods to find out what to do.

Gol fasted for three days, sitting out under the blazing rays of Atol during the day, and shivering in the cold at night. On the third day he took the sacred mushroom and flew with the Gods. When he returned to Earth he brought his answer back to the tribe. He gathered the elders together and addressed them. Most of the tribe, young and old, mingled round about to listen.

"Atol is angry with us and punishes us for our lack of respect. We have followed his worship and celebrated his festivals but we have no temple here in this new land. He demands that we build a cairn and offer an appropriate sacrifice for its inauguration. Only then will he send the rain and cease from parching the fields with drought."

The assembled people nodded their heads and murmured assent. Only Serin was dubious but she held her tongue till Gol had finished speaking.

"Each man in every family shall give one day in every two to help build the cairn. Only the very old and sick are exempt. We will build it here, at the field of the loch, where Atol can see our effort and smile on our labours. We will build it twice the height of a man and in a circle forty paces across. We shall leave an opening in the centre ready to receive the sacrifice when the cairn is finished."

Serin spoke out now. "And what shall be the sacrifice, Gol?"

"It shall be a maiden, a virgin untouched by man, beloved of the Gods, to be Atol's bride. All families shall bring their daughters here at the next full moon and one shall be chosen."

If any mothers quailed or girls flinched it was not noticed. The men nodded sagely. It was an accepted and acceptable sacrifice.

Gol went on. "The girl shall be queen and reign in the tribe until the cairn is finished. She shall bless the fields and the seed and you shall bring your animals for her to touch. She shall bring new fire to each household, and honour the dead and the dying. But she must be inviolate. If any man molests her, he shall be killed by the threefold death but his body left to the wolves. And a new girl will be chosen. Atol has said."

When the tribal leaders saw that Gol had finished, they led their families back to their homes. Some girls, already promised, would no doubt hurry along their weddings, and others would see to it that they no longer qualified for sacrifice. But virginity was prized in the tribe and an intact bride coveted by prospective husbands. There would still be many maidens for Atol to choose from.

Serin did not tackle Gol as soon as they returned to the family homestead. She chose her moment carefully, waiting till the bustle of the day was over and she and Gol were relaxing by the fireside. She called her daughter, Elif, to sit beside her and began combing her pale golden hair.

"See how your daughter's hair shines white like the moonlight. She will grow up to be a wonderful priestess for Alui, shall she not?"

Gol looked across at his daughter as if seeing her for the first time. "Yes, indeed she shall," he agreed.

"That is," Serin went on, "unless she is chosen by Atol to be his bride." She let the words hang in the air.

"But surely she is not a woman yet? She's too young. Her monthly cycles have not begun."

"Your daughter's cycles began this month and I took her to offer her blood to Alui at full moon. She is dedicated to the Goddess now. You were too busy with your rituals and offerings to notice."

Gol had never thought of his own daughter as a possible sacrifice. "Perhaps she will not be chosen. There are many other suitable girls. And even so, if she is, we must rejoice that our daughter has been so favoured to be the bride of Atol."

Much had to be done in preparation before the building of the cairn could begin. The land had to be levelled and many flat stones of even thickness collected and laid for a base. Sources of good rock had to be found and the men organised into teams to drag it on sledges to the building site.

At noon on the day of the full moon all the people came to the head of the loch to witness the selection of the sacrifice. Gol waited till he judged all were there.

"Atol is pleased to see your obedience and accept your offerings. Our great temple is ready to be built and the time is right to choose his bride. Mothers, bring forth into the circle all your daughters who are fertile and intact. If any girl is not, the man responsible must confess and take her out of the circle. A despoiled bride is not acceptable to Atol and he will punish us grievously."

A few mothers led their daughters into the circle. Some were weeping, some trying bravely to control their feelings. Gol watched with pride as Serin brought Elif into the circle to stand silently beside him.

A few girls waited, looking around the crowd, and, sure enough, one young man came forward and drew one out of the circle. There were some hoots of derision and laughter but Gol silenced them with a stare.

"If any other man knows that these girls are not virgins, he must admit it at once. Atol knows all things and he will punish both the girl and the wrongdoer with the most horrific of afflictions."

A few more men shamefacedly extracted girls. Some would no doubt be berated by the mothers and some, Serin noted with amusement, would have to face the anger of their wives. She was not pleased by this trial of chastity; surely the girls had to go through enough without this public humiliation?

When fifteen girls were left in the circle, Gol pulled a leather bag from his garment and held it up for the crowd.

"In here I shall place fourteen black pebbles and one white. Each girl shall take one from the bag and hide it in her hand until all have chosen. The one who picks the white stone will be Atol's bride."

A silence fell as, one by one, each girl fumbled in the bag. Gol raised his arms to the sun and shouted, "Reveal yourself, Bride of Atol!"

The gasps from the crowd brought his attention back. Elif stood, slim and still, her silver-gold hair gleaming in the sunshine, the white pebble in her open palm. There were sighs of approval from all around. The people saw at once that she was most fit to be chosen by a god: daughter of a priest of Atol, daughter of a priestess of Alui.

If Gol felt anything at all, he gave nothing away, but Serin could see that, beneath his hood, his face was grim. He knelt down before his daughter, acknowledging that now she was sacred, a goddess on Earth and queen of the people until her appointed wedding to the god.

He stood up and addressed the crowd. "Now, the Queen will come to live in the sacred woods to undergo purification and rid herself of all earthly memories. All who seek her blessing must petition me first and I will bring her to your dwellings and your fields. Ten days from now you may bring your animals here and she will touch them all with her fruitfulness. Then we will make the new fire and bring it to your hearths. We are beginning anew, and Atol will take pleasure in our devoted preparations."

Gol's confidence was now fully restored and Serin could see that he had not only accepted his daughter's sacrifice, but was intent on seeing it to its ultimate conclusion. For the moment there was nothing she could do.

It was the responsibility of Serin and her acolytes to attend to Elif and administer the purification rites. First they built a leafy shelter in the woods where she would live hidden from the rest of the community. They took her to the great gorge where waters funnelled through precipitous walls in a dark, foaming torrent, a place sacred to the Gods of the Underworld. There, in a deep pool at the base, they stripped off her clothes and scrubbed her body with lathery soapwort and washed her hair with boiled camomile flowers till it gleamed like the sun itself. They held her under the water till all the foam was rinsed away and she rose, spluttering and gasping but clean and pure for her new life. She was dressed in a tunic of white calf's leather which had been washed and beaten till it was soft as ducks' down. Finally they placed a fine, twisted gold torc around her neck and silver bracelets on her wrists and ankles.

Serin stroked and tended her daughter's body with all the love of a mother but, when the transformation was complete, she saw Elif as the goddess she would become: beautiful, remote, palely shining. She banished such reflections from her mind. She would not allow her daughter to pay with her life for the salvation of the tribe; she would find another solution. She decided that, as soon as she could, she would seek answers of her own in the mountains. She needed to re-establish the link with her goddess.

For the next few days, as Gol had specified, families sought the help of the Queen to bring fertility to their homes and crops. He would bring her, dressed in her fine clothes and shining bangles, to each household, where he would direct the rituals. Sometimes she had to bathe the bellies of pregnant women in pure stream water. Sometimes she had to place her fingers on the heads of cows or sheep or pigs. She even had to bless the wooden bowls where milk and butter were kept to ensure that they would never be empty. As death is also an important part of life, in some huts she had to oversee the passing of an elderly member of the family, or those stricken with illness. Strangely, unless the person was very young, Elif found these duties gently rewarding. She could feel a strength, a peaceful comfort, passing from her hands into the bodies of the departing. They were not leaving this Earth, but moving on to another life, just as the seed must be buried beneath the soil to grow into another plant. For herself, she thought little about her fate; she had accepted it.

After ten days Gol had organised the blessing of the tribe's animals. From all around, the people came with their herds of cattle, sheep, goats and pigs. They brought their servant animals, the horses and dogs, as well, because it was so important to have the protection of the Gods. You can imagine the chaos.

They had constructed enclosures and pens but there were far too many beasts to fit into them and, in any case, most people wanted to keep their animals to themselves. Sheep escaped and blundered about, bleating for their lambs. Herd dogs, tongues lolling, raced around their flocks, desperately trying to keep them together. Men shouted and whacked their cattle with sticks. Fights broke out between animals and people, and babies wailed, terrified by the noise and bustle. Clouds of choking dust rose from the tired earth. The smell of ordure and frightened creatures was overpowering.

Gol managed to impose some kind of order. He needed silence and dutiful respect while he made the sacred need-fire. He had done this many times before but it required the reverence of a magical rite. He had collected dry twigs and flakes of tinder mushroom in little piles, and glowered around the watching people till a measure of peace descended. He took up the stringed bow and began to work it backwards and forwards furiously, so that the stick, wound in the middle, twirled rapidly in its socket. Within minutes curls of smoke began to rise and sparks of charred wood fell on the tinder. He blew on the smoking bundle and placed it among the dry wood. A collective gasp of wonder arose from his audience as the wood took light. Well satisfied with his performance, he let others light the bonfires and set about organising the next part of the ceremony.

Families were instructed to drive their flocks to the circle where the Queen sat on a throne of green boughs decorated with flowers and leaves. As each animal passed before her, she held a twig of hazel over its head. Perhaps the creatures understood the significance of the ceremony, as they seemed to quieten and walk sedately beneath the wand. Then the animals were driven between the two bonfires which had been lit from the new fire. Of course, it took some time to complete the blessing, but at last it was finished and the people set off for home, cherishing baskets of glowing coals which they would use to relight their fires.

Serin was growing increasingly angry with Gol. It seemed that he was relishing his control of the ceremonies and was content to accept his daughter's fate. If she was to save her daughter, she had to do it herself. She announced that she was going into the mountains to seek wisdom and pray to the Gods.

Within a day's walk to the north, great silver-capped mountains raised their heads to the skies. They were sacred to the moon and represented a special place of retreat for those dedicated to the worship of Alui. Serin herself had lived there during her initiation and training and she returned periodically to regenerate her bond with the Goddess. Today she was hoping to find one special person, Adkara, the oldest priestess of Alui, who, long ago, had retreated into the isolation of these mountains to seek the peace of true knowledge. Serin was not sure where she would find her or if she was still alive.

On the first evening she trekked to the top of the very highest mountain. The weather was warm and very clear, the stars gleaming so brightly that you could reach out your hand to touch them. There was no moon that night but the stars gave enough light to make out the rolling peaks, silver waves on a velvet-black ocean. Serin sat motionless throughout the night, trying to empty her mind of wayward thoughts and her heart of recrimination. She must be at peace to open her mind to the Gods. When the first rays of the sun sparked fire in the east, she made her way down the mountain to search in the valleys below.

She found Adkara in a steep-sided glen where she had made herself a tiny shelter of stones beside a tumbling burn. She was sitting perfectly still beside the stream, listening to the pebbles chattering and the breeze whispering about her, but she turned her sightless eyes to Serin as she approached. Serin was shocked to see that her eyes were milky-white, turned moonstruck from so many nights spent gazing into the face of her goddess. She came forward to press her forehead to the gnarled skin of Adkara's hand.

"So it is Serin who comes to see me in her time of need." Adkara's voice was still strong and her mind astute. "My eyes can only see vague shapes but I saw you in my vision from far away. Come, share some milk and cheese with me. It is all I have until someone brings an offering from the valley. Then you can tell me what troubles you."

The two women ate lightly. Adkara ate hardly anything these days and Serin was preparing to fast before her soul-search. When they had finished Serin told Adkara about Gol's edict.

"Is it wrong of me to doubt the truth of his inspiration?" she asked. "You taught me to believe that the Gods control the land and its seasons and there is little we can do to influence these apart from worshipping and following the ceremonies. Or am I just being selfish as a mother keen to protect her child? Perhaps Atol *does* require my daughter's blood to bring life to our crops. I have come to seek enlightenment and perhaps a solution which satisfies all."

Adkara thought for some time. "I do not know the answer. You must find the truth for yourself, but I will also seek in my mind and my memories. There may be some way we can give Gol what he wants and pacify the Gods as well."

For the next few days Serin stayed with Adkara, fasting and praying and sitting out in the hills at night. No answer presented itself but the rhythm of her life slowed and she came to a measure of peace. On the last evening she led Adkara to the top of the silver mountain and together they watched all night long as Alui made her stately progress over the heavens and dipped below the southern horizon.

Although Adkara was very old and her eyes were blanched with moonshine, she could see more than most people and understood the secrets of the heavens. In the morning as Serin prepared to leave, she instructed her to sit before her and listen.

"I have thought long and deeply and prayed for Alui to give me guidance. She is angry with Atol for desiring one of her chosen priestesses and she has told me a way to save your daughter from her fate. But it depends on the will of Alui and you must follow my instructions exactly or you may be in danger yourself."

Adkara explained her plan in detail and Serin set off for home, memorising and rehearsing all that she had to do.

Work on the cairn was proceeding rapidly. A circular kerb of stones had been erected and the centre was being filled with loose rocks, leaving a lined chamber in the middle ready to receive the sacrifice. Serin suggested to Gol that they should aim for completion of the cairn in six months and perform the sacrifice in the darkness of the moon. Perhaps Alui would not wish to watch the ceremony. Gol agreed readily, thinking that Serin had obtained the approval of her goddess.

The months passed quickly. Elif continued to minister to the people, visiting the sick, walking the fields where the new crops had been sown. At last the chosen day arrived. Serin arose at dawn and took her helpers to tend to Elif. As they washed and anointed her and dressed her in her bridal robes, Serin strove to calm her agitation. So much depended on her performance today; so many little things could go wrong. Adkara had been sure of her plan but what if she had made a mistake? She was old and blind and maybe her mind had been turned by the moon into spiders' webs. But there was nothing else to do. Serin sighed and made a last beseeching prayer to Alui to guide her through today's ritual.

All the people had gathered at the cairn. Some had set out before dawn in order to arrive by the appointed time. For once they were solemn and silent, respecting the enormity of what they were about to witness. This was the holiest of rites, practised since the beginning of time to ensure the fertility of crops and animals and even the people themselves. Nothing must interfere with the procedure; no evil omen must occur; no untoward behaviour upset the Gods.

Gol was waiting silently by the sacrificial bonfire. Serin and her women led Elif out of the woods through the throngs of people, who bowed before her.

Serin spoke. "I bring you a daughter of the moon, untouched and eager to be the bride of Atol."

Gol accepted her words with a nod. As before, he instructed everyone to pass before Elif as she held the hazel wand over their heads.

Serin's anxiety grew. She had followed her instructions carefully and knew the day was right and the weather propitious, but Adkara had not been sure of the exact time. Serin had to find a reason to delay the rites. She searched the lines of men and women and spied a woman with a raspberry birthmark on her face. She stepped forward and pointed. "This woman is not acceptable for the blessing. She has displeased the Gods and is marked with their anger. She shall not pass below the wand."

There was consternation and whispers of fear all around and Gol was ready to refuse, but Serin forestalled him. "You cannot allow anyone unworthy to approach the Goddess. Their evil may be transferred to her and render her unacceptable. All our efforts will have been in vain. If you wish, I will withdraw all who may taint the purity of the maiden." She bowed her head to his sagacity.

Gol was furious at the interruption but he could not challenge her words without provoking the people's anger. The sacrifice must be kept pure. "Very well," he conceded. "You may examine everyone for imperfections and remove them from the blessing. But don't take too long about it," he hissed from the corner of his mouth.

Serin was satisfied. Here she picked out a man with a limp; there she indicated a child with a pockmarked face. Privately she asked her goddess for forgiveness in condemning these people to ridicule and possible hatred. She would do her best to make it up to them in the future.

So the line moved haltingly and with some resentful or fearful glances in Serin's direction. Had she done enough? She glanced fleetingly at the sky and sighed with relief. It had begun.

It was actually some time before anyone else noticed, but suddenly there was a shriek. "The sun, look at the sun – something is eating the sun!" Everyone turned to look upwards. Sure enough, by now, a sizeable bite had been taken out of the sun.

Serin mouthed a silent prayer to Alui and whispered thanks to Adkara. Her predictions had been accurate and now Serin must follow her instructions exactly; perfect timing was of the essence. She stepped forward and raised her willow wand, waiting for silence and attention.

"The ceremony must cease. This is a message from the Gods. Alui is angry. I feared that she would not merely hide her face from this desecration of one of her chosen. Perhaps she is also jealous that Atol seeks a new wife to share his bed. She is attacking Atol, and will eat him up if we do not stop this sacrilege."

Gol was speechless, completely confused. Nothing like this had ever happened before and, just for a moment, he doubted his own convictions. But he was priest of the sun, the most powerful God of the Sky. "No!" He gathered his wits. "Alui is a great goddess, but she is the wife of Atol and must defer to his wishes. He is stronger and will not allow her to triumph. We will light the sacrificial fire." He stood with legs wide apart and staff raised, almost as if to strike Serin, defying her to oppose him again.

Serin had not waited and prepared for this day to yield now at the crucial moment. She let her rage subside, her mind calm, and allowed the inspiration of her goddess to fill her with power. "Look around you. The light of Atol is fading. His reign is coming to an end. Look how the colours weaken; even the birds are singing their evening song. They are saying their last prayers to God before the eternal night which is to come."

There was total silence now in the crowd, all gazing in awe as the darkness grew. A lone blackbird in a nearby tree filled the air with piping notes.

Once more Gol strove to gain the upper hand. "Let us defy the darkness. We will light the fire and drive Alui back to her appointed place. I will make the need-fire."

Gol hurriedly assembled the bow and tinder. For once he felt insignificant as he knelt to begin the fire-making. This was magic, a magic which he had accomplished many times before, but, try as he might, he could not get the sparks to fly. Had someone tampered with the wood, dampening it? He instructed his men to bring another piece but it, too, would not raise a spark. Serin stood calmly by. Perhaps she was putting a curse on the wood?

At last she spoke. "See how Alui prevents the need-fire. She will not allow her daughter to be burned. Do not anger her more or she will kill Atol and bring everlasting night over this land. Do you think we can survive when light and warmth are absent? Not only will our crops die, but our animals and ourselves too."

Gol tossed the bow and wood away, but he was not defeated. "It is not necessary to light the fire with need-fire. Bring me a flint. It is holy enough for our purposes."

By now he was so incensed that his hands were shaking and even the flint would not spark effectively. Many people in the crowd were muttering. It seemed their priest was weak before the strength of the Goddess. At last, however, he raised a flame and flung the branch into the waiting pyre, which took light at once, crackling satisfactorily. The flames did not seem bright enough to dispel the gathering darkness.

Serin glanced at the sun. It was very nearly obscured. "Look at Atol. See how Alui has nearly destroyed him. You have never before known the power of Alui; she is mightier than Atol. Do you wish your foolish actions to bring about the death of your god?"

The silence of the crowd was broken by cries and prayers.

Then suddenly Serin shouted above the noise. "Look to the west. See – the shadow of death approaches. It is the end of our god; it is the end of our world."

As the people turned to the west, a great rolling shadow came towards them at enormous speed, like a huge dust storm with raven-black wings. It was indeed the coming of death itself. Behind it, stars peered shyly out of the gloom.

Serin knew her moment. "Now look at Atol. Serin has killed him. See him flame into oblivion."

As one, all the people stared upwards. The sun had completely disappeared but, from behind the dark disc which covered him, a bright aura of light radiated out in a last gasp of the expiring god.

Gol flung himself to the ground, wailing. Serin knew she had only a few minutes to restore order and complete her task. She stooped over Gol and pulled him to his knees.

"You may stop this now. Alui is not unforgiving. She will restore your god and give you back your light but you must cease this sacrifice; you must give her back her daughter. Now, before it is too late."

The screams began to subside and became a voice, one voice which repeated itself in many mouths. "Stop, stop, stop the sacrifice!"

Gol, looking up at Serin, pleaded, "Stop Alui – we cannot resist her; restore our god before she kills us too!"

Serin looked calmly around. Then she pointed to the sky. "Yes, Alui relents. See – she moves away and is bringing her husband back to life. There is a jewel in the sky which signifies her promise to us. She will not let Atol die."

The dark disc in the sky now bore a single star which grew slowly until the shape of the sun could be discerned again.

"But beware," Serin went on. "Alui will wait until she sees your intentions are honest before she releases her grip on Atol. You must extinguish the fire and free the maiden. There shall be no living sacrifices here today."

Dejectedly, Gol directed the dousing of the flames. He did not understand what had happened, but he had been defeated. His god was not the greatest god of all.

Serin relished her moment of triumph but she chose conciliation. "Alui does not object to the cairn, only the sacrifice. Why not continue the ceremony and place a gift from Alui in the centre of the cairn?" She stretched out her hand to Gol. "Show the people that, as Alui and Atol can be reconciled, so can we."

Gol glanced sideways at her. "Very well," he told her. "We will do as you suggest. What gift does Alui bring as a peace offering to her husband?"

Serin, although doubting the success of her plans, had prepared for this moment. She would use some magic of her own. She instructed one of her priestesses to bring forward a bag made of fine, supple leather tied to a long stick. "Behold the light of the moon on Earth," she cried, swinging the bundle on its stick around her head. Gleams and rays sparkled from the bag, lighting up the awestruck faces. When Serin judged that she had made a sufficient impression, she opened the bag and tipped several clear quartz crystals onto the ground. "These are Alui's sacred stones. They hold but a fraction of her light but they are dear to her. You may sacrifice them at the centre of your cairn."

Gol was satisfied and the murmurs of the people signified approval. A small fire was lit in the centre of the cairn and Gol reverently laid the moonstones in it. When the fire had burned down, a large sealing block was placed on the top and the hole in the mound filled up.

Now, perhaps everything did not happen exactly as I have told you. The story comes from the mists of time and has been passed down to me through many generations. Perhaps there was no Serin, and no man called Gol. If there was, do you think they became reconciled?

What is certain is that long ago our tribe chose to worship Alui. No, we did not forget Atol; indeed we gather at his cairn each year to seek his blessing. But we recognise the power of Alui and respect her moods. We know that she can extinguish the sun if she chooses and she may bring eternal darkness to the land if we ignore her wishes. So, my children, bring forward your offerings and remember never to underestimate the wrath of a slighted woman and the power of a mother's love.

Chapter Five

Axe

new technology

In 1998, local artist James Hawkins found a copper axe in his garden in Rhue. It is conjectured that the axe had been placed as an offering on a grave.

Fergal squinted against the morning sun to the pass at the head of the loch, where winter snow still dusted the high mountains. More traders would be coming that way today. Although most came by sea as usual, braving the perilous waters at this time of year, an increasing number took the easier land routes from the east and south. Of course, Fergal could see no sign of movement at that distance, although his eyes were as good as ever at spotting a deer antler on the skyline or the flash of leaping fish on the loch. It was at close work that his eyes failed him; tying line to fishing hooks, or carving intricate designs on bone needles or combs. Despite being only a few summers younger than him, Moura had no problem sewing and weaving by dim lamplight in the long, dark winter evenings.

Gloomily, Fergal pondered how long he would have left. He had led the People of the Loch for nigh on thirty summers and there must be a few who felt it was time for a younger, fitter man to take his place. Perhaps that Dunal, who was always strutting about showing off his muscles to the giggling girls! But Fergal had no worries there; he was still strong enough to drag a full deer carcass from the hill and his mind was as acute and perspicacious as ever.

"Come on, man! What are you doing standing there dreaming when there's work to be done?" Moura's voice recalled him from his reverie.

She had been a good wife to him, standing by him through the hard winters and times of privation, and accepting stoically the inevitable deaths of three of the eight children she had borne him. Now, his second son, Matu, would make a fine leader; not so strong and handsome as Darak, his firstborn, but wily and perceptive like his father. However, it was not the tribe's way to pass on the leadership to sons; leaders were chosen according to their merits and Matu would have to prove himself in competition with other contenders.

Reluctantly, Fergal pulled himself away from his meditations and turned back to the house yard where the whole family was engaged in exciting preparations for the trip to the Mart, loading baskets for everyone, right down to the youngest grandchild, to carry. At the end of winter, they had little enough produce to trade but what they had would be enough to purchase stock and gear and maybe even a few luxuries and exotic trinkets from faraway lands. Fergal hoped for a fine young breeding sow as he had developed a taste for salted bacon to supplement the rather dreary diet of fish and oat porridge that was their usual winter fare.

Soon everything was ready and the whole caboodle of children, drove animals and people, headed by the big workhorse dragging a fully laden sledge, set off to the shore. A motley assortment of shelters had already been set up by the first arrivals. Everyone from the lochside, and from other settlements further away, would be coming here today. It was not just an opportunity to trade goods and gawp in fascination at the latest inventions of the metalworkers and craftsmen, but also a chance to celebrate with old acquaintances and meet new ones. Many a marriage would be precipitated by encounters occurring over the next few days. For the children, it was a time of freedom as their elders were usually too busy, or drunk, to pay them much attention. So they roamed the makeshift camp, begging for tasty honey breads from the bakers, peering shyly at the jugglers and, when night fell, falling asleep with thumbs in mouths, cosy around the blazing fires, while the bards told their stories of brave heroes in the dim ages long ago or sang wistful melodies of lost islands in the far west.

As soon as the family arrived and set up their camp, the youngsters dispersed eagerly to find their own friends and engage in their own pursuits. Fergal helped Moura lay out the beautiful garments which she had spent so much of her time preparing for this Mart, before he set off to spy out what new tools and equipment were available and to sneer at the puny livestock which his neighbours had to offer. As leader, Fergal was by far the richest man in the area and had use of all the finest land for grazing, so it was only right that his animals would be better than the rest.

However, this was to be the beginning of a day of severe disappointments. A trading drover from far to the south had brought in a flock of strange new sheep, their wool soft and deep when Fergal plunged his fingers into their coats. They likely would never thrive in the cold, wet weather up here. But they were attracting a great deal of attention from the canny farmers, who would stick by the old ways and animals, but were always ready to speculate on what could be a very lucrative innovation. Fergal would try a few of these sheep himself if he could afford the trading price. To top this, a potter, newly arrived from the sea road, displayed some fine light-coloured pots decorated with interesting patterns. No one would look at Fergal's stock of plain but functional pots when compared to these. However, the greatest flurry of excitement surrounded one of the metalworkers' stalls. This year, for the first time, he had brought the strange new metal, which was reputed to be better, stronger and sharper than bronze. A single iron axe head was laid, for show not sale, on a sheep's skin. Fergal thought it looked strong and functional enough but did not have the fine sheen and lustre of the bronze and copper implements still on offer beside it.

It was as Fergal made his way back despondently to the family camp that he noticed the girl. A trader, whose dark skin and strange clothes revealed his origins in the far south over the sea, had set up his camp somewhat apart from the others. It was never the custom for the clan to take and keep slaves, but nowadays, traders like this one could make a good profit from strong women and children. Several were confined in a pen, morose and dirty like the other trade animals, but the girl stood alone, tied by the wrist to a stake at the side of the pen. It was not just the bright black of her hair and the lithesome curves of her body, only partially disguised by her loose-fitting dress, which caught Fergal's attention. Her eyes, black and smouldering with some emotion between hate and passion, pierced his heart like arrows of fire. Almost guiltily, Fergal turned away and hurried back to his camp.

All that day, while he bartered and haggled a good price for his goods, Fergal recalled the girl's eyes. At the end of the day, when most trading had been finished and the encampment was turning into a raucous assemblage of bleating animals and merrymaking people, Fergal found his feet leading him back to the dark trader's camp. The girl was not to be seen; all the slaves had been huddled away in tents for the night.

For the next few days, he took every opportunity to pass by, feigning lack of interest and averting his eyes whenever the trader looked his way. However, the trader knew his business very well and noticed that the tribe leader passed by just a little too often for chance. He made sure to show off the girl, as if to other customers, to her best advantage.

The slaves would be auctioned off on the last day of the Mart. Fergal made some excuse to Moura and made his way to watch the bidding. Most of the other slaves had been sold already. Generally they would be treated well and accepted as working members into the family groups. The girl was kept till last. For a considerable time it looked as if no one was brave or rich enough to put in a bid. Fergal scoffed as Earn, the chief from the loch over the water, opened the bidding with five sacks of barley. She was worth a great deal more than that and, anyway, what would Earn do with a fearsome young wife, when he could not even control his brood of wayward daughters? For some time, the bidding proceeded as comic entertainment for the gathering crowd, as one blustering farmer after another made ludicrous offers.

"Thirty bags of stones!"

"My old, blind cow!"

"I'd give you my old, blind mother, if she wasn't too decrepit to get down the hill!"

Without showing the least sign of impatience, the trader waited for the hilarity to subside. He had spotted Fergal in the crowd, and also a few others he reckoned would have more serious offers.

At last, a big man from the north put in a sensible bid of twenty bullock carcasses. There would never be many people who could enter the bidding at that level but a man from the islands, who owned five boats and made a good living from fishing, joined the competition and, for a while, the bidding swung between them. Open-mouthed spectators nodded from one to another as they bid amounts that most farmers would never see in their entire lives. Soon it seemed that the island man could go no further, and a slow smile of satisfaction spread over his opponent's face.

It was then that something came over Fergal. It was as if all his despondency in the last few days had erupted inside him.

"I give my bronze axe!" he shouted.

It said much for the People of the Loch that not one person gasped in horror. Each one of them knew what the axe meant and how valuable, beyond price, it was. The axe had been given to Fergal on his promotion to leadership and was the symbol of his power. It embodied the traits of a good chief – strength, sharpness and efficiency – and had been passed down from leader to leader through uncountable generations.

Fergal stood his ground, confident that no one could beat that. What had come over him he would never know, but he would not withdraw his offer. But all the Gods were against him that day.

"I give this fine iron axe and, as everyone knows, it can cut copper to pieces." The man who spoke from the back of the crowd was an outlander, obviously one of the new metalworkers or traders from the south.

Fergal could do nothing. As the bidding closed, he slunk away, suddenly overcome with a greater tiredness and defeat than he had ever felt before. The crowd parted silently to let him go.

That evening he avoided his family and Moura. She had heard of the incident, of course, and was not talking to him. He sought solace with a drunken group of farmers who had done well at the Mart and were busily drinking away all their profits. By the time he staggered away to make his lonely way up the hill, the family had packed up all the gear and gone home.

As he came out of the encampment he passed by the tent of the outlander and saw him stroking the hair of the dark slave. The guilt and humiliation in Fergal's heart, enflamed by the strong beer, blew all sense out of his head. He marched boldly into the circle of firelight.

"I fight you for the woman," he blurted out. The man was small and finely built. Fergal would have no trouble overcoming him. Such challenges were not uncommon in settling disputes and seldom ended in death or major injury. The fight ended when one of the contestants was too weak or wounded to continue.

Fergal, however, had underestimated this man. The stranger was no metalworker but a trained fighter, an auxiliary, who would sell his skills to any petty chief who wanted to exert his power over his neighbours. The fight was over in minutes, the stranger twisting and wrestling Fergal's face into the dirt. That should have been enough, but Fergal's passion and guilt were too much. He drew his axe from his belt and, staggering up, lofted it above the stranger's head. The man had turned away but saw the flash of metal in the corner of his eye. Instinct and experience made him grasp his own iron axe, and, as Fergal charged towards him, he swung it into his belly. Fergal crumpled to the ground, felled at one blow like a birch sapling.

Over the days when Moura lovingly tended her failing husband, poison entered Fergal's body and poisonous thoughts weakened his will to live.

On an early summer morning, when the song of skylarks trickled like a mountain stream and filled all the air with sparkle, the priests came to lay Fergal in his final resting place overlooking the loch. They dressed his body in his finest clothes and laid a large slab of rock over the cist so that none would disturb his last sleep. When everyone had gone home and the sun was dipping to the islands, Moura returned to the grave and laid his axe on the slab. There was no need of it now. Bronze would give way to iron and a new leader would care for the People of the Loch.

Chapter Six

The Broch Builder

tall towers and the Romans

The south side of Lochbroom boasts two examples of a type of building unique to Scotland: a circular, drystone tower, but it is disputed whether either of these can be called a broch. The earliest, at Rhiroy, although not a complete circle, shows evidence of upper storeys and hollow walls. The other, Dun Lagaidh, built on the ruins of an earlier vitrified fort, also displays some of the characteristic features of the broch. It is of circular, drystone construction, with a guard cell protecting the entrance passage and a staircase built into the wall. It was probably never very tall. Who was responsible for building these structures, and why, is still a matter of debate.

I suppose it all comes from inexperience. My mother died when I was born and I was brought up in an almost exclusively male household. I must have had a wet nurse and our family was rich enough to have had one or two female slaves, but I have no memory of soft arms about me and the comfort of feminine caresses. Not that I was aware of my lack; I was happy enough playing with older boys and following my father as he went about his work. As soon as I was old enough he took me with him even when he was engaged in long-term projects in further communities. I had to learn the trade. But you can see why I had little understanding of women and looked on them as fabulous goddesses quite beyond my humble ambition. All that goes a long way to explaining the events of my life, but not entirely. Fate dealt me a mixed fortune of tragedy and joy but, on the whole, I'd say my life has been happy. If you have work that is enjoyable and rewarding it'll take your mind off everyday troubles.

My family came from an island in the south but, as I said, my father travelled about so much that I never looked on any place as home. With the nature of the building work, we stayed in each community for a long time: long enough to make acquaintances but not enough to make friends. I never had a chance to feel settled before we were up and on the move again. No, I didn't mind that really; I was too busy helping my father and learning the skills of a master builder like him. You, Glikki, you of all people can understand that. You have to watch and listen and practise and, when you make a mistake, you have to be humble enough to admit it and then strong enough to try again. It takes years of dedication, and even then, if you don't have the natural talent, you'll only make a mediocre stonesmith.

My father went on working till he was quite an old man. In fact he only gave up when his gnarled fingers could no longer hold an axe. By this time I was old enough and fully experienced so I could take on the trade, but for many years he used to come and oversee the projects. I don't think he believed I would ever achieve his expertise. He died at work, you know; just keeled over while measuring a length of wood. We buried him there beside the building. I'll bet his ghost came to haunt the new owners, shouting at the slaves and berating the apprentices for idleness.

I went on with the work as before, moving around the country to the very far northerly islands or sometimes to the south, wherever there were chiefs keen enough to display their status and wealth with grandiose towers. Yes, you could say I am cynical about it: you're bound to get that way when you see poverty and death ignored for the sake of pointless demonstrations of power. But it was my job to supply the symbols of that power and, to be fair, there were positive aspects of the work itself: skilled craftsmen were employed; youngsters like yourself learned the secrets of the trade.

The commission on the loch was quite a modest one. Big towers were going out of fashion by then and my client, while wishing to emphasise his position as chieftain, was satisfied with a smaller but still imposing structure. So I came here in the summer of my thirty-ninth year. I'm sorry I don't remember you then; you were only a little boy. Well, you may have been ten but you were too young to help with the heavy work and I had other things on my mind.

Of course I noticed Brana. No man could miss her! I don't think you would call her beautiful in a conventional sense but she was striking, with an aura of sensuality which excited men and antagonised women. She was tall, taller than me but strongly built. Her hair was black, with the dark and sheen of a raven's wing (I think that's why she got her name), and her eyes blue; blue like the sea on a calm day. She was promised to the son of a neighbouring chieftain. He was everything I am not. He was tall, handsome, boastful of his prowess in battle, and Brana adored him. I don't think he was very bright but women aren't much interested in intelligence in their men. She paid me no attention at all. Not then, anyway.

So I got on with my work. When Brokko, the chief, had approved my plans, we chose our site on the top of a rocky knoll on the south side of the sea loch. The place had been fortified before by Brokko's ancestors and there were considerable ruins spread about the west end of the hillock. The rubble was a useful source of stone for our building but required clearing and flattening to make the foundations for our tower. Although it was to be a modest building, as I said before, with low walls and no upper storey, I took pride in putting all the skill of my years of training into the construction.

I well remember the Day of Sacrifice. All the people of the loch were there, dressed in their finest clothes, and all the artisans assembled to begin the building work. Brana was proud and utterly glorious, celebrating this manifestation of her father's power. The priests came up from the shore with the sacrifice, whose terrified bellowing nearly drowned out their chants and the mournful cry of the sacred horns. But the death was good and the blood seeped into the foundation stones cementing the building firmly to the life of the earth. As daughter of the chief, Brana had been chosen to lay out the true circle, and I helped her walk the cord round the centre peg. I doubt if she was aware of my nervous guidance and the reasons for my shaky hand. We celebrated that night with a great feast on the shore beside the loch, and the lights from the bonfires gleamed redly on the black waters and the sparks mingled with the stars. There was much to eat and drink and, I've no doubt, many couples sanctified the dark shadows with their own festivities.

After the inauguration ceremony we set to the building work with enthusiasm and it proceeded quickly. There was such a quantity of good building stone in the ruined fort that we didn't need to mine it from quarries elsewhere. I was much impressed by the old stronghold: its sheer scale was incredible. It must have taken many people many years to construct, bringing suitable stone from local quarries and erecting the huge walls. I had to admire the skill and audaciousness of those architects so long ago. Maybe they were sorcerers and magicked those stones into place. I don't know how they managed it otherwise. But, like all things, it came to an end and someone had destroyed the walls with a fire so severe it fused some of the rocks together. I often wonder who did that and why. Anyway, I often sent a prayer to the souls of those long-dead builders for supplying me with such ready quantities of material.

This was such a minor project that I had not brought my usual small team of stonemasons and woodworkers with me, but we were able to find men with sufficient skills locally. The chief expected service from his people in the form of labour so we had no shortage of strong, if reluctant, farmers for the main workforce. By the end of the first season we had most of the solid wall completed to head height, with the entrance passage, guard cell and passage for the stairs begun. I remained here over the winter and took advantage of any good spells of weather to continue the work. The Gods were kind to us in the following summer, so we were able to finish the wallhead to the upper walkway and stone parapet. Brokko called in his people before the autumn harvest took them back to their fields and in no time at all we had the roof in place and thatched. The whole tower was finished and we called for the blessing of the Gods with the final sacrifice.

I should have left then, but I had no further commissions and, really, nowhere else to go. And by now the Gods had conspired to tie me here forever.

As I told you, Brana's betrothed, Senako, was one of those young men who felt the need to display his prowess in battle or the hunt. Brana was never more delighted than when he came visiting with spoils of the chase, or bloody scars inflicted by fearsome boar tusks or irate neighbours. She would sit entranced, her eyes dazzling, while he recounted how he had insulted this or that chief, or punished a grovelling peasant for his lowliness by slaughtering his sheep. There never seemed to me to be much bravery in that. But one day he overreached in his stupidity and led a band of equally arrogant youths in an attack on a wily local chief. He got himself killed for his efforts.

Brana was distraught. They had been due to marry that autumn and she was now without her betrothed; her beloved. After days of tears and wailing she retreated into herself, silent and withdrawn, pale and waning like the dying moon. Nothing consoled her; she would talk to no one.

Except me.

To this day I do not know why she chose me as a confidant, although I thank the Gods for it. Maybe she felt I was so quiet and insignificant that she could trust me. Maybe she sensed my sympathy and could come to me without fear of dismissal. At the end of the day, when the work was done, she would come and sit beside me and whisper all her fears and sorrows.

I can't say I particularly cherished her fulsome praise of Senako's bravery and beauty, but I tried to give her consolation by listening and nodding my head where necessary. She felt gratified and, I think, began to see in me someone more than a mere manual labourer. I don't flatter myself that she ever saw me as desirable but I was a worthy enough match. I am the master of my guild, from a family of guild masters. Brokko certainly saw it that way when I went to him to ask for her hand and, if he felt disappointed in her choice, he was diplomatic enough to show no trace of it.

We were married six days later.

Now, now, Glikki, my boy, I am not about to divulge the intimate details of my married life. Of course I had had women before, but not the kind whose face you'd remember in the morning. So making love to the woman I loved, who was also the most beautiful woman in the world, was quite beyond anything I had ever experienced. I wish you just as much joy in your marriage. She was sweet and soft and gentle, and so considerate of my advancing years that she did not press me to fulfil my husbandly duties as much as might be expected of a younger man. But I think I acquitted myself in that respect to everyone's satisfaction. Years of arduous work build up strength and stamina. In fact I performed so well that, before the Samhain festival, Brana announced that she would give birth to our first child in the spring.

We settled into a most comfortable life. I had built a good home for us by refurbishing the ruins of an old tower nearby. Brokko had had it demolished when he took over as chieftain of the loch. No doubt he couldn't stomach the symbol of a previous chief so near to his own. It had once been a beautiful, well-constructed building of considerable height. I often wondered if one of my own ancestors had built it long ago. So it still retained some of its best features, although the upper storey had gone and the raised wooden floor had been taken out. Since some of the structure was unsafe, I demolished a section of wall and the lintels of the entrance passage rather than rebuild them. This provided a good, strong base wall for the new roof and furnished a very pleasant house for us; nothing too grand to compete with Brokko's edifice. And so began the happiest time of my life.

As befitted her rank, Brana had little to do with housekeeping, but we kept servants enough for that. We spent our time with necessary tasks and leisure pursuits. I had never had time for anything but work in the past, so I suppose this was my first holiday. I can't say I particularly enjoyed the drinking and carousing with Brana's young friends, but I did love the evenings spent with visiting singers and bards who recounted tales of heroes of old and the machinations of the Gods. I didn't care for our hunting expeditions, either: I've never understood the pleasure in watching life drain away from a guileless creature. Brana loved it. She would tramp for miles over the hills, searching for deer, and when the quarry was located, it was often she who delivered the final spear thrust. She particularly adored the boar hunt. I think she admired the bravery and ferocity of the animal. I can still see her, standing still and slender in the sheltering trees, while the beaters forced the prey towards us. Her eyes would gleam with bright fire and the filtering light made blue-green colours in her hair. It was joy in itself to look at her. But she soon became too great with child to indulge in the hunt and had to confine herself to home. She didn't take kindly to that.

I worried about the unborn child, of course. I'd never had much experience with pregnancy and childbirth. So I became utterly frantic when Brana went into labour very early. I expected the child to be far too unformed to survive, and I felt it might endanger Brana as well.

But my fears were unfounded. The labour went quickly and without difficulties and the midwife was able to hand me a perfectly well-formed, healthy son, whose puckered face and bellowing lungs testified to a strong character and lusty vitality. I was, of course, completely besotted, so it was maybe just as well that Brana insisted he stay with his wet nurse nearby until he was old enough to be weaned. I saw him every day, and took no greater pleasure in life than in cradling him on my knee. What a grasp he had in his tiny fingers! I was sure then that he would make a fine builder to follow me; maybe even as great as his grandfather.

Ah, beware, Glikki, of tempting fate; the Gods take pernicious delight in upsetting one's plans.

I was not so engrossed with my new family life that I could ignore events around me. You would have had to be a blind mole scrabbling in the earth to be unaware of what was happening: the whole country was in a ferment.

We had heard about the Romans for as long as I could remember. When I was a lad they slaughtered our priests on our holy island and laid waste to many lands in the south. Sometimes we heard of brave heroes who fought against them, and a warrior queen who led her tribe in battle. They made fine stories for a cold winter night about the fire. But, on the whole, the Romans were a curious and remote phenomenon. For the last few years we had heard of the army's encroachment north under the leadership of a strong, determined governor called Agricola. (Do you know his name means 'farmer' in their tongue?) Every summer he would advance a little further, destroying settlements where he met opposition and forging alliances where chiefs were too spineless to resist. In the winter they would fall back to the comfort and safety of their established camps in the occupied territories.

That summer even we, who live at the very edge of the Earth, felt the threat of the Roman advance. No one talked of anything else. The men as usual rattled their weapons, such as they had, but the women advocated retreat into the hills should the army come this way. Personally, I credited the Romans with more sense than to try to penetrate the wild mountains of the west, and for what: a few desolate strongholds and a pitiful, impoverished population?

Then we began to hear reports of a great leader, Calgacos of the Caledon tribe, who was calling on all the peoples to unite and form an army to oppose the Romans. Already he had gathered many thousands. He even sent an ambassador here to urge our tribe to ally with the others. His arrival on horseback, with a small troupe of mounted warriors, caused great panic and consternation amongst us. Brokko had brought as many of his people into the tower as he could and barred the door until he could see the standards of peace. Even then he would not invite them inside, but met them on the broad field below the tower. Soon, however, having allayed his fears, he brought them indoors and furnished them with food and drink. The formalities of hospitality completed, the ambassador spoke to us of his mission. I wonder if I can remember his words.

"You think you are safe from the Romans here, in your remote highland fastness. But no one is. They will march through the valleys and attack with their war galleys from the sea. We must stop them before they conquer and subjugate the whole land. Last year we taught their governor a lesson and trounced one of their legions. They ran off yelping like curs to their winter encampments. Agricola will come again but he will be tentative, not so sure of himself this time. We must meet him with all the might of our assembled tribes; teach him that this country must remain free from Roman tyranny and send him back to Rome with his tail between his legs."

His words were rousing and I do not think there was a man amongst us who was not ready, then and there, to march out to battle. Except perhaps myself. Brokko was eager but he was also practical. First he wanted to make things secure at home, and he needed time to gather all his men from the surrounding hills and valleys. We had little in the way of weapons to supply them all, so he set our smith the tasks of collecting as much bog iron as could be found and forging swords, spears and axes. I helped him in his work and found it a very satisfying occupation. Other men fashioned arrows and bows, and everyone donated what weapons they had. We assembled everything we could, from farm implements to fine old bronze swords, and, by the time of the new moon, we were ready.

Brana was in a fervour. She would have liked more than anything else to have marched off with the army, but Brokko was adamant. She must stay here and look after her young child. Thwarted in her plans, she turned her assault on me and urged me to take up weapons and join the fight. But I would not. I have never fought with anyone in my life and have no skill at all in these matters. I would have been more of a hindrance than a help in any battle. She was disgusted with me, of course. She took every opportunity to chide me for my cowardice, and shunned my company the rest of the time. It suited Brokko, though, that I stay behind: he needed a reliable man to protect the family, the other women and children, should the unthinkable happen and the Romans break through our opposition and march north.

There was tremendous excitement when at last our men marched off to war. We all – women, children, old, crippled and unfit like myself – accompanied them to the head of the valley, singing and cheering, though many were trying very hard not to weep. It is not good fortune to send a man to battle with tears: it presages doom. Except for Brana. She was strung tight like a bow, shouting and cheering with the rest, but with tears pouring down her cheeks all the while. I could not tell whether she was crying from frustration at being left behind or shame that I was not among the band. Afterwards there was no doubt that it was the latter as she would not speak to me or share my bed.

Life that summer was very strange. With most of the men away it fell to the old, the young and the women to carry out the everyday tasks of house and field. Everyone was busy but, at the same time, there was a lassitude and expectancy about the place which affected performance and moods. It was as if all life had marched south with the army, and we who were left behind were merely keeping time on the spot. Tempers frayed and fights broke out over the most trivial of things. I suppose only the children were unaffected, although they spent what free time they had battling titular Romans with wooden swords and spears. No one wanted to be a Roman, and our men always won. It is so long since I was a child, I've often wondered what unspoken law compels a child to obey the command, "You're dead!"

We waited eagerly for news and, whenever a travelling merchant came down the valley or a strange boat appeared in the loch, everyone gathered to hear what was happening in the south. We had regular reports. Men from all the tribes of the land had flocked to Calgacos; the first time that our people had shown such unity, being permanently addicted to internal raids and petty warfare. Instead of leading them south to attack the enemy right away, he sensibly waited, gathering more recruits all the time, for the Roman army to come to him.

I should think Agricola had reports of the vast force which was assembling ahead of him, but he continued his advance unperturbed, sending his fleet forward to pillage and strike terror into settlements on the coast. The Romans have a most efficient if slow method of moving through enemy territory. While the soldiers march through the day, bands of scouts and surveyors go in front to find the best position for the next evening's encampment. Each soldier carries a spade and some stakes and, on reaching the chosen site, they set to digging a trench and erecting a palisade. Before night falls the entire army is safely protected behind the walls of a defensible camp. It does seem tedious but you have to admire the wisdom and practicality of such a method of warfare. That is no doubt why they are masters of the world and we, who have the bravest and most spirited of warriors, must hide on the edges of the land behind our mountain ramparts.

Our army waited. We waited, almost holding our breaths with collective anticipation. We did not have to wait long. Bad news, like a raven's flight, travels straight and fast.

Our army had been defeated. Thousands of men were slaughtered and the scattered survivors were limping their way home through the ruined countryside. We did not know whether the Romans would be marching stolidly behind them to complete the massacre, or would be halted by the approach of winter.

Despite our fears, most of our men came home in better spirits than expected. The survivors returned singly or in small groups, within a few days; others dragged their weary, wounded bodies into the valley many moons later. Anxious women and children waited every day at the foot of the pass, apprehensive as to whether approaching warriors would furnish joy or misery. Only a few were known to have been killed; some were wounded and some were missing, presumably either dead or captured by the Romans. They would end their lives in slavery. Of 108 of our men, eighty-seven returned. This was not such a great defeat as reported.

When Brokko came back, at the head of the largest band of men which he had been able to gather from the battlefield or on the route home, you would have thought he was a triumphal hero. He rode a magnificent stallion which he had captured from the enemy cavalry, and was fired with enthusiasm and optimism. Agricola had won the battle, but not the war. He was on his way back to winter quarters and, Brokko was confident, would not try the strength of the northern warriors again. That evening everyone came to join the feast around the fireside and hear the story of the great battle. This is the gist it.

"It took us fifteen days to find the army. At first we marched on established tracks through the hills, not knowing exactly where to go, but soon we met bands of other warriors heading east to join the forces. When you pass the middle of the country, the land changes completely: it becomes flat, with many bogs and marshes and huge forests of enormous trees. Even the sea to the east is different. It laps sluggishly against dark, forbidding cliffs instead of breaking in towers of spray like it does on the rocks here. I can't say I would like to live there but it must be easier to grow crops and nurture animals. And the people are quite different too. Although they speak the same tongue, it's often difficult to understand them: the words are sometimes strange and they say them in a funny way. But we were all engaged in a common enterprise and tried to ignore our differences for once.

"When at last we found the great army, it was a magnificent sight. Stretching out over the huge plain were masses of booths and wooden shelters; warriors with sparkling weapons jousting in the sun; horses being exercised and chariots wheeling in mock races; the grey smoke from a thousand campfires hazing the brilliant colours of the tribes. If I live for another forty seasons, I shall not see such a rousing spectacle again.

"We pitched a camp at the edge of the crowd and went at once to offer our allegiance to Calgacos and the other tribal leaders. He is not such an imposing man as I expected, neither tall nor particularly strong, but when he spoke you could tell why he had come to leadership and how he had accomplished the unprecedented feat of gathering all the warring tribes together. He looked at you with calm blue eyes, assessing your worth and peering deep into your soul. He accepted my tribute and thanked me for my warriors, and then, as if I was his counsellor and friend of many years, explained what was happening to the enemy and how we were going to fight the mighty battle which would trounce them. You could trust a man like that, and follow him to the ends of the Earth.

"Our people had tried to avoid engaging the enemy, preferring to harass them here and there and retreat into the mountains. Now Calgacos knew that we would never stop the Romans until we had defeated them decisively in a pitched battle. But he would select his battle site carefully and wait for the Romans to come to it. He chose the slope of a rolling hill behind a flat plain. Our warriors would be ranged in ranks on the hillside and our war chariots could meet the enemy advance on the firm, flat ground in front. It was a good plan and it should have worked, but we underestimated the strength and discipline of the Roman soldiers, to our loss... to our heavy loss.

"At last our scouts reported that Agricola had pitched camp within striking distance of our battlefield. That evening we sacrificed twenty white bulls to the Gods and the priests read the omens: they favoured our endeavour. There was much feasting and rejoicing. Early in the morning Calgacos roused all the tribal chiefs and told them how to dispose their men on the hillside. We girded our weapons and armour, such as had it, although many preferred to fight naked in the traditional way, and waited in our allotted places. We were well to the rear, near the end of one of the crescent-shaped lines on the hill. Calgacos had reserved the front and middle sections for the strongest fighters and seasoned veterans. So we had a good view of the battleground and the enemy army. It was pitifully small: only a thin line of infantry at the centre, with horsemen disposed on each flank. We were sure it would be defeated long before we were needed.

"Our leaders raised the war cry, which resounded as a great bellow along all the lines, firing our blood and terrifying the enemy. Battle commenced with an exchange of missiles. Not much damage was inflicted on either side, but the rain of spears terrified the horses pulling our war chariots and they bolted in all directions over the plain. Agricola then sent forward some of his foot soldiers to attack our centre lines. These were not Romans but, enlisted in far countries, had been fully trained in the tactics of hand-to-hand sword-fighting. We supposed he was happy to sacrifice them and keep his legions in reserve. All we could see from our stance on the hill was a confused melee of fighting soldiers and careering war chariots, now joined by the enemy cavalry which had swung in from the flanks. You must understand that all of us who waited on the hillside were fired with the spirit of Lugh and, eager to join the fighting, rushed down onto the plain. The battle should have been won then.

"I don't really know what happened. I had made my way, hacking and slashing, right into the middle of the field, and suddenly there were fresh Roman horsemen blundering into our midst. Agricola must have sent them in from his reserves. We were confused, trying to cope with this new onslaught and deal with the foot soldiers who maintained a solid line of defence. Signalled by horns to change tactics, the cavalry swung round behind us and we were now trapped between their formidable advance and the indomitable infantry. It was disastrous. I weep to remember.

"Our men lost all heart. There seemed to be no way to kill these clever opponents. Some of us rallied together and fought to the death. Others, believing our cause was lost, fled the battlefield and sought refuge in the woods. Our little group, more by luck than by skill, had fought our way to the centre of the field where Calgacos still held out with his Caledons. He was wounded sorely and his men were urging retreat rather than glorious if pointless death. Our small band joined them in fighting furiously to cover his escape. Single-handedly I slaughtered more than twenty men and captured a horse whose rider I had killed. We put Calgacos on the horse and led him far away from the battle. I'm not ashamed to have fled. We saved the life of a great man who will one day lead the tribes again to oust the Romans from our country. He was very grateful for our help and, in recognition, gifted me the horse, the same which I brought home with me."

Well, Glikki, you can understand that Brokko's account left us in some confusion. Who could claim the victory? On the face of it, the Romans, since they had killed so many of our men and scattered the rest. On the other hand, many of our men and Calgacos himself had escaped to carry on the opposition in future years. It all depended on what the Romans did next.

Soon the news reached us that Agricola was slowly leading his army south, no doubt boasting of his triumph and taking hostages and tributes from the vanquished tribes. Maybe next season he would return but, for the time being, we would be left in peace. Or so we thought.

I had been down by the stream helping our blacksmith, as I often did in those days. Clyfar was a fine craftsman, skilled in working both bronze and iron. He had been much intrigued by the gear Brokko had brought back with the captured horse and was attempting to copy its complicated three-link bridle bit. The first we knew was when a youngster came running, breathless, from the beach, screaming of many great dragons coming in from the open sea. Indeed, it looked so to be. Passing through the outer islands was a fleet of ships, their sails flapping like wings in the breeze. Clyfar and I knew at once what they were, for we had heard of how the Roman ships had accompanied Agricola and his army, sometimes forging ahead to terrorise the coastal settlements. But we had not expected to see them here. We spread the alarm and Brokko sent men to warn his people, urging those who could to hurry to the safety of the tower and the rest to seek refuge in the hills. Luckily most of the animals had already been gathered close for the winter, so it was easy to drive them to hiding places. Although the ships were scudding in on a brisk north-wester, we had plenty of time to make everything ready and then wait, watching from the top of the tower, to see what this massive fleet would do.

The Romans must have good sources of intelligence, as the ships sailed straight into the loch right up to the bay in front of our tower. There they lowered their sails and put down anchor. It was a magnificent sight. There were upwards of a hundred ships, each, I'd estimate, more than fifty paces long with places for two and even three banks of oars. We could see men with helmets and spears, so there were clearly soldiers as well as sailors on board. How could we withstand an attack by such as these? We would just have to hope that the walls of our tower were high and strong enough to repel their assault. Perhaps Brokko now regretted that he had not ordered a higher building.

Presently five of the ships drew into the shore and were hauled onto the beach. Soldiers, fully armed and equipped with shields, descended the planks and marched up to the small plain before the fort, where they ranged themselves out in three rows, presenting an unbroken wall of shields towards us. All of this was accomplished silently and efficiently. Two men, wearing more elaborate gear and obviously leaders of the force, stepped in front of the lines, along with a tribesman of the south, undoubtedly to serve as interpreter. When the younger of the two spoke, his voice carried clearly with strength and authority but, of course, we could not understand. He would stop every so often and wait for the interpreter to relay his words. This is what he said.

"We come here in peace to offer you the advantages of allegiance with Rome. Your peoples have been defeated but we have no desire to cause more bloodshed. If you are willing to meet with us and pledge yourselves to the Emperor, we will promise you access to trading routes throughout the continental lands and the middle sea. You will become part of a great civilisation, and benefit from the rule of law and the prosperity which it will bestow." The young man raised his arm as if to encompass us all, and the sun glinted off his armaments and glimmered on his bronzed skin. He was not like any of our people, but tall and dark with powerful limbs and a strong face. I did not fancy the idea of meeting him in battle.

Brokko, however, was not to be cowed, or won over by promises of riches. "We want nothing which Rome has to offer. Our trade and our wealth are sufficient for our needs and comfort, so we are not fooled by your empty words. We know that allegiance with Rome means subservience and we will bow to no one, emperor or king. We are a free people, and we will remain a free people till long after Rome has been trampled to dust under the feet of her enemies."

Brana, looking at her father with approval and admiration, came to stand by his side on the parapet of the tower. Oh, how I wished she looked at me with the same affection!

The young Roman, for I had no doubt that he was a full citizen of that country, listened passively for the translation of Brokko's words. Then he inclined his head and spoke more aggressively. "Do not doubt that we have the power to annihilate your meagre forces. We can destroy the walls of your pitiful tower with our war machines and slaughter every one of you. But we have no wish to do so. We would prefer if your people joined us peacefully of their own, *free*, will." I was not sure if the interpreter had placed an ironic emphasis on the word 'free', or if he was passing it on faithfully from the young man. He went on. "I will give you till sunrise tomorrow to think about our offer and discuss it with your men."

Much to everyone's surprise, it was Brana who responded. She was wearing her hunting leathers and held her boar spear in her hand. She looked every inch the warrior goddess with her raven locks streaming in the wind. "Do not think that my father, the chieftain, speaks alone. There is not one man or woman here who does not support him, and there is not one man or woman who will not fight to the death to oppose you. And do not doubt that each one of us will take ten of your soldiers into death with us."

The leader looked long and hard at Brana before speaking but, when he did, there was no doubt in the irony of his words, even if we could not understand. "I am slain already. I had no idea that the beautiful Diana herself resided in this lonely northern wilderness. But, Lady, though your words of provocation pierce my heart, I may pierce you yet with a spear of my own." He laughed, and then his words grew harsh again. "You have until tomorrow morning."

I had never seen my wife redden with confusion. She had expected fierce retaliation, not humiliation. She hid herself behind Brokko and did not speak another word, then or for some time after.

Brokko did not need a day to make up his mind; nor did he need to consult with the people. No one wished peace with Rome. The next morning, as the sun lifted itself from the mountains, the five ships drew into the beach again and the soldiers filed out. The leader waited until he could see Brokko on the parapet and then shouted, "Well, have you reached a decision?"

"There was no deliberation needed. We will not bow to Rome and we will resist your armies. For, even if you kill every one of us here today, more of us will stay alive to fight you tomorrow." Brokko flourished his spear above his head.

The Roman seemed saddened, but resigned. "Very well, if that is your wish," he said. "But remember there is more to be gained from peace than war. You will live to regret your decision when you see the benefits accrued to the southern tribes who have chosen to ally with Rome. We came to you in peace and we will leave you in peace."

In answer Brokko flung his spear, aimed carefully at the man's heart. The Roman stepped aside agilely, letting the spear bury its head in the turf. Then, with no more than a silent sign to his men, he led them back to the ships.

We could not believe that that was it. Would they now bring the rest of their ships to the shore and begin an assault on our castle? We could not hold out for long, particularly if they had brought their siege artillery. I had heard of these: catapults which hurled enormous boulders;

huge machines like taut bows whose arrows would pierce armour and bodies alike. But nothing happened. The fleet remained anchored below our fort. We could see some small boats, launched from the ships, being rowed to the other side of the loch. Perhaps they were in need of fresh water, or hoped to find some unattended flocks. They remained in the loch all day, and that night we could still see the twinkling lights from their lamps reflecting in the dark waters. I went to bed exhausted and, when I woke in the morning, the fleet had gone.

And so had Brana.

No one noticed at first. She had not spoken to me for days, and kept out of my way. She had seldom spent time with her son and usually left him to the care of his nurse. So it was not until the evening meal that I became anxious.

It turned out nobody had seen her all day. The men searched everywhere in the vicinity, but retreated into the tower as darkness fell. She would have to come back of her own accord.

I became increasingly worried. Had she wandered into the mountains and been attacked by a boar? Or, more likely, had she been captured by the Romans and carried off into a life of slavery? But then why had she left the safety of the tower, and how? The tower door had been secured with its wooden bar. Someone must have let her out and barred the door again. Alternatively, she would have had to lower herself down from the parapet with a rope, but the tower watch protested their vigilance all that night. If I had been a superstitious man I might have thought she had called on her ravens to spirit her away. But most of all I wondered why she had gone. Was she so ashamed of my unmanliness that she felt any life was better than the one here with me? And what about our son? Did she feel nothing for him?

As the days passed we searched further and further afield and, as our people gradually came back from their hideouts in the hills, I asked everyone if they had seen her. No one had. The days became moons, and the seasons changed. I never saw or heard of her again.

So ended the short time of my married life. I was left with an infant son to rear and nurture by myself, but that was a joy rather than a duty. I did not wish him to grow up like me, unfamiliar with women, so I made sure he had someone to nurse him when he was very young, and plenty of girl companions to play with as he grew older. Of course as soon as I could I took building commissions around the country, and always took him with me. He was a blithe child, always singing, with a voice as sweet as a bird's. That is why we called him Meisalko, the blackbird. He learned to walk very early and, as soon as he was able, would totter down the beach to look at the sea. It seemed to fascinate him, and he would try to copy its rhythms with a wordless song of his own. When someone introduced him to a harp, he tried to pluck the notes with his podgy baby fingers. I made a miniature one for him, and he was soon able to pick out tunes on it. Whenever our bards sang songs or recited stories, he would listen carefully and try to reproduce them later. He was so clever, quick of mind, and skilled with his hands, I was sure he would make a better builder than ever I had. But why do we wish so for the unattainable? Why do we expect our children to conform to our desires?

I think you were coming with us by then, Glikki, as a labourer on our projects. You know how Meisalko showed little interest in the work. Oh, he would listen and follow instructions carefully, but there was no enthusiasm and he never tried to initiate his own ideas. As soon as darkness fell and the day's work finished, he would brighten immediately and take himself off to the sea to sing songs to the waves. But he was a biddable child, and grew into a strong and skilful worker. I could not find fault with him, and yet I could not praise his labour. Every time it was you who asked to complete some of the wall in a different way or suggested novel ways of supporting the roof. His heart was not in it, so it came as no surprise, when he passed the rites of manhood, that he chose not to follow my trade. Instead he elected to sit at the feet of the bard and learn his songs and music.

Oh yes, of course I was disappointed, but I respected his choice and, if he studied hard and developed that talent he had displayed so young, perhaps one day he could become a master of his art, which, after all, is valued more highly in our world than mere building.

Our ways parted then. I to travel over the land as before; he remaining here beside the loch. I saw him often enough as every winter I returned to our home, but we grew further and further apart. He would enthuse for hours about the new melodies and skills he was learning, but had no interest in my latest engineering task. I was proud of him but we had little in common. So life went on, satisfactory in many ways, if mundane.

Now I come to the part of my story which gives me the greatest pain, even after all these years. Nothing prepared me for what was to happen, although perhaps I should have seen the signs of the Gods sooner.

It happened on a day like any other in the early spring. I had just taken a commission in the south – chieftains there were ordering broch towers in the threat of further Roman incursions – and was preparing to leave on my travels. Meisalko had taken himself off to fish from the rocks on the seaside. We never knew exactly what happened. Did he slip on the rocks, or did a sudden wave pull him in? Did the God of the Sea require his sweet singing to cheer his cold undersea halls? They found his body, pallid and bloated, several days later, washed up on the beach.

We built his platform on the heights of the mountain and held his funeral rites as the sun went down. Our bard sang a lay of Meisalko: that he was transformed into a blackbird and would henceforth sweeten the feastings of the Gods with his music. And indeed when the birds came to peck at his body, I fancied that there were blackbirds and ravens and even the great sea eagle perched on his bier. After his bones were clean I took them to join his true love, the sea, but I kept his skull. It is there, in the wall, in the niche I had reserved for my own head when the time shall come.

You were a great comfort to me then, Glikki, but soon I learned that the Gods, in their divine irony, had given me a greater gift by far. When I still expected my son to follow in my tradition, I had been blind to your talents and zeal. Now at last I saw what a superb engineer you were born to be, greater by far than myself. I was overjoyed when you asked to be initiated as my apprentice and, over the years you trained at my side, I learned more from teaching you than I believe you did from me. You have given me the greatest happiness in my life, and now, as it draws to an end, your bright future will light my way into the dark.

But listen to my words, Glikki. You are adept now, but you can become greater yet. Do not ever stop learning or seeking knowledge. There is a future for you here: chieftains will always want castles of some kind. But I say you should leave, travel the world. Go to Rome to learn the secrets of their engineering: how they float great temples on top of slender pillars; how they move water in pipes on tall bridges. And there are other lands, further yet, where I have heard they have built huge mountains out of stone to protect the bodies of their rulers. There they have mastered the science of the stars and mathematics beyond our meagre understanding. When you have learned all of these things, you may not wish to return to our dark and lonesome land but, if you do, you will be the greatest builder of all. Then build in memory of me, the old man who first taught you the secrets of stone. That is all I ask.

I am tired now, Glikki. The fire is growing dim. Put another log on it and then come to sit beside my bed again. You are a good lad. You have been more than a son to me.

Glikki closed his master's eyes and crossed his withered hands on his chest. Tears were not necessary because the old man had lived well and accomplished much. He had given Glikki his first inspiration, and had taught him diligently throughout his life.

His name might not be remembered but his buildings would stand as memorials to his skill and expertise. As long as there were architects and builders in the world, so long would his towers be objects of speculation and admiration.

Chapter Seven

*Martin
of the Island*
Celtic Christians

Isle Martin, the closest of the Summer Isles to Lochbroom, boasts an unusual cross-marked stone amongst others in a small graveyard. It is supposed that the island was the retreat of an early Celtic Christian monk called Martin. Annat, an abandoned settlement on the north side of the Scoraig peninsula, may mark the site of the 'Mother Church' from whence he came.

An Old Man's Prayer

My Father in Heaven, listen to an old man's prayer.

I praise Thee as the giver of life, the creator of all things. If I am worthy, if my sins are forgiven, I will join You soon and the company of angels and the souls of those who departed before me. But pity those who are left behind. Bring redemption to the sinners and lead them into Your holiness. My needs are small but I beg You to provide me enough bread to sustain me for a little time more: it will not be long. And forgive my sins.

I have few sins left, thank the Lord, but, perhaps, the sin of complacency. Oh, wasn't it different in my youth, when my head was full of notions of grandeur and my body pulsed with life? I was going to bring Your word to the ignorant, travel the world spreading Your message of joy and peace to the heathens. What was that all about? Here am I, on a desolate island with only a few novitiates who would, no doubt, prefer to be out in the fields than listening to my empty platitudes. I wonder if I even brought one soul to God.

Aye, I was sinful enough then. It is hard for a young man to keep his mind on the spiritual when the body yields to such consuming pleasures. Och, remember how hungry I was, on bended knee at morning prayer in the church, and all my mind could think of was breakfast. And remember the cheese that I stole nibbles of in the dairy. *Oh, me absolve, Pater!*

Now I often forget to eat.

And remember the young women... such lissom bodies, such glowing hair, bending to the stook in the sunshine. I did not always choose to be celibate; it would have been no sin to marry and bring up children in the way of the Lord. But You chose otherwise for me, Lord.

I did not understand then why it was necessary to give up the pleasures of the flesh. Surely You made our bodies as they are. How then could satisfying those bodily desires be sinful? Praising God by fulfilling our natural functions as the birds do, singing Your hymns at sunrise and dusk, or the beasts bowing their heads to the grass in the fields.

But I understand now. It's not the forswearing of gratification which is important. It is the need to concentrate wholly on Your worship. There is no place for the mundane in spiritual contemplation, and those whose lives are riven with temptation had best leave the Church.

I nearly did, too. But You brought me back. Each time I was tempted, You showed me how much greater is a life of service in Your Church.

But isn't that a kind of sin itself: to seek fame and Heavenly reward in righteousness? Well, I don't know. I'm only an ignorant old man and I never did find fame anyway. I'll soon know if I've merited a reward in Heaven.

I suppose the greatest of my sins was pride. I felt so privileged to read and write, and loved to trace the words of Scripture and embellish them with fanciful, intricate designs. I should have been doing it to the glory of Your name but I confess I just liked the work for its own sake: to dip the pen in the ink, and scribe a perfect letter; to hide beasts in the curlicues of a design; to inhale the smell of parchment; grinding and mixing vivid colours for the illustrations. I thought I was so adept, such a master, that my Gospels would be praised and revered down all the depths of time after I am long dead. How vain I was! But my books are all left behind. I shouldn't think anyone looks at them now. No matter.

Father, I kneel before You and my knees hurt. Did You love me more when I was a young man and flung myself before You and beat my head against the ground? I must not complain, but my old bones ache more now in my posture of reverence than they ever did then. Do You understand that? And my thoughts go flying off in all directions without keeping to the point.

Now then, where was I? Yes.

Forgive my sins, and forgive those who have sinned against me.

For I never was able to forgive them myself, no matter how I tried and prayed. I nursed the wounds they inflicted like open sores and, as soon as they began to heal, I would scratch away the scabs again. But old age brings the cure of forgetfulness. I can no longer remember their offences, and even their faces are fading from memory. Perhaps, if I grow older yet, I will learn to trust them again. Love will be a lot harder. *Mea culpa.*

Let me not be tempted by evil thoughts.

I know I am not good. It is so easy for my mind to stray. But perhaps my thoughts are not evil, just a little bad. I am not able to look on the ways of men with equanimity. But it is right to balk at injustice and prejudice. Forgive me for also condemning stupidity and ignorance. They know no better, and some are taught to be that way.

Oh, Lord, I cannot learn to love the false preachers. They come with honeyed words and promise salvation for those who will follow the law slavishly. They teach that righteousness is better than humility; that the chosen few will trample on the unbelievers. They speak the words of the Devil, so how can I love them? Father, can You help me to love them even while I denounce their teaching?

Oh dear, I have rambled off again. But I am near the end.

For Thine is the kingdom, the power and the glory.

Amen.

The Sermon

Listen to my words, my children, but listen critically. I glimpse the Truth as a light far off; it twinkles and is sometimes obscured but it becomes clearer as I grow older. These, my sayings, are only guiding points; you must all find your own way.

Speak little, listen a lot – this is wisdom.

Listen to the children talk, and know innocence.

Behave always as if you would be an example to others; actions speak louder than words. You may hide unworthy thoughts in your head; only God will know them. When you have learned to act well towards others, strive also to rid your mind of evil intentions. Anger, envy and lust will eat away at your soul as a worm an apple.

Love the smallest of God's creatures and do them no harm. What are you to a whale?

If a man steals an egg from your nest, give him a hen; his children may be starving.

Do not prefer the brother who sits at your table to the stranger in a foreign land; we are all children of God.

It is very hard to love our enemies; we are not gods... yet.

Trust all who come to you for help; it is better to be thought foolish than mean of spirit.

You may fast for two days and two nights, you may punish your flesh, and yet not achieve enlightenment. The Truth will come when you least expect it.

Practise abstinence against the day when there is nothing left to eat.

Strive not for riches or fame; the poor man lies beside the king in the earth.

Humility is a virtue above all, but do not let yourself be humbled by others.

If your neighbour falls, you must pick him up; likewise if he falls from grace. It is not for you to judge or condemn.

If you desire approval, give praise; if you wish admiration, show appreciation of the works of your friends; kind thoughts will show in your face and make others smile at you; compassion, love and joy are the most infectious of emotions.

When a foolish man talks of evil things, do not correct him. He will not believe you anyway.

His Song of Praise

(Sung to the tune of 'Be Thou My Vision')

Sun of the morning, bring life with your light;
Moon, guide our footsteps through shadows of night;
Stars, glitter gently, ye jewels of the sky:
Praising the Maker, the Creator on high.

Storms in the winter, when thunderclouds boil;
Soft rain in springtime calls seeds from the soil;
Summer's caresses and autumn's reward:
Each season's blessings give praise to the Lord.

Horse in the meadow bows his head in a prayer;
Fish in the ocean, and birds in the air;
Flowers of the machair and fruits of the tree:
Each living creature offers worship to Thee.

Purple the mountains and silver the seas;
Golden the barley that sways in the breeze.
Solomon's palace no riches can bring
Than this little island, and I am its king.

All of the beauties of sky, sea and earth
Have given me joy from the time of my birth;
Now, as life's sunset brings end to my days,
I offer my whole heart, my worship of praise.

His Blessing

My fingers on your brow for blessing.
May the seven angels of the Spirit protect you,
And the two guardian angels stand behind your head.
The blessings of the saints upon you:
Valiant Michael to guard you from ill;
Bride, aid-woman of Mary, to watch your hearth;
Columba, most beloved, to love and keep you.
A blessing on your kine in the fields;
A blessing on your flocks on the machair:
Protect them from fairy and banshee,
From elf and water horse.
May your milk be sweet in the churn,
And your bowls filled with buttermilk and honey.
Peace of the Father over you,
Peace of the Son throughout your days,
Peace of the Spirit comfort your heart,
Now and for evermore,
Now and for evermore.

Chapter Eight

Ulla's Steading

the coming of the Vikings

The name Ullapool is of Scandinavian origin and means Olaf's or Ulli's Steading. Sometime in the ninth century Norse settlers arrived in Lochbroom. Stray finds in the sand dunes at Achnahaird indicate a possible undiscovered Viking settlement nearby, and steatite bowls may testify to their presence on the Summer Isles and in Lochbroom itself.

Ulla never believed the story Inga and her mother told her about the troll in the rock. Ever since she had been a precocious toddler, they had impressed on her the dangers of straying past the strange-shaped boulder which marked the edge of the family settlement. Torvik, Ulla's older brother, described the fearsome appearance of the troll and delighted in portraying at length how he would crunch her bones and smack his pebbly lips if he ever caught her wandering in the twilight. But Ulla reasoned that, since trolls would turn to stone at the first rays of sunshine, she had nothing to fear from them in daylight hours.

When she was little more than six years old, Ulla grasped the opportunity, when Inga was milking and her mother fussing over her weaving, to escape out of the homelands. It is true she ran past the big rock without glancing at it, but after that she walked steadily along a well-trodden path leading into the forest. At first everything was peaceful and ordinary. The spring sunshine glinted on wildflowers and butterflies flitted here and there. Birds, busy with nest-making, scrabbled in the bushes, and

Ulla paused to listen to a robin trickling his song from the topmost branches. Then she chased a particularly colourful butterfly deeper into the trees. Of course, as always happens in the old tales, she was soon completely lost. This did not worry her unduly. She expected that her disappearance would have been noted by now and someone would come to fetch her. They might even send the big hound, Bodø, to track her. The fjord where Ulla lived cut into high, steep-sided mountains, leaving only a narrow coastal fringe of fertile land. Beyond that wild woods stretched almost to the mountaintops, where a person would certainly be attacked by a bear or eaten by a wolf. She decided that the best plan would be to wait where she was rather than forging on into greater depths of forest. A small stream gurgled through tumbled rocks and, if Ulla had known better, she would have realised it was the one which flowed down and through her home fields to the sea. The sun shone warmly onto a patch of soft green grass beside it. She lay down there and presently fell fast asleep.

By the time she woke, the sun had left her grassy glade and only little pools of light danced among the shadows. She shivered with cold and stood up. It was then she saw the little man. He stood at the edge of the woods and seemed to blend in with the colour of the grey trunks. He was gnarled and warty and it appeared as if lichen was growing on him; strands of green moss hung limply from his heavy brow. Ulla began to be frightened, but he did not move at all. For a moment she wondered if it was only a rock and a trick of the light had given it life. Then he slowly raised his arm and pointed. For a brief moment

Ulla stood rooted to the ground with fear, but suddenly strength flowed back into her limbs and she ran.

As luck would have it, and because she was naturally running downhill towards the sea, she soon found herself in familiar territory. She ran as fast as she could past Troll Rock and then had the presence of mind to slow down to regain her breath before bursting into the steading. She was somewhat disappointed to find that no one had noticed her absence. A pedlar had arrived and everyone was eagerly examining his wares: exotic luxuries like a new knife blade for her father, bales of fine cloth for the women.

Ulla never told anyone about her encounter with the little man, and she did not stray past Troll Rock again. But she often thought about him and wondered what he had been pointing to in the deep grass at the edge of the stream. Had he wanted her to look at something? As time passed and she grew older, the memory faded from her mind like a dream.

Some years later, on a fine winter's morning, Ulla had managed to finish her chores early and decided to try to find the glade in the woods again. This time she followed the stream from its gentle meandering through the flat fields at the sea's edge to where it tumbled through fallen boulders at the feet of the snow-capped peaks.

In a surprisingly short time she found the clearing in the woods again, but there was no sign of either little men or troll-shaped rocks. It was difficult to make out details but at last she thought she could identify the spot where she had fallen asleep, and where the man had stood. She traced the line of his pointing finger to a jumbled pile of stones which had previously been hidden in the long grass beside the stream. She could vaguely make out a circular shape; perhaps it was a ruin of the old people, or a fairy mound. She began to move rocks and dig a little in the dirt below them. After about an hour's work she had found nothing. Maybe it had just been a dream. She sat back on her heels and tried to see again the little man with his beetling brows and insistent finger.

The clearing grew very quiet, and even the gurgling of the stream seemed to fade. A beam of light from the sun gleamed through the tree branches and fell upon something she had not noticed before. To the side of where she had been hunting, a large, flat rock lay on others. She could see a dark void beneath. The rock was far too big for her to move but the hole was just big enough for her to push her hand in. Tentatively she squeezed it in and felt around inside. Her hand touched something hard and cold which moved when she pressed it. Steeling herself not to shriek, she grasped the object and began to pull it out of the hole.

What she held in her hand, smooth and translucent in the sunshine, looked like a leaf made of stone. Clearly it was not, but was some kind of tool or weapon made long ago by the old people. Perhaps someone had been buried here and, as a last tender thought, this little knife blade had been placed inside his grave. Or hers. This could equally have been the last resting place of some old woman, maybe even Ulla's great-great-grandmother. For some time Ulla squatted on her heels, trying to imagine who the person might have been and what use she might have made of the stone tool. Whatever it was, the little man had meant for

Ulla to find it, and it must have some purpose in her life. Recalling that it was time she got back home, she wound it inside her dress and made her way back to the steading. She kept it a secret – hard enough to do with an inquisitive big brother prying into her affairs – and made a leather pouch for it, fastened on a thong, hidden inside her dress. It gave her a feeling of comfort to have the bag, with its mysterious talisman, warm against her chest.

Ulla was picking wild strawberries in the meadows behind the farm when the raiders came. She heard women screaming, men shouting and the clattering of iron swords. Her instinct was to run deeper into the woods, but instead she crept through the trees to the edge of the meadow where they had begun to cut the first winter hay and hid under one of the drying racks. From this viewpoint she could see what was going on. Some fierce-looking strangers were moving about the farm. The screaming and shouting had stopped, but they had not set fire to the houses and storage barns. She expected they were herding up animals and hunting for booty. In these days, population growth and a shortage of productive farming land were putting pressure on everyone. Younger sons who found themselves without an allotment of land often set off on raiding sprees like this, usually to further lands across the seas but sometimes closer to home.

When it was completely dark, she made a circuitous route around the settlement to the fjord, expecting to see where they were loading supplies into their boats. But there were no boats. Perhaps they had left them in the next inlet and come overland. That would be why they had managed to attack the village without warning. On the other hand, she could see no sign of people carrying off goods in any direction. She decided she had to get closer. Keeping in the shadow of walls and moving from one hiding place to another, she stole into the steading. At one point she nearly ran into trouble. She had to cross an open space between one building and another, and ran low and fast into a deep shadow. She sank down gratefully into the darkness, whereupon she suddenly felt warm breath on her cheek and a touch on her shoulder. She let out a little cry, fearing discovery, and then with a flood of relief realised it was Bodø, tied up inside his kennel. She flung her arms round his neck and cried silently into his warm fur. Evidently they had considered him more valuable kept alive. She offered a silent prayer to the Gods for this piece of good fortune. His kennel would make an ideal hiding place. No one would look inside the kennel of an angry and distressed dog.

By the time morning came it had become clear that the raiders were not leaving. On this occasion, the rich farmland and plentiful stores had tempted them more than portable booty. They meant to stay and keep the farm for themselves. She had no idea what had happened to her family, her father and the rest of the men. Those who resisted were probably dead; those who were compliant and valuable might be kept on to work the land. She had to get away.

She waited all day in the kennel. As she anticipated, no one came near Bodø. They would let him starve for a while till hunger made him more manageable. At last, in the deep night when all sounds of activity had died away, she said a tearful farewell to Bodø, and crept out of her hiding place. She slunk back through her route in until she was out of the meadows and into the woods. She had no idea where to go – perhaps along the coast to the next steading, where there would be friends and safety? – but at least she had escaped.

She walked straight into the man.

He had been standing so still in the dark beside the trees that she did not see him until he stepped out and grabbed her. The raiders must have expected a few stragglers to have escaped, or even that a counter-attack would be attempted, and set him as a guard. He bundled her up in his arms and carried her, struggling wildly, into the big house.

The firelight lit a circle of about a dozen men and some women, eating chunks of pork and quaffing her father's prized beer. Ulla's stomach growled with hunger at the sight: it had been a long time since her last meal.

Her captor threw her triumphantly onto the floor at the feet of the leader. "A little morsel to complete your meal, Bjorn."

"Not many pickings on that. But she'll make a field worker when she grows bigger. Well done, Bjarni; come join the feast as a reward. Someone else can take over the guard duty now."

One of the women tied Ulla's hands and feet and bundled her into a corner. "Dare move and ye'll get hammered," she hissed.

Ulla curled into a miserable ball. The big fire warmed her chilled limbs, and perhaps they might give her a bone to gnaw in an hour or two.

So began Ulla's years of captivity in her own home. She did not find out what had happened to her family. Perhaps the raiders had buried them hurriedly or, more likely, thrown their bodies into the sea. They had kept Inga and some of the other servants, who probably missed Ulla's father's benign management but would, after all, find little difference in their toil and servitude. The change in ownership of the farm had been accomplished in a day with no outward sign of violence, but a deadly cauldron of hate and resentment brewed in Ulla's heart. She would finger the talisman on her chest and pray that the Gods would visit terrible retribution on the usurpers. She could do nothing and showed nothing, accepting her chores with a silent but sullen resignation and waiting for the opportunity to escape. It never came, so she began a process of escape within, sinking into the background, effacing herself, so that often for days no one noticed or spoke to her at all. She found that, if she carried out her tasks efficiently without complaint, she could avoid the beatings that some of the less canny servants incurred. And she was not, as yet, of any interest to the men.

She dreaded growing up and, when the first signs of womanhood appeared, did her best to disguise them, binding her breasts to keep them flat and making herself as unattractive as possible. She deliberately let her golden hair grow lank and matted, rubbing dirt into it and ignoring the lice. She never washed the dung from her hands and face, and endeavoured to nurture a particularly rancid smell. Most of all, she just wished to be invisible, and it seemed to work. It worked with everybody, that is, except Gorb, the big one-eyed blacksmith who worked his forge in his hut beside the stream. Perhaps his one eye was more perceptive than two, or, more likely, none of the other women were attracted to his charms, but he began to take an interest in Ulla. She could feel his gaze on her and would finger her talisman, wishing for her cloak of invisibility. His close association with iron probably made him immune to her magic and he would follow her about, smirking through the gaps in his blackened teeth and making suggestive gestures. All she could do was keep out of his way as much as possible.

One day she set off to the woods to collect mushrooms. She was trusted enough by now that they let her do that. She liked it, as she could quickly fill her basket, and then luxuriate in the peace and break from continuous toil. She often returned to her glade beside the stream and wished for the troll to come and carry her off to some trollsome heaven.

He never did, but Gorb did. He had spied her going into the woods with her basket and hidden in her little glade. When she settled down to rest in the pool of sunlight, he jumped out and pinned her to the ground. There was absolutely nothing she could do; he was a strong, determined man. He laughed at her biting teeth and lashing limbs. They excited him even more. So she adopted a tactic that might put him off: she lay back and feigned unconsciousness. It did not deter him at all. She felt him groping, tearing her clothing, hissing at the crawling lice, but then heard a sigh of wonder as he discovered her small, perfect breasts hidden so carefully below her bindings. He tore frantically at the rest of her clothing and, probably fearing too sudden an outcome, thrust himself hurriedly between her legs. She felt a searing pain, but gritted her teeth and moved not a muscle. It was over in a few seconds. He grunted, got up, rearranged his clothing and went off, leaving her lying motionless, dead for all he knew.

The clearing grew completely still; the leaves ceased moving in the breeze. The trill of birdsong and the chattering of the stream faded away. Ulla felt her body growing into the grass, seeping away into a welcome death. She lay there without moving for a long time. But at length she felt the weight of her talisman on her chest, pressing on her, and it felt as if it was growing warmer. Somehow it seemed too hot to bear. She sat up and pulled it away from her body. And then everything returned: the stream bubbled through the rocks; the branches waved overhead. She was sore and soiled, but she was alive and she would have revenge.

Gorb looked for her frequently after that. When he trailed her through the woods, he stumbled and breathed heavily, so she always knew when he was following. There were too many people about in the settlement for him to catch her unaccompanied. But he was a clever, vicious creature and appeared to enjoy the chase. If she was milking alone, he would drag her into a haystack and gag her with a dirty rag. He would lie in wait in the woods in the hope she would come that way. Her life became a perpetual torture of fear and expectation and there was nothing she could do. Making an appeal to the women would provoke derision, and she certainly didn't want any of the men to know what she was hiding so carefully. At least Gorb had not told anyone else of his discovery, probably wishing to keep the secret for himself. There was only one way out – Gorb had to die.

So, as the year faded into a glorious autumn, she plotted her revenge. The death had to be so perfect that no one would suspect murder. Either Gorb must disappear completely so that his body was never found or she had to make it look like an accident. Could she tie a great weight to his legs and drown him in the sea? How could she ever manage that? He was too strong and devious a man for her to overpower on her own. Somehow she had to use his advantages to work against him. Finally she formed what she thought could be a workable plan. It would require careful preparation.

Above her glade in the forest, the stream fell in a steep waterfall into a deep, dark pool. She had often walked that way, and had worn a path close to the edge above the tumbling water. By working away with stones and sticks, she created a gap above a slippery glissade which slid straight into the pool below. Then she built a light bridge of sticks covered with soil over the gap, so that it appeared that the path was continuous. For added effect, she even placed tentative footmarks over the bridge, being careful not to use her full weight. She created a hiding place where she could wait, screened by bushes from anyone coming up the path. Finally she found herself a great round stone, just light enough for her to heave above her head. All she had to do now was accustom Gorb to following her into the forest. Every day she would set off at the same time with her basket to pick mushrooms. She did not always go in the same direction, in case he got into the habit of lying in wait. She even let him catch her once or twice.

When her preparations were complete, Ulla had one more thing to do: she must perform an outsitting. On a night of the full moon, she waited till all was peaceful around the houses and set out into the forest. She had no clear idea of the ritual involved, knowing only that magical rites and incantations were needed. But she would do her best to conjure up the spirits of the dead. When she reached her glade she took out her stone talisman and laid it on the ground. Her magic needed blood. So she took the knife again and, wincing with the pain, cut a circle into her flesh on the inside of her left calf: a symbol of the sun. But then she whispered a warning to Tyr: "Help me now and I will praise you all the days of my life; fail me, and I will erase you from my heart just as I do this symbol." Carefully she cut a cross over the bleeding circle on her leg. She let the blood drip freely onto her knife, feeling a little faint but nonetheless determined. Then she began to chant, calling on her mother, her father, all those who had been killed by the raiders. All night long she continued her ritual but nothing happened; no one appeared to her. When the first light of dawn showed in the east, she bound the wound on her leg with yarrow and returned her knife to the pouch around her neck.

In the mid morning she told Inga that she was going to search for mushrooms along the coast fields and set off in that direction, but she doubled back, passing the door to Gorb's hut, and walked towards the forest. Had he seen her? As soon as she was in the shelter of the trees, she rushed to fill her basket with field mushrooms which she had collected the day before and left in a cache in a hollow, and continued up the path by the stream. She strained to hear if he was following her. As soon as she reached the waterfall she laid her basket on the other side of the bridge and, on a last-minute inspiration, placed her stone knife gently in the middle of it. If her plan worked, she would gladly sacrifice her talisman. She retreated into her hiding place and waited.

Ages seemed to pass. Perhaps Gorb had not seen her. Perhaps he was too busy working today. But at last she heard him puffing up the hill. She tried to still her body, shaking with anticipation. She had to do everything right now, as she had planned. She watched him approach the bridge and then he stopped. What was wrong? Did he not see her basket? Did he suspect something? She could hear his breath heaving but could not see his face. Slowly, slowly, she stood up from the bushes and hoisted the big rock above her head. Had he seen the stone knife? Silently she mouthed a prayer to all the gods she knew, and especially the little man of the woods.

Gorb bent forward and, as if in slow motion, reached out to grasp the knife. With all the strength she could muster, Ulla brought the stone down on his head. She could feel his skull crack and saw brains bursting out, but he did not cry out or move. For a moment of complete stillness, Gorb remained bent over the bridge. And then, slowly, he toppled. Head first he crashed through the dirt and sticks. His body slid and bumped its way down the slope, collecting, she hoped, more cuts, bashes and grazes on the way, and finally dropped, with a satisfying splash, into the pool below.

Ulla waited for many minutes to see if he would move, but his body floated face down, spreadeagled on the top of the water. She straightened up and carried her rock well downstream and then threw it into the deepest part of the water. Gobbets of gore rose to the surface and spread in slow, red rings. They were soon swept away in the current. Coming back, she checked to see if he had moved, but he was definitely dead. She cleared away any sign of her bridge and hiding place, collected her basket and, by a roundabout way, went back to the fields.

For the best part of a day, no one missed Gorb. He had never been particularly popular. When his body was found in the late evening, everyone assumed he had lost his footing and tumbled into the stream. If anyone wondered how he had managed to bash his head so hard or why he held an ancient stone knife tightly in his death grip, they did not speculate aloud. He was buried without great ceremony under a pile of stones beside his hut. No one mourned.

Although Ulla's life was considerably better since Gorb's disappearance, she made up her mind that she had to escape. When the pedlar returned to the settlement, she rushed off to the river pool, stripped off her grimy, ragged clothes and washed the years of dirt from her body. She scrubbed her head with sand and pulled her fingers through the matted lumps in her hair. The sun was very warm on her body and the cool, clear water lapped her gently. For a long moment she forgot the purpose of her ablutions. Then she dried herself off and pulled on her filthy clothes again. She did not want to make herself too obviously attractive.

The merchant, whose name was Skól, was still surrounded by a gaggle of women. Ulla had to wait till evening before she could get him on his own. He was sitting outside beside his packhorse, tidying his merchandise, when she approached him. Casually, she let the dirty scarf around her head slip down to reveal her soft golden hair. He continued with his work and did not appear to notice her. She felt for the talisman around her neck and then remembered that it was gone – she could not make her magic now.

Without looking up, he said, "So what do you want, little girl? A length of new cloth to replace those rags which you favour, or a pretty bead to shine in those golden locks you've hidden so well?"

Ulla was somewhat disturbed by his unexpected perception, but she was not deterred from her purpose. "Take me with you when you go," she said.

He finally looked up and scrutinised her for a moment. "And what would you offer me for this service?" he said.

Ulla had no experience in the arts of seduction but she had watched the other girls often enough. She bowed her head, but peered up at him through her long lashes.

To her chagrin he let out a great guffaw of laughter. "No, Ulla – yes, I know your name and I know who you are, but I am too old for such delights and, in any case, even when I was young you would not have suited my taste. But I'll take you with me just the same and maybe one day you'll be able to repay me for my trouble."

Ulla had no possessions to pack, and made only one preparation for her departure. She went to Bodø in his kennel. "No, I can't take you with me," she said. "They would come after me to find you, but I am of no value at all."

He licked her face as if he understood her words, and she buried her face in his shaggy mane. Perhaps she would never find such a friend again.

Skól had a shrewder idea of her value to the settlement than Ulla herself had, as they left in the dead of night and travelled far and fast into the interior of the country. In a land surrounded by water, most journeys were made by sea and inland areas were covered by deep forest with only a few paths. Skól knew all of these, and within days they were many miles from Ulla's home. By now he had run out of stocks and needed to return to the trading centre to replenish his supplies.

In these days, Kaupang could hardly be called a town, being just a jumble of huts on the coast. But it was, nevertheless, a centre of trade and commerce for the area. Ulla felt breathless with wonder when she saw the boats of all sizes and shapes from all sorts of exotic countries, and the markets selling everything from gloriously coloured silk cloth from the east to walrus ivory from frozen lands in the north. The smells and the colour and noise animated her, and it was some time before she could direct her mind to the next part of her plan.

In the time she had been travelling with Skól, she had come to respect and care for the old man. He was gentle and reflective and he had not once questioned her motives or behaviour. But for some reason she was reluctant to share her intentions with him. So she bided her time and watched the activities and movements of people around the harbour. It should not be too difficult to find what she was looking for.

Indeed, it was no effort at all. Behind the docks was a jumble of sheds, warehouses and market stalls, but one building stood out among the rest: it was a more imposing structure with a wooden walkway in front. Ladies could be observed sitting or sauntering along this walkway and, from time to time, men would go in the front door. Ulla left Skól busily negotiating business and slipped into the building.

Inside was very stuffy and dark and it was some time before she was able to make out the furnishings. There were heavy hangings on the walls, benches strewn with gaudy cushions, but nobody at all to be seen.

Presently she heard a gruff cough from the corner. "What do you want? We want no beggars in here." What she had taken for a particularly large, brilliant cushion took shape into the fattest woman Ulla had ever seen.

"I want to work here," she said.

The cough turned into a spluttering laugh. "In case you haven't noticed, this is a whorehouse. My clients are not interested in scrawny, filthy children. Come back in a few years when you've grown up."

"I'm older than I look," said Ulla, and to illustrate the words slipped her dirty clothes off her shoulders and shook her long, golden hair free of its bindings.

Disappointingly, there was no reaction from the fat woman. "And do you know how to pleasure a man? I want no tears, or second thoughts or blundering; this is a professional house."

"I am not inexperienced." Ulla lifted her head with as much pride and bravado as she could summon.

This evidently satisfied the woman, as she shouted out to someone. Another woman, as skinny as the first was fat, sidled in.

"Get this object washed and burn those rags. See that she is scrubbed free of lice and fleas, and check that she harbours no infections. We'll see if any of my more discerning clients take an interest in a piece of lean, fresh country meat."

The work, if you could call it that, was little worse than any other disagreeable, dirty job; somewhere between emptying the chamber pots and cleaning out the cowshed. Ulla would have liked to feign unconsciousness as she had with Gorb, but she knew that the men expected some enthusiasm. The other girls told her little tricks, and advised her on the ways to cope with more unsavoury customers. She did her best, giving as much pleasure as possible to the gentler men and dealing as quickly as possible with the others. She did not intend to be here long.

It took longer than she expected. Nice young men do not marry whores. No handsome jarls on white horses come galloping up to rescue beautiful if misunderstood prostitutes. Ulla cultivated the most promising of her clients, letting them know that she had been sold into the whorehouse and worked here very much against her will. None of them took the bait. When at last she had convinced Olaf, a kind, quiet farmer lad, that he was utterly besotted with her, he confessed that his family held rich lands in the west and he was expected to marry a woman of equal standing. Ulla learned that love is tempered with expediency most of the time.

Her deliverance came from an unexpected and fortuitous direction. On his infrequent visits to the city, Skól would come to see her. He usually paid for her time, wanting nothing but conversation, and she found the visits relaxing and comforting. On one occasion he brought someone else. At first Ulla did not recognise the tall, blond young man, and expected he was a friend of Skól's that she had to entertain. But something about the sardonic smile he gave when she approached brought memories flooding back.

"Torvik, is it you? I thought you were dead like all the rest." She did not dare fling herself into the arms of the teasing big brother she had lost so long ago.

"Yes, Ulla, it's really me. I escaped when the raiders came and, well, after many adventures, came here to the centre of civilisation and culture." He had lost none of his ironic sense of humour. "But I too thought you had been killed. It's good to find I have a little sister again."

Skól left them to cry and hug and talk about their respective lives. Torvik told Ulla that he had come to Kaupang to petition the King for restoration of their family lands and holdings. He had done remarkably well as a merchant seaman and was now in a position of some influence in the tiny world of Norse nobility.

Harald Finehair was King of Norway in name rather than fact, but he was keen to establish his right to that title by promoting law and order in his country. It was very important that the hereditary ownership of land be recognised and protected. So he was sympathetic to the two personable young petitioners who came to him. He also wanted to be seen as a strong and just monarch who would ruthlessly punish any of his people who perpetrated land raids within the country of Norway, notwithstanding the fact that he had been guilty of just such behaviour in the past. He agreed to lend Torvik a small band of men to oust the raiders who had taken over the family steading.

In return he expected Torvik's loyalty and support in his ambition to subdue his enemies and unite all of Norway under his leadership.

Torvik told his sister later about the successful expedition. "We rowed into the harbour with muffled oars in the darkest hours of night. No one could have expected anyone to get past the reefs and shoals, but I had sailed through them all my life and there was just enough light to see. Those fools had grown complacent: they didn't even have a lookout. We just walked in and slaughtered them in their beds. We spared our old servants, of course. You'll be able to see them yourself soon."

Ulla made no comment about the violent nature of the attack. It was justified retribution. She was glad that they could return to their old home and begin to repair the damage which had been done to the land and their reputation.

Ulla found it hard to settle. Luckily no one knew of her life in Kaupang, but somehow, after all the tragic and varied events in her life, she did not feel like the naive young girl who had braved the trolls in the rocks so long ago. As Torvik was away most of the time she was left in charge of all the management of the house and farm. It was challenging and enjoyable, but it was lonely too. There was nothing for her here – Bodø had died long ago. When Olaf, her shy young farmer, arrived somewhat shamefacedly at the steading with gifts and a proposal of marriage, she accepted. At least he knew her past and still wanted her. She might not find such an understanding man again.

Ulla's wedding was a quiet occasion compared to the usual extravagant festivities and merrymaking of a Norse marriage. She had no relatives, apart from Torvik, to join her celebrations and she was reluctant to invite all the neighbours in case someone recognised her from her time in Kaupang. As the heiress to a considerable fortune, which she was bringing to the union, she could insist that the feast was small but sumptuous and the guests limited to those she knew. Olaf understood her misgivings and respected her request.

Olaf Ketilsson was the son of a minor chief from Utstein on one of the south-west fjords of Norway. His father had supported Harald Finehair in his campaign to subjugate the area and been rewarded with a manor estate. As the fourth son, Olaf was not likely to possess lands and a hall of his own and, by the time of his marriage to Ulla, his eldest brother had succeeded to the family lands. Ulla took to Arnkel immediately: he was large and strong like her husband but jolly and exuberant, given to practical jokes and all-night bouts of singing and drinking. Arnkel's wife, Gróa, was another matter. As small and mean as her husband was fat and generous, she made it clear that she was the sole mistress of the household and Ulla must occupy a very lowly position within it. Luckily she did not suspect Ulla's background or she would have set out to make her life miserable, but Ulla resumed her well-tried tactic of silent obedience and acquiescence, so Gróa could do nothing more than sneer and berate her for idleness.

Indeed, Ulla enjoyed her life well enough. She was no longer mistress of her own house and had to sleep on a curtained bench in the main room of the hall, but she welcomed the fact that she only had to share her bed with one man, who was gentle and considerate too. He never beat her, and, she found, if she could give him pleasure enough in bed, he would make no other demands on her. If she sometimes thought back to the fading memory of her early childhood or the colour of life in Kaupang, she did not let it prejudice her relationship with the kindly man who had taken her for his own. And by the fourth month of their marriage, she was able to announce proudly that she would present him with his first son in the spring. Olaf was overjoyed and took the news as a reason to build a house more suitable for a growing family on a small holding which his brother bestowed on him.

Ulla loved her little house and, more than anything else, she loved to be the mistress of it, wearing the household keys on her belt and managing her small flock of sheep, her hens and her two old and laggardly servants. She never forgot that she had been a servant herself once, and treated them with unusual respect and kindness. They thought her soft in the head. Very soon the tranquillity of her home was disrupted by the arrival of a squalling, red-faced infant who demanded food all day and never slept at night. Olaf whispered in her ear that the scheming god Loki must have crept into her bed one night. It was not the custom to name a child immediately after birth – many children died in infancy – but, privately, Ulla called him Arnkel after her lusty brother-in-law. Soon another boy, Kali, arrived in the household. Ulla felt her life was consumed by the continuous tasks of feeding the infants, washing their soiled clothes, preparing meals for everyone, caring for animals, cleaning, laying in stocks for the winter, and weaving cloth whenever she had a minute to spare. She enjoyed tending a small garden where she grew leeks, cabbages, beans and several medicinal herbs – she considered this more pleasure than work. But sometimes it was necessary to stop for a moment to straighten her back and look out over the silver waters of the fjord and imagine longships in the clouds winging their way to distant lands. Life had settled into a daily and a seasonal routine, and Ulla expected that it would continue just the same until they rolled her up in a sheet and placed her in a grave with her knife and brooches and spindle whorls by her side.

The Norns had other ideas. Three years after Ulla's marriage, the community was disrupted by the arrival of her brother Torvik, leading a fleet of three longships. Ambitious and clever as always, Torvik had risen in the estimation of King Harald, following him in his latest round of expeditions and conquests. Having been trounced in the decisive Battle of Hafrsfjord, the King's enemies had fled to Orkney, Shetland and the islands in the west, from where they perpetrated raids on mainland Norway. Seriously annoyed by this behaviour, Harald sailed to the west to subjugate these rebellious upstarts. Torvik had made a name for himself in this campaign and been rewarded with rich lands in Orkney. He came armed with tales of sword fights, rich plunder, fine green farmlands where oats and barley flourished, and huge whales rising from the deep to blow fish-tainted spume and turn a baleful eye on the astounded seafarers.

The entire community crowded into the great Hall of Arnkel to hear Torvik's tales of adventure. Eyes sparkled in the light of the central fire, mugs of ale and mead were quaffed, and slaves scurried about serving haunches of pork and mutton to the voracious travellers. Even the children were allowed to sit up, cuddled in arms, listening spellbound to stories of great monsters and feats of daring and courage in the fabled ocean of the west. Ulla, too, listened enthralled. Here was a life which she had scarcely imagined, a life of constant peril and excitement. If only she had been born a man instead of a woman and could venture out on the prow of a sleek dragon ship to fight fierce battles in foreign lands! She glanced at her husband, who stood smiling gently, drinking sparsely as was his habit. He would take only a passing interest in Torvik's stories and, in the morning, return to his fields of oats and his cattle. Arnkel, on the other hand, was already making plans to fit out two ships and join this year's expedition to the west. Ulla was in no mind to wheedle or cajole her husband and she knew that he would not respond to direct confrontation, so she decided to appeal to his reason and love for his children.

When the tales and the carousing were over and everyone had retired to their beds or snored drunkenly by the fire, she broached the subject with him.

"We've two sons now and a third on the way. There'll never be anything for them here; your parcel of land is too small and there's no more to be shared. There is fortune and land to be found in the west. If you join this expedition you could win a future for our sons."

"So, little wife, you've tired of me already, that you would have me go on dangerous exploits and perhaps never return?"

Although Ulla could not see Olaf's face in the dark, she recognised the sad humour in his voice and considered it enough encouragement to continue.

"Well, it's true I could do with more space in my bed as well as in my house, and bigger fields," she laughed. "But it seems to me that there is space aplenty in the southern lands; enough for you and me and our children. Why not join Torvik and your brother this season and find us a new home?"

"I've no quarrel with the people who live there." She could hear the trouble in his voice. "I don't want to kill or steal from those who have prior right to the land. I'm not a warrior, Ulla, and I'll be satisfied enough to die in my bed from old age. Why should I leave everything I love to risk my life and make enemies in an alien place?"

Ulla had one more point to make. "When the fighting is over, they will need peacemakers, people who can negotiate with the native chiefs for peaceful settlement. And they will need farmers, like you, to break in new land and husband it. You needn't fight at all; just wait at the back till the battles are won and then step in."

In the darkness Ulla was unable to see what effect this suggestion had on her husband, but felt it prudent to let the matter lie for the moment.

Whether won over by her appeals for their children or moved by reason, by the next day Olaf had reluctantly agreed to join the war force and himself captain one of his brother's boats. Ten days later, the small group of five boats, each equipped with warriors, their weapons, shields and stores, and even some horses, set out for Orkney where they would join the vast fleet of Earl Sigurd and Thorstein the Red. Ulla watched them set off with a strange feeling in her breast – apprehension, excitement, premonition? Whatever would come, she felt that life was about to change forever.

The summer passed as summers do with a host of mundane tasks and petty troubles. With most of the men away, women took on the work in the fields, tending crops and animals, mending fences and even taking small boats out into the fjord to fish. Ulla liked this most of all and elected to do it whenever she could. She loved the response of the boat to the steering oar and the thrill of pulling aboard a line splashing and sparkling with silver fish. She stroked the bulge of her womb where her next son lay and knew he would be a man of the sea one day.

Everyone hoped fervently that the ships would return before harvest time. But the summer sun had been good and the crops were ready early. Although very near to giving birth, Ulla joined everyone, old and young, in the fields. Oats and barley had to be scythed and stooked; flax was cut and prepared for the long process of making linen; hay for winter feed was hung out to dry, like so many lines of washing, on wicker fences. By the time the ships returned home, all the harvest was in and a new crumpled red face squalled from the crib in the corner of Ulla's house.

Ulla found herself relieved and happy to see her husband again. He had grown lean and brown and, although he never said a word about fighting and killing, his sword had several telltale nicks on the edge. In their bed that night she discovered a joy in lovemaking that she had never known before; a discovery of new pleasure in a familiar setting. Afterwards she lay cocooned in his arms and wondered at herself. He was not asleep.

"So you missed me after all, my little one. Didn't you know I had to return to make sure you hadn't taken another to bed? And don't you want to know about the new home I found for you?"

For an answer Ulla nuzzled and nibbled his neck, which nearly distracted him from the story. But at last he took it up.

"We crossed from Orkney to the mainland and conducted our campaign by land. The people mainly escaped to the hills or behind the walls of their forts, but here and there we met with organised resistance." He paused and then began again. "Earl Sigurd and Thorstein the Red fought battles and subdued the people through all the mainland of Caithness and as far south as the lands of Moray and Ross. All along I looked out for a place where my Ulla would like to settle and make a home, and I found it, on the west coast of Ross. There our ships met us at the end of a deep fjord which cuts into the mountains. We hauled up on one of the islands which protect the entrance to the fjord. It was a good anchorage protected from the stormy west winds, and we had repairs to make, wounds to tend, and needed fresh food. We soon found that the people who live around the fjord are not at all happy to share their riches with us, but they have poor weapons and are no warriors. Their houses are no more than rough shelters, and the few who call themselves chiefs live in the ruins of ancient stone towers. Torvik would like to say we conquered them but I'd say we made a pact, without a drop of blood shed on either side. Anyway, in return for the privilege of hunting in their woods, we agreed to leave all their people in peace. We didn't stay long, but I saw enough to think that you might like it too."

When Ulla did not respond at once, he went on.

"The land would remind you of home but it is gentler, softer; the winters are so warm that the animals can stay out in the fields. There is plenty of space for all our children."

Ulla was content but a strange fear had crept into her heart. Why did this man she had wedded for expediency care for her so kindly? Surely the Norns who meted out fate and justice would repay her ingratitude? In reply she could only bury her face in his neck where he could feel the hot tears of her happiness.

Olaf would have preferred to set out with his men the next summer to establish and build their new home, but Ulla would have none of it. As soon as the decision was made, she wanted to pack up all their belongings and children and leave right away. Olaf prevailed on her to wait and use the winter to build up stocks and collect all the things they would need in their new home. Torvik would also accompany them with his three boats: he had a fancy for making a base for Viking raids in the southern lands. Arnkel, on the other hand, was happy to spend the rest of his years surrounded by his hunting dogs and drinking cronies, and retelling tales of his brief moments of adventure. He did agree, however, to loan them one boat with crew as long as it was returned at the end of the season. By the time the first buds of spring were showing on the trees and everything was prepared for their journey, Ulla was tense with anticipation. She sailed out of her homeland without a backward glance.

Their ship was not a warship but a *knörr*, one of the big wide-beamed boats which the Norsemen used for trading. The central hull could carry a large amount of cargo and, on this occasion, it sounded and smelt like a small farmyard. There were three milch cows, a bull calf, goats, sheep, chickens and even two piglets and a pregnant sow, along with bags of seed grain, equipment for farming and tools for carpentry and ironworking. They were not going to an empty land, but they expected to be self-sufficient and even produce enough surplus to trade. In addition, three other men, with their families, servants and slaves, had decided to settle in the south, so all four boats in their small flotilla were full to overflowing.

Their journey was not a long one by Norse standards but they were venturing out into the open ocean without a sight of land. Ulla was exhilarated by the lift and fall of the waves and the taste of salt spray on her lips, and was somewhat disappointed when worsening weather forced them to shelter in the Orkneys and delayed them for a few days. She took no pleasure in visiting the hall of Earl Sigurd, where the men caroused and the women eyed her distrustfully, but it gave them the opportunity to ask the Earl for permission to settle on his lands on the western mainland.

Early one evening, before the main business of feasting and drinking had begun, Torvik introduced his sister to the Earl and presented their request.

"My Lord, I have served you well, helping you win battles and conquer the country so that now your lands extend throughout the islands and far south to the very domain of the Picts. Now I would like to establish a base on the western coast, and my sister and her husband, who also fought in your campaign, wish to make a home there."

This request suited Sigurd very well. His rampageous braggart of a colleague, Thorstein the Red, had been killed by the Picts in Caithness. His mother, Aud the Deep-Minded, had escaped to Orkney with her wealth and a large retinue and was presently imposing her strong character on Sigurd's household. Sigurd had neither the resources nor the temper to entertain more guests. Furthermore, the western and southern lands were frontier territory and it would be useful to have a strong base somewhere on the west coast. Privately, Sigurd did not expect them to be able to hold the land for long.

"I will grant your request on condition that you, Torvik, maintain control of the area for me," he said. "In addition I will grant your sister whichever land she wishes to settle on as long as she and her husband pay me levy and allegiance. I need an outpost on the western seaboard which can command the inland routes from the east and also service our ships on their voyages to the south."

These conditions were no greater than they expected, and they accepted readily. Ulla was anxious to leave: the indomitable Aud, who was a devout Christian, insisted that all the women, whether converted or not, observe proper moral behaviour and humility, and looked with disapproval on the riotous drinking of the men. It was not a comfortable household. Torvik and his men were also eager to be away in search of fortune, so, as soon as the weather permitted, they set off again.

From now on they were always in sight of land and Ulla watched the unfolding vista of cliffs and crags on the Sutherland coast. Most of it looked forbidding and inhospitable but, occasionally, they caught tantalising glimpses of sandy beaches and the suggestion of low woodland reaching down to the shore. Further inland, strange-shaped mountains rose above a crumpled landscape.

It was only a few days' sailing before they reached a group of small islands at the entrance to a big sea loch and pulled into the anchorage on the sheltered side of the largest island. Ulla could understand why the Norsemen called it Tanera, Harbour Isle, because, in addition to the perfectly situated bay on the east side, there were several inlets and indentations around its coast which could give protection from stormy weather no matter what the direction. It was a perfect temporary base for Viking raiders, but it might not be so suitable for permanent settlement and to support four growing families. There were few trees for building, no animals except seals to hunt, and only a few patches of land which could be made over to pasture. It would be adequate for the present but they would have to find somewhere with running water, trees and good areas of flat land. Ulla looked longingly inland where the narrowing loch disappeared into the haze below snow-tipped mountains. But this land was already occupied. Sometimes on still days, she could make out blue smoke wisping from camp- or household fires, and she often sensed that eyes were watching anxiously to see when these unwelcome strangers would leave.

Olaf lost no time in deliberation. They must plant their crops soon or they would miss the season, and they still had to prepare the ground. Before Torvik left, the three longships sailed leisurely into the loch and anchored below the fort of the local chieftain on the southern shores. They made no attempt to land but hung white-painted shields on the sides of the boats as the recognised sign of peaceful intentions. Before long a small band of men came down from the fort and approached the beach. Olaf was well aware that the success of their venture depended on the next few minutes. Behind him was displayed the full power of Norse superiority in war, but he would only achieve permanent settlement with the grudging cooperation of the local people. Ulla had demanded that she accompany him; they were, after all, about to negotiate for her own home. So the two of them, along with a captured slave as an interpreter, rowed the small boat ashore. They came without weapons but carrying baskets of goods for trade: bales of wadmal, the coarse woollen cloth which served as clothing and sails; some finer linen material; brooches and pins in silver; walrus ivory combs and various iron tools and implements. They laid these out on the beach and waited to see what the reception would be.

The local chief, Lagaidh, was a man of pragmatic intelligence. He was well aware that the Norsemen were now in control of all the islands to the north and west and along most of the mainland coast. There was nothing to be gained by direct opposition, but a great deal by accommodation and trade. The goods on display were by no means the richest but Lagaidh knew they represented much more: access to permanent trading supply lines. He had little to offer in exchange but, by clever manipulation and bartering, he might be able to control, and in the process cream off some profit from, the flow of goods through his area. But something else attracted his interest. Ulla was the first Norse woman he had ever seen. She was taller, more slender and clearly more spirited than native women. Her fine clothes and jewellery indicated that she must be a person of some standing. He wondered if she was on offer as well.

The interpreter explained that the strangers had no warlike intentions but wished to settle in this land. Lagaidh made a show of reluctance but was privately pleased to grant them the islands in the loch. His people had no use for them anyway. A pact was struck, sealed with blood, and Lagaidh watched the strangers depart to their longships, his mind occupied with thoughts of profit and speculation about the availability of nubile young Viking women.

Having made a show of strength, Torvik set off with his ships a-Viking. It was not likely he would return till worsening weather put an end to all sea trips.

Ulla and Olaf settled down to the back-breaking tasks of working untamed land and building more permanent houses for themselves and the other families. For the time being, everyone chose to remain on Tanera but, in the future, some of the smaller islands might prove suitable for habitation. Building houses proved to be the biggest problem. Stone walls were easy enough to construct but there were no trees to provide support for a turf roof.

An expedition to the mainland would have to be made, and they would have to barter some of their precious provisions in return for the necessary wood.

As it happened, they found Lagaidh, the chief, more than willing to allow them to cut all the wood they needed and even hunt for welcome supplies of fresh meat, in return for a few tools and lengths of wool and linen. Clearly the Norse people possessed goods which were considered luxuries in this primitive land. Ulla stored up this knowledge for future reference.

For several days all the men cut wood from the extensive forests at the head of the loch. There were fine trees here, many of them tall and straight, suitable for ships' masts, and others of differing types more suited to other uses. For the time being, they only needed spars for roofing, but they took note of the wealth of timber available. When they had sufficient wood for building, along with offcut branches for fuel, they rowed the fully laden *knörr* back to the island.

The summer progressed with unremitting toil for everyone. Even the children were engaged in the lighter tasks of tending animals, sowing seeds and weeding the growing crops, whilst the adults completed the houses. Along with one large building for living quarters, there were two for animals and crop storage. They would need more houses when Torvik and his men returned.

For Ulla this was a time of joy and fulfilment. Her sons delighted her as they grew from babies into individuals and she found increasing pleasure in the company of her quiet, careful husband. She had always thrived from hard work but now it was especially rewarding as it contributed to the construction of her home. All the families watched the growing crops with interest and some apprehension as the success of their venture depended on what they could produce in their first year. Despite its warmer winters, this country seemed to have much cooler and wetter summers. The oats grew well, but frequent winds and rainstorms flattened much and there was little sign that they would ripen in time for the harvest. Ulla despaired most of all over her flax field. There was just not enough sunshine to encourage growth. On the other hand, all the animals thrived on the rich green pasture and produced record numbers of healthy offspring. Obviously the new land was a fount of fertility, as Ulla found she could expect another child in the spring.

Torvik returned with his men and boats in time to help with the harvest, such as it was. Their raiding had been successful but, privately, Olaf disparaged the booty: you can't eat silver bullion and fine silks, and pretty jewellery won't keep a body warm. How were they going to feed a community which had just quadrupled in size? It was Ulla who suggested that some of these riches could be traded for crops and hunting rights on the mainland. She had not forgotten the acquisitive light in Chief Lagaidh's eyes. And so it proved. Torvik's warriors could work off their high spirits and energy hunting for deer but, more importantly, lucrative relationships began to be established between the Norse people and some of the locals. Several of Torvik's men were eager to return to their families in Orkney, so he dispatched them northwards in two of his longships. It looked as if the community might have enough to survive the winter.

As it happened, the disaster occurred because of a shortage of another kind. In a community consisting of many lusty young men, a few married women and some native female slaves, strife is bound to occur. Ill feeling had already developed because one woman had left her husband for another man. Torvik, following his impulsive, reckless nature, solved his own problem by carrying off the daughter of a family from the nearby peninsula. The girl, beautiful but insipid (Ulla thought privately), seemed perfectly happy with the arrangement and the attentions of her handsome lover but her family were furious and brooding vengeance. They waited, however, till the time was right.

Mindful of his promise to Arnkel, Olaf had returned the loaned *knörr* and its crew. Before sea conditions worsened, Torvik made a last trip to the Hebrides to purchase meat, meal and other essentials to tide them over the winter. As far as watchers from the mainland were concerned it appeared that the settlers had been abandoned and were unprotected by either longships or warriors. What they did not know was that Torvik had sailed with only a skeleton crew and most of his seasoned Vikings remained at Tanera. That, and the vigilance of the guard dogs, saved the community from complete massacre.

The attackers had chosen a night with no moon and an overcast sky. Anyone with little sea lore, and mindful of the shoals and reefs on this rocky coastline, would never venture out to sea on such a night. But the locals were experienced seamen and there was just enough light to make out the pale curls of waves breaking on rocks. They landed their boat on a beach a little to the north of the settlement and crept quietly to surround the houses. There must have been fifteen to twenty men armed with swords, spears, axes, and variously protected by purloined, borrowed or home-made helmets and shields. It was their obvious, if misplaced, intention to wipe out this nest of heathens and send a message that the men of this land were not about to submit to the rule of any foreign invaders.

One guard dog heard their stealthy movements and set off all the others barking. Frustrated in their attempt at surprise, the attackers moved in straight away to each of the houses and battered the barred wooden doors with their axes. By now the occupants were fully alert and reaching for weapons and armour. One of the more enterprising locals had had the presence of mind to bring torches and a pouch of coals. They set fire to the thatch hoping to burn the inmates to death. Ulla smelled the sweet taint of burning heather and shrieked a warning. The Norsemen erupted from their houses like rabbits from a burrow and assaulted the ferrets in true berserker fashion. Screaming like a Valkyrie and flourishing a spear above her head, Ulla plunged through the doorway. This apparition, enlarged by the light from the flames, was enough to emasculate the remaining attackers. The other women, too, furious at having their homes destroyed, rushed to join the fray or grabbed buckets of water to douse the flames. The battle, if it could be called that, was over in a matter of minutes. The attackers, realising they had made a fatal mistake, retreated swiftly to their boat, leaving at least one of their number dead and a few more escaping with severe wounds to their heads as well as their pride.

Of the Norsemen, one man, Stein, was dead, and two of the houses had lost their roofs entirely, but no women or children were injured and all the animals were safe due to the quick thinking of a young lad who had herded them out of danger as soon as the attack became apparent. Taken objectively they had suffered lightly, but the damage to their relationship with the local people was immense. When Torvik returned a few days later, he demanded a punitive expedition to the mainland. He gathered all the families and his crew together – their small hall was full to bursting – and addressed them.

"We must avenge our brother's death. We must teach these people a lesson. These lands are ours, won by the conquests of Thorstein the Red and Earl Sigurd. We rule here and we must administer justice. We can't let the people think they can challenge us."

Roused by these stirring words, the assembled warriors shouted and cheered, grabbing handy weapons, as if ready to set off right away.

In his quiet, confident way, Olaf had become acknowledged as leader of the settlers. He stood up now, his arms folded, and waited until the authority of his presence had quietened the men. He nodded to his fiery brother-in-law. "Yes, Torvik, we must ensure that justice is upheld in our new lands. But you, yourself, are responsible for the first injustice – or, I may say, criminal act – which set this train of events in motion."

An air of tension spread through the hall as the assembly speculated on Torvik's reaction to this allegation, but he merely glared at Olaf and waited for him to finish.

"You stole a daughter, and, whether you consider her of less worth than a horse or a bag of silver, her relatives place greater value on her life. They now have lost a man's life, and we, too, have lost a man. We are matched but for the matter of the woman. If justice is to be observed we must either return her or pay compensation for her abduction."

Nodding of heads and murmurs of concurrence signalled a certain amount of agreement. Ulla noticed that all of the settlers were supporting her husband's argument, and she smiled at him to offer encouragement.

Torvik was not to see reason. "The woman is mine and stays with me. But we must punish these people for their audacity. I say we strike back with fire and sword immediately, before they have time to slink away to their lairs in the mountains. Teach them to respect our right to rule."

Many of the men voiced their support for this plan of action, but there were others, perhaps blaming Torvik for the whole incident, who grumbled their dissent.

Olaf chose his words with care. "Respect for a right to rule is not won through fear, but by just and reasonable administration. Remember, Torvik, you will sail back to your lands in Orkney or Norway. We have chosen to make this place our home and must suffer the consequences of our initial behaviour towards the people. Already they believe us to be pillagers and rapists, taking by force that to which we have no right. I think we could make this an opportunity to show our compassion, our reasonableness, our desire for peace; to show that we have much more to offer for compliance than violence and theft."

Although Olaf spoke quietly and without force, his words carried great weight and solemnity. Ulla looked at her husband with renewed admiration and respect. His words also won the minds of the listeners for, although there was still fierce argument from the most hot-headed of the Vikings, by the end of the evening, it had been agreed to settle the business by peaceful negotiation instead of more bloodshed.

Although Torvik would never admit it to her, Ulla could see by his behaviour that he recognised the wisdom of Olaf's argument. Torvik was not the kind of man to settle either here or in Orkney, and even less likely in their family lands in Norway. He would rove the seas and eventually die by the sword or perish lost and forgotten in some unexplored far-off land. In some ways she was very like her brother, but she had chosen a different way of life. Now it was as if he stepped back and distanced himself from the others in the community. Although he accompanied Olaf in the peace delegation to the mainland, he left the talking to him.

Olaf settled the matter to everyone's grudging satisfaction. Torvik would pay the girl's family 150 øre of silver: ring money, hack silver and jewellery. Since both sides had lost a man in the battle, it was not considered necessary to pay recompense but, as a gesture of conciliation, Olaf offered to support the deceased man's widow and two young children. Whatever the woman thought of this arrangement, it seemed to be satisfactory to her family and she would certainly have no shortage of suitors willing to take her as a wife.

Winter set in in earnest. For days on end the wind blew fiercely and huge waves burst on the exposed western rocks, sending showers of salty spray right over the island. On the mainland, blizzards coated the mountains with snow. But ever so often, quite suddenly, the sea would calm, the sun would break through the clouds and bring distant views into sparkling clarity. To a people used to locking their doors against the winter freeze and dark, these days were an unexpected joy. They could get out and tend to the animals and even make occasional trips to the mainland to cut wood or hunt. There is no doubt, too, that some of these expeditions led to closer relationships with the natives, as there is not a Norseman living who will refuse a place by a warm hearth on a long, dark night, or a jug of the local brew with pleasant female company. They all found they had much in common.

Only Torvik seemed to be dissatisfied with this way of life. He busied himself during the day with manual projects such as housebuilding or repairs to the longship which they had hauled up onto the shore, but at nights he usually drank himself into a sodden stupor or lustily dragged his wife, or any other available woman, off to his bed. Ulla observed this and eventually decided to broach an idea she had been nursing for some time. She approached him one bright morning while he was caulking the hull of one of their small boats.

"Torvik, I will never return to Norway now," she stated emphatically. "I would like to surrender my share of our family lands in return for a *knörr* with a cargo of trade goods. I've a fancy for a life of commerce. Will you do that for me?"

Although Torvik was a man of action and impulse, he respected Ulla's opinions. If he loved anything or anyone in this life at all, it was probably his shrewd little sister. And his thoughts of late had been turning in a similar direction: the sedentary life he was leading did not suit him at all. So he took little time for deliberation.

"I, too, wish to give up our lands. I will never settle anywhere for good, but I would like to make Orkney my base and trade far and wide throughout the Norse dominions and even further." A thoughtful look glazed his eyes. "We should realise substantial return from the sale of our combined lands, enough to build several ships and purchase cargo. Let's make a partnership, you and I? We can begin small – you handle the trading of goods in the islands here, and I will bring Norse specialities. But who knows how it will go on? A fleet of ships trading the sea roads and merchants travelling far to the east and south, Rome and Istanbul."

Ulla smiled to herself. She had lit a spark which might, with luck, bring some meaning into her brother's life. But she sought to curb his enthusiasm. "Don't go too fast, Torvik. For the present let's agree to sell our lands and purchase one or two *knörrs*. We can leave it to the Norns to determine our future."

While winter storms prevented him from putting to sea, there was nothing to be done, but Ulla was delighted to see her brother making plans. He even stopped drinking to excess, and treated his wife with more consideration. Olaf commended this change for the better and approved Ulla's project, but he had been making some plans of his own. He proposed that, as soon as spring arrived, they make a move to the mainland. The island had only ever been a temporary settlement and the time was now right to look for more permanent accommodation. Ulla approved this plan; she would like her next child to be born on the mainland.

On a calm, clear day shortly after the winter solstice, they called on Lagaidh in his gloomy, dilapidated tower. By now he had become accustomed to these visits and looked forward to them as much for the chance of furtively ogling Ulla as for the likelihood of some lucrative deal for himself. On this occasion, though, he was not so keen on their proposition: once these invaders had a foothold on the mainland they were likely to take control of everything as they had done elsewhere. It was Ulla who changed his mind. Through their interpreter she explained that, once established on a permanent farm, they hoped to set up a trading link, bringing luxury goods from Norway and even further afield in exchange for timber and locally grown produce that might be needed on the western islands or Orkney. She proposed that Lagaidh should handle this end of the market. Although she could not speak the language yet, she could by now understand enough to guess that Lagaidh was interested in this proposal. He made a show of extreme reluctance but finally agreed to let them have a small piece of land of his own choice. Neither Ulla nor Olaf mentioned the fact that, as all this country had been conquered by Earl Sigurd of Orkney, they had a right to any land they wanted without permission of the local chieftains.

Now, the best land in the area lay at the head of the loch, where thousands of years of silt had washed down from the inland valleys and covered the stony beaches left by retreating ice. Lagaidh had no intention of giving that up: years of work and strenuous effort had gone into making it productive, and it also controlled one of the routes overland to the countries in the east. Halfway down the north side of the loch, a raised beach was cut by a substantial river. The land was stony and the few peasants who lived there in their meagre hovels struggled to make a living. Lagaidh was not unduly worried about dispossessing them of their land; the plight of common folk did not concern him. In fact it was Olaf who sought to deal equitably with them. He would let them stay and work their patches of soil in return for their help in setting up and working the farm. He emphasised that they would not be slaves but would be free to leave if this arrangement did not suit them. Bemused by this favourable offer, all three families agreed to stay and would in time no doubt learn that this big blond Viking with the gentle eyes was true to his word; not at all the berserker they had been led to believe.

So it was settled. In the spring Olaf and Ulla would move to the mainland with all their goods and animals. Of the other Norse settlers, one family agreed to come with them, but Einar chose to settle on a nearby island and Ivar elected to remain on Tanera: it would remain an important staging post and harbour for Norse ships, whether on Viking expeditions or engaged in more legitimate pursuits.

Ulla lost no time in preparing for the move. Although the winters were long they were very mild and she could see no reason to wait for spring. Two of their houses had been destroyed in the attack and only offered temporary shelter, so it made more sense to concentrate effort on rebuilding on the mainland. She was also anxious to retain the labour of Torvik's men before they left on their summer roving. In a week she had everything ready for the move but, as luck would have it, the weather turned and fierce storms kept everyone cooped up indoors for days on end. Tempers frayed and arguments and fights broke out. It was none too soon before the sun came out at last, the wind dropped and the sea calmed to a rolling swell. Those who understood the ways of the weather predicted that this would last for a day or two, so Ulla insisted that they take the opportunity at once.

Understandably it took several trips to ferry all their belongings, people and animals to the mainland. Their single longship was not designed for such transport. Once ashore they erected simple shelters for the people and stockades to confine the animals for the present. And then the weather set in again. The men grumbled, the children whimpered and even Ulla, listening to the wind howling outside their booth and watching the salt-ridden rain driving in from the sea, wondered if she had been too hasty. But she was learning the pattern of weather here: nothing lasted for long and it could change completely in a matter of hours. Soon they were able to crawl out of their sodden shelters and assess the potential of their new home.

It looked surprisingly promising. The stony base made for good drainage and there was a layer of sandy topsoil in places. It would need a lot of work and the addition of organic material and nutrients to make it fertile. But shortly after their arrival they made an unexpected discovery. Olaf had noticed some limestone pebbles brought down by the river and, hunting for the source, soon found large areas of limestone outcrop in the valley behind the settlement. This was a treasure of untold wealth. The stone could be ground down and used as fertiliser on the fields. Lagaidh must have been unaware of its value, otherwise he would never have agreed to let them have this land. Quite apart from its usefulness on the soil, limestone could be another trading commodity.

Ulla was more concerned about the siting of their hall and outbuildings. Although it was exposed to the western winds, she chose a spot on the top of the terrace above the river. It was close to sources of stone and timber and would not be prone to flooding either from the sea or the river itself. She had discovered that one of Torvik's men had a particular talent for housebuilding, and the two of them talked for hours and pored over drawings of possible layouts. Although they would begin in a modest way, Ulla wanted there to be plenty of scope for other buildings and outhouses as the settlement developed. She would like a separate byre and servants' quarters. A small stream could be diverted for a lade for a mill. They would need a house for ironworking. She even fancied a bathhouse. At last it was agreed to begin with a substantial hall for the family, and a byre. The rest could be tackled later.

While Olaf set to work preparing fields for crops and enclosures for the animals, Ulla supervised the building. The main farmstead would be shaped as a long rectangle containing a large living area with a central hearth and benches around the sides. A smaller building to accommodate the servants and slaves would be partitioned off for wintering the cattle. Torvik's men, glad to be busy after so much idleness, lugged heavy stones up from the river to construct the drystone walls with an earthen core. This part of the work was completed in a surprisingly short time. Then they had to cut timber for the roof spars and turf for the roofing itself.

Olaf decided to prepare their first crop fields in the floodplain of the river. It was the only place where the stony base had a shallow covering of silty soil. After ploughing the fields, he organised his farmworkers and enlisted the local people to collect seaweed and grind down some of the limestone for fertiliser. This was an unfamiliar practice to the natives, who seldom did more to fertilise their fields than spread farm manure. Olaf did his best to explain to them that the seaweed and lime contained some kinds of magic food which would encourage growth. The land would also need years and years of manure and rotted vegetable material to turn stony sand into fertile soil. The people listened and observed sceptically: they would wait and see the results of all this effort. In particular, Olaf worked on the small flax field. He was confident the barley and oats would flourish well, but their experience on Tanera had showed that flax needed extra fertiliser and lime. Flax was an essential part of the Norse economy: not only did it supply linen for cloth, particularly bridal wear, but the seeds yielded linseed oil, and the stems and leaves, tough fibres for cord. As it was unknown to the natives, the products would be very valuable. A sacred symbol of the goddess Freyja, flax was considered 'women's seed' and careful ritual had to be observed during its planting.

On a Friday, the day dedicated to Freyr, the God of Fertility, and his sister Freyja, Ulla donned her best clothes: a linen shift and woollen overdress, held up by two oval bronze brooches, her white headscarf and fine leather boots. She wore her silver arm rings and a necklace of glass and amber beads. All the men and boys were dispatched to outlying fields: it was very important that no male watched. Ulla led the grown women to the flax field and began to sow the seed, a gentle rhythm swaying to right and left, offering a silent prayer to Freyja to ensure the success of the crop. As soon as Ulla had completed a row, the other women joined in, some perhaps offering prayers for their own fertility. Tonight, when the men returned, they would have to attend to that.

Olaf also worked on a small vegetable plot beside the farm where Ulla could grow her cabbages, beans, and medicinal plants such as plantain, meadowsweet and henbane. The animals were allowed to roam under the constant supervision of young herders. There were a few wolves in the mountains – you could hear them howling eerily on still nights – and even foxes and eagles were a danger to newborn lambs and kids. Olaf noticed that the animals which ranged into the valleys behind the settlements thrived better than those at the coast. He resolved to establish a summer shieling up there next year.

After the fierce storms of the winter, this spring was a delight. From early in the year the sun shone for days on end and the snows on the hills melted very quickly. Ulla took it as a portent that the Gods favoured their new home. Certainly the crops grew very well, the flax too, and the animals flourished on the new green grass. Ulla's latest son came into the world quickly and with a minimum of fuss, and Ulla named him Thorir; she felt sure he would be a fine warrior one day.

By now Arnkel, her oldest son, was four years old. He was tall and blond like his father and followed him everywhere, deeply interested in the farm work and tending to the animals. Kali, who was just learning the freedom to roam, was outside in all weathers, climbing on the rocks to look for fish in the pools or running up the hills hunting for birds' eggs. He made friends quickly with the native children and soon looked indistinguishable from them, with his dark hair matted and wild and his skin tanned oaken brown by the sun. Ljót, merely one and a half, toddled about the house interfering with the women's work and constantly climbing up on laps to be cuddled; he was a very affectionate lad. Nursing Thorir by the hearthside, Ulla felt privileged and fortunate to have such healthy and exceptional sons.

Torvik remained with them for only as long as it took to finish the main buildings. As soon as he felt they were established, he loaded up his longboat with timber to trade in the outer islands and Orkney and set off on a roundabout route, first to pick up his other boats and crew in Orkney, and then to Norway. Everyone felt a little concerned that they were now unprotected from either vengeful natives or roving Vikings who had no compunction about attacking their own people. Olaf determined to build a ship for themselves some day, and ensured that a watch was always kept for invaders by land or sea. He was confident that his people were strong enough to fend off all but the most determined raiders but, in fact, his preparations were unnecessary as this part of the country was settling into a relatively peaceful period, with control by the Norse acknowledged by all. Although greatly outnumbered by the natives, the settlers could muster support from Orkney and the Hebrides to quash uprisings. It was easier and more lucrative for wily local chieftains like Lagaidh to bide their time and wait till the incomers were assimilated into the population by natural process.

The summer passed so quickly with all the innumerable tasks that they were well into the autumn harvest before Torvik returned. He came sailing grandly up the loch with his own longship and two new *knörrs* which he had purchased in Norway along with cargoes of staple and luxury goods: wheat, honey, malt, iron weapons and tools, whale bones and walrus ivory from Finnmark, rich cloth from England, and fine jewellery of gold and silver. He had already made good trade in Orkney and the Hebrides, and now he gave one fully laden *knörr* to Ulla as her share of the proceeds from the sale of their lands. She was delighted to see him, and took a childlike interest in rummaging through the stock. She selected for herself only a few items which would be of use to the community and took the rest to Lagaidh on the other side of the loch.

If Lagaidh had ever regretted his decision to let these people settle on his loch, he rejoiced in his good fortune now. His only fear was that he could not procure enough of value to trade. But Ulla explained that wood from the vast inland forests and young stock animals would always be needed by settlers on the other islands. Lagaidh proposed that they take the most luxurious goods overland to the eastern sea coast where a thriving market was becoming established at Dingwall, the seat of Norse government for the area. Every horse or ox they could find was loaded up and Ulla, Olaf and Lagaidh, along with enough well-armed men to protect their supplies, set off to the east. It was not a long journey by any standards but they made two days of it, resting overnight by a sheltered inland loch.

The market was a poor affair compared to what Ulla remembered of Kaupang. But she greatly enjoyed meeting other Norse settlers and dealing with merchants from all parts of the known world. While Lagaidh appeared taciturn and unresponsive, she soon learned that he struck a hard bargain and always knew when someone was intent on cheating him. For his part, Lagaidh ascertained that Ulla carried an intelligent as well as pretty head on her shoulders. They returned from the market with greatly increased wealth as well as mutual respect.

Before the winter, Ulla determined to take the *knörr* herself to trade the rest of her goods in the outer islands. Olaf was not particularly happy about this arrangement, especially as Thorir would have to accompany her, but he knew there was no point in complaining. The journey went well, with good weather and favourable winds. They were able to ply their trade all along the coastline of the bigger islands and to many of the small islets which made up the chain. The Norse, who had settled in the Hebrides, scraped an existence from marginal land and were eager for basic supplies like timber, and the exotic goods Ulla had to offer. So, by the time the harvest was in, Ulla had returned with fine tales of her adventures and even more useful goods for further trade.

The harvest had been most abundant. All the crops, even the flax, had done exceptionally well and their original stock of animals had increased tenfold. They had more than enough to see them through the winter, and Ulla wondered how she would ever find the time and hands to process the flax and wool ready for weaving. She enlisted every woman in the community and even let it be known that any local women who wanted to help would be richly recompensed for their labour. Not many took up this offer at first but, as soon as they saw the fine materials and jewellery which their predecessors had earned, others came over the hills to join them. Ulla was soon in charge of a small industry.

The wool was easy to work: all the women were adept in preparation and spinning. But flax required a long and complicated process to render it into thread. First the plant had to be soaked in water for seven to twelve days. Then heckles with long iron spikes were used to strip fibres from the skin of the stems and leaves ready for spinning. The finest threads would be used to weave clothing, coarser material for sails, and the roughest made good tough ropes. But a certain amount of expertise was necessary to achieve this, and only the Norse women, who had learned from childhood, could produce the finest linen. Ulla did not expect any more but was happily surprised at how quickly some of the local girls mastered the process. By wintertime many of them went proudly back to their huts in the hills with new skills and fine gifts to display.

Unlike the previous winter, this one was less windy and stormy but unremittingly damp. The occasional snows soon melted into puddles of slush. Most days it rained with a fine, penetrating drizzle which soaked through clothes and fur, and indoors coated everything in a grey layer of mould. Olaf checked their stores of grain daily and ensured that fires were kept burning in the grain store to stave off the worst of the damp, but inevitably some was ruined. At least the animals could be kept outside in enclosures which he had built by the farmstead, and he only brought the cattle into the byre in the coldest weather. But everyone, animal and human alike, seemed to suffer a depression from the perpetual dullness. Only Ulla took a delight in stopping to watch the swirls of mist fingering the mountains; she was much too busy to be depressed. All day, when she wasn't tending to the children or supervising cooking, she would be weaving; mostly functional cloth, but occasionally a length of fine linen for a special dress or headscarf. She took the greatest pleasure in pressing cloth into crisp pleats with a glass smoother on her whalebone plaque. As the final part of the linen-making process, this was a sacred task, and she whispered an incantation to Freyja to bless her household with fertility. Olaf, for his part, spent what spare time he had working iron in the small smiddy which he had built by the river. He was strong and skilled with large farm implements and weapons, but he also took pleasure in producing more delicate objects like shears and lamps. The winter passed very quickly.

Their next summer was as sunny and warm as the last. Olaf began to clear the lands around the farmstead and used the big ox to pull the heaviest rocks aside. He spread lime, seaweed and manure and ploughed them into the soil. He replaced wooden fences with stone dykes to protect the growing crops from the animals which were still allowed to roam freely. But, as soon as the weather allowed, he sent the flocks and herds to the hills and valleys for the best pasture. They only kept enough cattle, sheep and goats close by to provide their present dairy needs.

Ulla knew she had much to do at home but she had a strong desire to establish her trading links. Truthfully, she felt cramped by her mundane existence; she wanted to feel the rise of the waves beneath the deck and look on other faces and lands for a while. If Olaf knew this was the true reason for her wish to travel, he kept the insight to himself. Thorir was now weaned and there were plenty of surrogate mothers who would be delighted to care for their boys. Ulla promised that she would not voyage far or be away for long.

First of all, Ulla had her *knörr* loaded with timber which Lagaidh's people had felled, and enlisted a small crew for the voyage. Trading vessels relied on sails rather than oar power, so did not require as many rowers as traditional longships. This made them slower and reliant on wind direction and the weather, so she was apprehensive about the voyage. The ship was so fully laden that they could not portage it over narrow necks of land and had to wait for calm seas before rounding dangerous headlands. The most daunting passage occurred where mighty ocean rollers pounded great red sandstone cliffs at the tip of the north-west mainland. Any vessel had to keep well out from the shore before turning into the strait which separated it from Orkney. Even here they would not be out of danger as the Pentland Firth was notorious for whirlpools and contrary currents. The sailors kept up a constant chant to Njord, God of the Ocean, to protect them from the vagaries of the sea but, privately, Ulla put more faith in the expertise of her helmsman as he steered the ship to best advantage of the wind and waves. The knuckles of his hands were white where he gripped the steering oar, and his eyes flicked constantly from the sea to the set of the sail. Either his skill or the favour of the Gods brought them through and they were at last able to pull into the harbour on mainland Orkney where Torvik lived. Luckily he had not yet left, so, after selling the timber, they agreed to set out together to Norway to see what new treasures Kaupang had to offer.

The town had grown hugely in the seven years since Ulla had left. Imposing stone buildings took the place of the tumbled shacks and warehouses, and proper wharves had been built for the many ships docked there. Ulla was not disappointed to see that there was no sign of her previous place of work. In a corner of the big market square she found a bronze trader she remembered and fervently hoped he did not recognise her. "You know the old man, Skól. He used to buy brooches from you. Is he anywhere about?" she enquired.

"Skól?" he huffed, squinting curiously. He was obviously trying to place the familiar face. "No, haven't seen him in years. I guess he's dead," he added bluntly.

Ulla turned away quickly in case he recalled who she was. She asked everyone around the market but no one had seen Skól and few remembered him. As there was no particular reason to delay their visit here, Ulla transacted her business as quickly as she could whilst negotiating the best bargains. She wanted to visit some of the nearby farms to purchase horses; there were few in Scotland and most of them were weak, spavined beasts. She required some good, strong Norwegian horses as breeding stock and for the heavy work around the farm.

Torvik took her to a stud farm near the town. Here she was able to purchase four sturdy horses: three mares and a stallion, enough to breed from for the present. It was in a small paddock behind the farm that she saw the big black stallion. He was unlike anything she had ever seen before, bigger but altogether finer boned, with a proud head and a fierce eye. The farmer explained that he came from fabled lands far to the south and east and, no, even if she traded all her goods and mortgaged all her belongings, she could not afford to buy him. He was a king's horse and would father a line of kings' horses. Maybe if she came back in a few years… Ulla had to be content.

Torvik and Ulla parted ways. Torvik set off south; Ulla sailed for home. She felt the same thrill she had felt on her first voyage into the open ocean, but the salt on her cheeks was as much from tears at her homecoming as the sting of the spray. She stood at the prow of the boat to spy the first sight of the hills behind the loch. At last the sailors turned the sail to catch the westerly wind and the boat skimmed into the beach below the farmhouse. Her family were overjoyed to see her and she wondered at how much the boys had grown in her short absence.

So Ulla's life stretched out into a pattern. Busy throughout the year with work on the farm, she tried to make one trading trip in the summer, but left most of their combined business to Torvik. She was richly fulfilled and her memories of deprivation and hardship wafted away like mist on the hills.

Three years after their arrival in the loch, Ulla gave birth to a stillborn daughter. As she cradled the tiny body in her arms, she wondered at the beauty and waste of life. The child was perfect: a touch of lavender on her almost-transparent eyelids; long brown lashes and a fuzz of dark newborn hair; even the fingernails on her tiny curled fingers were complete miniature versions of an adult's. Here had been a potential person, a little girl laughing and playing in the sun, a lover, a mother with a new baby of her own. Yet she had not even breathed her first living breath of air. Her entire world and life had been encompassed in the shelter of her mother's womb. Ulla was reluctant to let them take her daughter away to bury in the cold, hard earth, but the labour had been long and difficult and she soon sank into a troubled unconsciousness.

A shadow passes over her face. When she looks up she can see blue sky through pale green leaves. She can hear the tumble of water and feel a light spray on her cheeks. Below her the water falls away into the pool below. Looking down, she sees the body lifeless, floating on the water, and tendrils of blood spreading out from it. She feels the weight of the brain-encrusted rock in her hands, and drops it. It slithers and bumps its way down to the pool and lands on the body, submerging it.

The body rolls onto its back and she can see his eyes, wide and staring. The eyes blink.

Ulla's recovery was slow, and ever after she felt that part of her core health and inner being had been wrenched out of her with the child. She was only twenty-four years old but felt, somehow, that Death had brushed his hand over her head. However, there was still much living to do, and living children to attend to. Ulla was far too busy to dwell on her feelings and, if nightmares disturbed her sleep, she generally did not remember them in the morning. The community faced troubles enough.

Their first years in the loch had been very fortunate. Good weather meant fine harvests and easy travelling. Both the farm and Ulla's trading enterprise had flourished. Relationships with the local people were warm and mutually lucrative. Then the weather changed. Cold temperatures and lack of sunshine hampered crops; those that grew were flattened by summer storms. They harvested little hay that autumn so, when severe snowfalls forced them to bring the animals indoors, they could not feed them. Of course, this was not unusual for Norse people, who had never been able to winter animals outside and had, consequently, killed many of them in the autumn and preserved the meat. They endured several seasons like this, but they had built up plenty of stocks and were rich enough to trade with countries which had more plentiful harvests. But Olaf was dispirited to see the results of all his hard labour pounded into the earth with the fierce rain showers.

Tension was brewing amongst the people. Ulla was not aware of it until Arnkel slinked into the house one day, trying to hide a black eye and bleeding nose. She made nothing of it but privately quizzed Kali about the cause of the fight. Neither boy would say what had happened, but they were proud to boast that the opposing faction had come off much worse.

It was Ljót who gave the game away. Ulla chose an intimate moment when she was combing through his hair to seek out the nits and lice which pestered everyone in this close-living community. "What happened to Arnkel?" she asked quietly.

"Oh, it was just big boys. They were calling names and Arnkel hit them."

He volunteered no more, so she pressed him further. "So what did they say, Ljót? What names were they calling you?"

"They called us pagan bastards and said you are a heathen whore, Mother. They said we'll all die and go to the land of Hel because we have Odin and Freyja and Thor and all the rest, and not the One True God. But Arnkel fought them back, and I think their leader has a broken arm now," he added triumphantly. Then he deflated suddenly. "Mother, do you think we will all go to Hel?"

Ulla ruffled her son's shaggy locks and reassured him as best she could. "I'm sure if you're a good boy, brave and just and kind to weaker people and animals, whatever god there is will look well on you and reward you. Don't listen to what the other children say."

The incident passed and there seemed to be no more trouble between the youngsters, but Ulla felt uneasy. She had been aware, of course, that the people here had a different religion and often despised the Norse for their pantheon of gods and superstition and magic. Itinerant preachers had passed through the settlement from time to time and had spoken to the servants and slaves, giving them strange ideas of a loving god who valued everyone – earl, servant or slave – equally. Ulla had no particular problem with that: her years of servitude had given her a strong empathy with those less privileged and she always treated everyone fairly. Then one day two of the servants, old Freydis and her son Bork, came to her with a request.

"Mistress, you have always been kind and generous to us. Everyone, even the lowest herd boy, knows that they are very lucky to work for you. We – all of us servants, and the slaves too – ask a boon of you… which I'm sure in your kindness of heart you will consider."

Freydis was normally either taciturn or grumpy, but had no fear of speaking her mind. So Ulla surmised these effusive words heralded a request of some import. She put down the weaving plaque she was working on.

"Well, Freydis, go on. I'm listening."

"You will know that some of us have become Christians, and many more are thinking about it. We would like… we need a place to worship, and we'd like you to ask the master if we may build a church for our devotions. We will build it ourselves in our own time and not waste any of our work time. It can be very small and we don't need good land for it; any old stony bit would do."

Freydis had to gasp for breath after this swift outpouring. The strain of obsequiousness becoming too much for her, she violently elbowed her son in the stomach. "Go on, say your bit," she snapped.

Bork was too shy to do more than stutter his obviously rehearsed speech.

Ulla was amused by this performance but kept her face straight. "I will consider it myself, and then speak to my husband," she said.

She found that Olaf had already heard of the request and was well disposed to the idea. "I have no objection. It seems appropriate to take on the gods of the new land we live in, but I will keep to the religion of my forefathers; they believed in the god who made the sun and rules all things, men and beasts, and that seems the right belief for a farmer. Tell them they can have their church."

It was indeed a very small building, smaller than the bathhouse which Olaf had finally built beside the river. But the servants crammed in on the day they called the Sabbath and the young preacher spoke to them, and they sang songs. Ulla often stopped to listen but the tunes seemed plaintive and the words meaningless. She preferred the rousing Norse songs of wild seas and brave heroes. She felt a vague disquiet when she saw the preacher passing by in his long, sombre robes with his strange shaven head. It was all very well adopting the customs of a new land, but the Old Gods had been kind to them and might not take kindly to being abandoned.

A green light filters through the leaves. The tumbling, rushing water drowns out the sound of birdsong and the sighing of the wind. It is very peaceful. She feels the old magic talisman in her hand, and brings it up to her face to study it. It is glowing, growing brighter and hotter. Suddenly it is too hot to bear. It falls from her hand and bounces into the pool below.

The body twitches. It lifts and turns its head fully round to stare into her face. She screams.

Ulla awoke drenched in sweat but, when Olaf questioned her about her nightmare, she could tell him nothing. The dreams were becoming more frequent and, although she had tried drinking a draught of wild thyme and camomile last thing at night, she slept no more peacefully. She stayed awake and worked later into the night but, although it helped her to sleep soundly when she eventually went to bed, she felt even more drained and tired in the morning. She was also becoming worried about Olaf.

Last winter he had been ill. He lay in bed, coughing and feverish. This damp land gave everyone colds. Ulla dosed him with an infusion of willow bark to bring down his fever, and thyme and fennel to control his cough. He soon recovered and was up tending to the farm in no time at all. He was left, however, with a persistent cough. Throughout the summer he worked as usual and made no complaints about his health. Ulla was unaware of the times he got up in the night because he didn't want his coughing to disturb her already fitful slumbers. She thought nothing of it until one day, at the end of the autumn harvest, she saw him stand up from tying a stook of hay. Somehow she had not noticed before how thin he had become. He was of course as tall as ever, but his strong, muscular limbs had deflated like bladders expelled of air. She said nothing, but made sure he ate second portions of every meal and made hearty stews and soups for him to eat during the day. It helped at first; she thought he was growing fatter and stronger, but by winter the deterioration was noticeable to everyone. He could no longer keep his malady a secret, as every time he lay down to sleep, he would be racked with violent coughing. He could only sleep when Ulla propped him up on several cushions.

Ulla searched through her herbal remedies but she had little better than thyme, which strengthened the lungs, and fennel for the cough. If she had been in Norway, she would have sought the help of a seer who would use her magic powers to divine the reason and remedy for the sickness. But here there was no one she could turn to. She did what she could but he continued to worsen. Soon he could no longer work on heavier farm tasks, and even his tall frame appeared shrunken and wasted. Ulla could not believe the change in her strong, handsome husband; someone or something was draining away his vital energies as a spider sucks the life from her prey.

By the depths of winter, Olaf retired to his bed, propped upright as before to stop the fluid gathering in his lungs. Ulla tended him night and day and left the house and farm work to the servants. At last one morning she noticed that the colour had returned to his cheeks. He woke up and said that he felt better – maybe he could manage a little walk out to see how the animals were doing? Ulla helped him into his clothes, marvelling at how thin his wrists had become; they were no bigger than her own. Leaning heavily on her shoulder, he was able to make his way slowly out to the animal pens. It was a bright, cold day and their breath misted the air. He looked for a while, making sure that everything had been attended to during his illness, and then he turned to Ulla. Fondly, he stroked her cheek.

Suddenly he was convulsed with a violent bout of coughing. A large gob of bloody phlegm shot out of his mouth. Ulla shrieked for help and they carried him back into the house. He did not move from his bed again. Despite all her concoctions and ministrations, Ulla could do nothing to allay the deterioration. Over the course of the next few days, Olaf grew weaker and weaker. His breath, interspersed by severe coughing, rattled in his throat. The high colour which had lit his cheeks turned to a grey pallor, and he brought up spittle speckled with fresh blood from his lungs. About a week later, in the deep of the night, Ulla at last managed to get him to sleep by applying a warm compress of henbane in vinegar to his forehead. He seemed peaceful for a while, but suddenly he turned and a huge effusion of scarlet blood and mucus erupted from his mouth all over the sheets and bedclothes. Ulla rushed to get a basin of water to clean it up. She did not at first notice that the rattling breath had stopped.

As befitted a man of good family and a leader of the new community, they buried Olaf near the farmstead which he had loved so much, under a mound of stones with his favourite hound and his sword, axe and shield, together with a sickle, an adze, his blacksmith's hammer and tongs, and his drinking horn.

Life must go on. Ulla threw herself into the management of the farm. Although it was winter, there was still much to be done. Animals had to be fed as there was not enough fodder outside. The seed crop had to be checked in case it got damp. As soon as the weather allowed, the big ox had to be yoked and the fields ploughed. The servants and slaves were generally efficient and accustomed to their labour, but someone had to oversee everything and determine when and what had to be done. All this was in addition to her usual work in the home. Arnkel and Kali were by now old enough to be of great help but Ulla found the responsibility weighed heavily on her shoulders. She could not do all this and continue to run her trading enterprise. She considered all the options and decided on a plan.

As the time of the Winter Nights festival approached, Ulla instructed her women to make preparations for a feast. Everyone was to be invited, even the lowliest hen girl and the native slaves, and neither food nor ale or mead was to be spared. She selected fine gifts for all from her stock of trade goods. On the day of the feast, fine snow had fallen but it was not enough to hinder the travel of all their neighbours. As the farmhouse was too small to hold all the company, Ulla had great fires lit around the courtyard and the food spread on tables outside. A sombre atmosphere was soon dispelled by the warmth of the fires and the cheering influence of good food and liquor. Eyes sparkled with conviviality and drinking horns were raised in praise to the departed host and his generous widow. When everyone had eaten their fill, but before the matter of serious drinking had begun, Ulla stood up and signalled for silence. There had been much speculation about the reason for this magnanimity, so everyone listened attentively.

"I have invited you here to honour the memory of my husband Olaf. He was a man of peace who treated his friends and servants with kindness and his enemies with respect. I ask you to drink a toast to him."

This request was greeted with much cheering and beating of tables. Ulla was somewhat surprised at how much popularity her quiet husband had gained in so short a time. She had to wait till the enthusiastic toasting and reminiscing had died down.

"But there is another reason I have asked you here today."

The last murmurs died away and a hiccupping youngster, who had been experimenting with ale, was dragged off by his mother.

"I cannot manage all the work on the farm myself and my sons are, as yet, too young to take over. I must appoint someone to oversee the labour. And I must entrust each area of the farm to those who are most conscientious and best able for the task. I cannot decide now, but I ask each person to work diligently over the summer at their chosen occupation. By the time of the end-of-autumn feast, I will grant all slaves their freedom and release all bondmen, and I will choose those who have proved most reliable to remain and take charge of the farm. Anyone who wishes to leave may do so; anyone who has been lazy or shirked from their duties will be sent on their way. Any freemen or women who wish to work for me will be paid for their labour and treated in the same way."

A stunned silence greeted this speech. No one had expected such. At last the silence was broken by Bork, who jumped onto the table and raised his drinking horn. "Let us drink to the memory of our good master Olaf Ketilsson, but also to his fine wife and our mistress, Ulla Grimsdottir!" he shouted.

Pandemonium broke out, and thereafter toasts came fast and furious. What was left of the feast was attacked again, and most of the guests drank themselves into a stupor. Ulla had drunk lightly, so, when the carousing had finished and the bonfires died down, she picked her way through the sprawled bodies, covering some with a cloak here and there. She went to bed well satisfied with herself.

Throughout the year Ulla instructed what had to be done and observed how well it was carried out. She took note of those who went beyond her instructions and accomplished more. Her words had stimulated even the idlest of the servants but there were a few who did not rise to the challenge. She would dismiss them when the time came. She sent word to Torvik in Orkney that she would not be able to trade with the *knörr* this year and he answered her in person, sailing in with two *knörrs* laden with goods.

Ulla was more pleased to see her brother than she would admit. Torvik, for his part, grieved to see how worn his little sister had become. She was only twenty-nine years of age, but recent events had aged her. He pressed her to find out what was troubling her, but she told him nothing. At length he set off with her *knörr* as well and promised to fill it with appropriate goods and return before the end of summer.

This season the weather was good, the farm flourished and a good harvest was gathered in. At the autumn feast Ulla announced that now everyone had their freedom and could leave if they wished. She would speak individually to those who remained. Unsurprisingly, few left. There was little future for freed slaves in this part of the world. She confirmed the positions of most of the farmworkers, but granted some more authority. She chose Bork to be overseer of the farm. He was quiet and young but had proved his loyalty and efficiency. In many ways he reminded her of Olaf. Indeed, he set out right away to reorganise some of the winter preparations, but always consulted with her before instituting new practices. Ulla was satisfied that the farm was in good hands.

Before the winter solstice, she received a surprise visit.

Lagaidh had observed events among the Norse settlers. After her husband's death he'd expected Ulla to take a new one from among her own people, so he had been intrigued when he heard how she had engineered the management of the farm. Although he was not shy or reticent by nature, he felt somewhat daunted by Ulla's independence and spirit, so he had waited until now to make his proposal. He brought gifts which he thought might please her: a fine gold arm ring for her vanity and a breeding sow for practical purposes.

Ulla received his gifts and proposal with grace. He was neither young nor handsome and she knew him well enough to know that he was not particularly gentle or considerate, but he was a shrewd, strong leader of his people. She could see that there were many advantages to the match. It was too soon after her husband's death to enter into a new marriage, she told him, but she would think about it over the winter and give him her answer in the spring.

The winter was relatively mild that year, so Lagaidh was able to come courting from time to time. Ulla smiled to herself frequently to see this uncompromising man acting the fawning suitor. If the role did not fit him, he was at least making an attempt, and she learned to appreciate and look forward to their serious conversations. When spring came she was happy to agree to their marriage.

It was out of the question that they should live in the cold, damp tower on the other side of the loch, so Lagaidh, along with all his household, moved into the steading. Accommodation was cramped at first but they set about building new quarters for the servants. Ulla found herself comfortable with the new arrangement. Her boys did not, as she feared they might, resent the man who had supplanted their father; in fact, they looked up to him with some awe and admiration. Lagaidh could manage the farm and the trading, and if, sometimes, when he was asleep, she imagined other arms around her, she did not let it disturb their relationship.

Spring passed to summer and the trading season began again. When Ulla announced that she was about to set out to Norway with the *knörr*, Lagaidh objected. Although he was aware she had made several trips before, he expected his wife to remain at home and look after the children and the household chores. By gentle and logical persuasion, Ulla finally managed to arrange a compromise. They would both go on the trip and leave the farm management to Bork.

They set out first to visit Orkney and Shetland where they could trade timber, furs and hides. Then they crossed to Norway, principally to sell their furs but also to have a glimpse of the latest luxuries which Kaupang had to offer. Ulla was amused to see her stoical husband amazed by the bustling life and business of the port. But she had another wonder to show him.

She had always remembered the fine stallion she had seen on her visit to the stud farm. When they had finished their business in Kaupang, she took Lagaidh there. The stallion was gone by now, but had left a fine selection of progeny. The price was high but Ulla was a rich woman; she bought a pretty grey for herself and a grand stallion for Lagaidh. They would breed an extremely desirable line of horses. For the time being the horses would remain in Norway; they would pick them up on their way home. But first they were intent on sailing south to England and the mighty town of Winchester. The *knörr* was loaded with skins and furs, walrus ivory, eiderdown, bone combs, bronze and iron crafts, beads and steatite utensils – luxury items to tempt the court of King Alfred.

If Lagaidh had been impressed with Kaupang, he was dumbfounded by Winchester. The city had been ransacked by the Danes some years earlier, but Alfred had fortified it with a strong wooden barricade and ditches and was now embellishing it with many stone buildings and Christian churches. It was still principally a trading town, but Alfred was intent that it should become the symbol of his sovereignty over the kingdoms of Wessex and Mercia and, in due time, capital of the Anglo-Saxons.

As minor traders, Ulla and Lagaidh had no expectations to meet the King, but very soon Alfred learned of their arrival and summoned them to his court. As well as being a skilled military leader and literary scholar, Alfred had a profound curiosity about foreign peoples and lands. He would not miss this opportunity to quiz visitors from the far north. They conversed through an interpreter.

Overawed and confused by the language, Lagaidh had little to contribute. Although he now spoke Norse, he was not fluent and there was no one to interpret his native tongue. Ulla told the King about her early life in Norway and her voyages around the islands. He was most interested to learn of the shapes of the land, the names of mountains and the sailing times between ports of call.

He asked her to draw a view of what she thought the land might look like from above and indicate the names of the places she had visited. This concept was alien to Ulla, but she tried to envisage what a great eagle would see as he soared amongst the clouds. Alfred's clerics helped her draw the outline and wrote in the names she gave them. In the end it was not much of a map but it seemed to satisfy the King. He invited them to visit a few more times when he had specific questions to ask. He was not interested in the goods they had to trade except for very unusual or exotic items, but the ladies of his court were delighted by the fine furs and beautifully carved bone pins and combs. Ulla and Lagaidh soon traded all their goods and filled the *knörr* anew with the luxurious materials, glass flagons and wine which the English imported from the Continent.

Ulla was impressed with the genteel civilisation of English life, but found she was missing the wild mountains of her home, and her children. As soon as they could, they set sail for Norway again to sell some of their goods and collect their horses. They returned home with them and made no more trips that summer.

So life continued. Summers were busy with crops and animals, and they made at least one trading trip each year. Winters, when all the chores were completed, were times of entertainment when everyone could gather round the fire in the hall and listen to songs and sagas of brave heroes and their adventures. Ulla would look with fondness on the bright heads of her four children; they were growing up into fine young men. Only sometimes, when a dark mood took her, did she think of the perfect, beautiful daughter they had put under the rock on the hill. She had no more children with Lagaidh. She thought something had changed inside her when her daughter was born.

The body bobs gently on the surface of the water. Seeping blood spreads out and colours the pool with scarlet. The head lifts and turns, looking straight into her eyes. He pulls himself up and drags himself out of the pool. He is not angry; he wears a leering grin on his face. He stands and lurches up the path towards her, dripping water and gore. Vines have tangled her feet and blocked her mouth; she can neither run nor scream. He reaches out for her.

Lagaidh had never had much time for female sensitivity but he was concerned that his wife suffered such fitful sleep and nightmares. When she would not explain the reason for her dreams, he suggested that she talk to the priest whom he had brought with him. Although she was not Christian, he might provide her with some solace. Ulla did not agree at once; she could not see that any god could provide her with answers.

Brendan was an old monk from Iona who had seen his youthful missionary zeal tempered by the mundane task of ministering to the religious needs of a small community. What he had lost in piety he had gained in understanding and compassion. If Ulla would not speak to him of her own accord, he tried to be available to her whenever she needed advice or conversation. Ulla slowly came to enjoy their times together as he was an erudite man, learned in many spheres, and had travelled to Rome in his youth. He could tell her about marvels of the ancient world and the strange philosophies of the Greeks and Romans. For his part, he was surprised by her intelligence and curiosity, but disturbed by the deep trouble which he could sense within her soul. He did not tell her anything of his religion until she began to ask questions. After that they often talked about it in the evenings when Ulla sat up late to finish her weaving.

One night, after a particularly gruelling day in which Thorir had fallen and knocked himself out on a rock, Brendan and Ulla sat by the dimming embers of the fire. Thorir was asleep at last, with a large compress wrapped about his head and his wooden sword clasped in his arms.

"Tell me more about your god," said Ulla quietly. "Is he all-powerful and terrible as Odin? Is he strong and just like Thor, or a bringer of fruitfulness and plenty like Freyja?"

Brendan thought for a little before he spoke. He guessed there was more behind Ulla's question than simple curiosity. At last he began. "He is all and more of these things, and yet none of these. You should not think of Him as one of your Old Gods, My Lady. They are as men are: proud and selfish, quick to anger; seeking vengeance and punishment for real or imagined slights. Try to think of God not as a person, but a spirit, an ideal of pure goodness and love. And as God is, His Son came to be: one who loved so much that He gave His life to save others from their sins."

Ulla frowned and said, "This I don't understand. I understand the idea of making sacrifice to a god; we sacrifice animals, and once human beings too. But why should a god be pleased at the sacrifice of his own son, and how can it bring forgiveness for our sins? It doesn't make sense."

Brendan smiled and inclined his head. Sometimes it was very hard to explain the intricacies of doctrine, especially to sceptical non-believers. "It is hard to understand, but think of it in two ways, Ulla. Firstly, God loves us so much that He gave the life of His Son for our sakes. But think of the sacrifice of Jesus as an example: if you truly wish forgiveness, you must be prepared to sacrifice yourself to God. You must come with penitence and humility to confess your sins."

Brendan could see that Ulla was unconvinced. He would give her time to ponder his words and wait till she came to him.

Ulla's dream came every night now. She sat up late and, if Lagaidh demanded that she come to bed, she would wait till he was asleep and then creep out again. She could not work as the fire was too dim and she could not light a lamp for fear of waking everyone. So she sat upright, gazing into the patterns of the flames and dozing from time to time. During the day she took a little nap when she could but she dared not lie too long or the dream would come. She was not sleeping enough for an active life, and her health began to suffer. She grew thin and gaunt and, although the paleness in her cheeks was considered comely, it annoyed Lagaidh. He had expected to marry a strong, sturdy, wholesome woman, not a fragile wraith. Instead of sympathising and trying to find out what was wrong, he berated her for what he considered idleness and weakness.

Brendan watched concernedly and could see that Ulla was close to breaking point. At last, one afternoon when everyone was out and peace had descended on the household, he drew her aside from her work. "Come for a walk with me, Mistress. The bluebells are just showing in the woods. It would do your heart good to look on them."

They walked through the woods beside the river. Ulla wondered at the contrast of the vivid indigo in the bluebells, the viridity of the beech leaves and the yellow of the gorse. They sat down on a grassy bank beside the stream and watched a dipper bobbing up and down on rocks in the water. Brendan spoke quietly.

"You are very troubled, My Lady. I see a shadow which follows you and there is a beast which gnaws at your heart. Won't you tell me what's wrong? Perhaps it is a sickness I can cure."

Ulla glanced at him wonderingly. She had come to respect and trust this old man; maybe he was like the father she could only vaguely remember. Tentatively, she began. "I have done a great wrong, Father. I think if you knew, you would not be sitting beside me so sympathetically. And the Gods are punishing me; they have taken away those I loved and they will give me no peace till I pay with my own death."

Brendan took her hands in his. "Ulla, I judge no man or woman. I am not worthy to do so. Tell me. Tell me everything."

The words came slowly at first, as water seeps through the mud and boulders of a childhood dam, then breaking and pouring through like a torrent. Ulla told him her story, from her enslavement, to her rape by Gorb and his murder. She even told him of her years as a prostitute in Kaupang. At length, drained by the emotional release, she drew her tale to a close. "So what do you think of me now – a whore and a murderess?" she whispered.

Brendan had listened silently to all she said, and sat for many moments before he spoke. "Now I understand. I see the reason for your trouble and, maybe, I can provide a way for its resolution. Your Norse gods are cruel and vengeful. When Gorb died his family believed it to be an accident and they were unable to seek recompense or revenge. But you and the Gods," he corrected himself, "*your* gods know, and they seek retribution."

Ulla nodded. "This I know. I know every time I dream. For each time he reaches out his hands to me, I wake up. If ever I don't and he catches me, I will die."

Brendan took her hands again. "There is another way, my daughter. Your gods will extract revenge and your guilt will weigh you down until you can bear it no longer. But the Christian God is a god of forgiveness. If you come to Him with a contrite heart, confessing your sins and promising obedience, He will forgive you and absolve you of your guilt. All that it requires on your part is true belief and repentance."

Ulla looked at the ground, saying nothing. Brendan could not tell if she understood or accepted his words. He tried again.

"Ulla, the scar on your leg. I don't know how such a strange wound came about, but I do know that it is in the shape of the cross, the ringed cross of the Celtic Church. It can be no coincidence that you bear the mark of Christ on your body. I believe that He has chosen you as one of His own. It is a sign, and you should not ignore it."

He had no way of knowing what a confusion his remarks raised in Ulla's mind. She had made the cut on her leg in a ritual act of magic; a magic which had served her well, but had led her to a dreadful deed. How could it be the symbol of another god, a god which she had never even heard about at the time? Did it mean that even then, the god of the Christians was watching her? Did it mean that he approved or disapproved? Did it mean that he could forgive?

They had many talks like this in the following weeks. Brendan told her the stories of Jesus' life and some of his teachings. She particularly liked the stories of the sinful woman who washed Jesus' feet with her tears, and the woman taken in adultery. Often she would whisper to herself, "*Let he who is without sin, cast the first stone.*" By the time of the harvest festival, she had agreed to be baptised.

Brendan was pleased. Lagaidh was delighted. That Ulla had turned to the true faith was a first step towards civilising these Norse heathens, and would be an example to others.

When she came to her baptism, Kali came with her. She had not insisted that her children join the new religion; she considered faith to be a matter of individual reflection and choice. But Kali had listened to Brendan's stories too and liked the Christian god better than the gods of his fathers. Brendan took them to a pool in the river and immersed them fully in the water.

No dove descended upon Ulla's head when she emerged from the water, but Brendan drew her up and said, "You are born again in the love of Jesus Christ and your sins are forgiven. I give you the Christian name Ruth, as a woman who came to a new land and married a man of a different people. May you live in peace."

Ulla's nightmares never returned.

Bluebells gleam deeply under the trees on the banks of the river. She walks slowly down towards the sea. The little man stands by a rock. He has not changed; he is just the same as before. The lichen droops on his brow and his limbs are gnarled and knotted. He raises his finger and points. He points beyond the shore, beyond the near islands, far out towards the west. Then he beckons her. She understands and follows him.

There is no record of the time and manner of Ulla's death and no memorial marks her final resting place, but she has left her legacy in the name of a village and in the genes of those who still live in Ullapool.

Chapter Nine

The Battle of Garvie Bay

clan warfare

The MacLeods of Lewis seized the lands of Coigach from the Nicholsons in the fourteenth century. By the sixteenth century, inter-family feuds, violent killings and petty warfare wrecked the fortunes of the MacLeod family. Legend tells that a battle was fought between the men of Coigach and the Lewismen at Garvie Bay. Accounts of the outcome of the battle differ but, at any rate, Kenneth Mackenzie of Kintail complained in a letter to King James that the Lewismen had wasted his lands in Lochbroom 'with fire and sword in such barbarous manner that neither man, wife, bairn, horse, cattle, corn nor bigging [building] has been spared, but all barbarously burnt and destroyit...'

Do you think the days of mighty heroes are past; all withered away to legend and fairy tale? I tell you that we old men can remember one whose strength and courage could equal that of Osgar of the Fians, and another whose wit rivalled that of Fionn MacChumail himself. I will tell the story of Donald MacDonald; we call him Donnie Ghobha, the smith of Achnahaird. I will be as Oisean to Osgar to tell of his brave deeds and tragic death. Now listen.

Old Ruari MacLeod of Lewis had nine sons. When his heir was drowned, our great chieftain here – Torquil Cononach, long may we sing his praises – seized his chance to claim his rightful heritage, imprisoning his father in Stornoway Castle and forcing him to resign his lands. Old Ruari, the cunning fox, reneged on his agreement, but at last he granted the lands of Coigach to Torquil, retaining Lewis for himself and his other sons, who were equally duplicitous.

Torquil made his base here in the castle in Ullapool, but ever strived to win back the Lewis by launching raids on his half-brothers. At length a younger brother, known as Torquil Dubh for his heart was as black as his hair was raven, determined to retaliate and lay waste his brother's lands in Coigach. He assembled a war party of seven hundred or more of his clansmen and set off from Lewis in a fleet of galleys.

Now in those days, John MacKenzie McDonald McEan, the tacksman of Achnahaird, who was a prudent and conscientious man, maintained a watch beacon on the point of Reiff. Such was the lawlessness then that there was much fear of piracy and interference with legitimate trade and travel. Each day a watchman scanned the seas for signs of unwelcome sails.

This was the middle of winter and attacks from enemies were not expected. The watchman was busied in teaching his son to weave withies for lobster creels. His son, no doubt bored with the occupation, looked out over the Minch to the far sea. "Father, what do you see there on the horizon? It looks like a flock of great birds with many coloured wings skimming over the face of the sea."

The watchman at once gave his attention to his son's indication. "Aye, it looks like birds but my eyes are not sharp and young like yours. Tell me what you see."

"There, below the hills of the Lewis, I see specks but they do not fly high like birds; they stay spread out above the waves. I think they are coming this way."

At once the father sprang to his feet. "I doubt that these are birds of the sea, but birds of ill omen they may well be. We will watch a little longer till we can make out what they are."

It was not long before the father too was able to distinguish the sails of a considerable fleet. "It is as I feared: our enemies from across the water are come upon us. We must raise the alert. I will light the beacon to warn our people here but you must run as fast as you can to the tacksman's house and warn him to gather the clansmen. He must also send word to our chief in Ullapool that a warband is approaching from the islands. He will know what to do. Go now – run like the wind, for many lives may depend on it."

The boy, whose name is not remembered, stayed not a moment. He was off like the fleetest deer, or Caoilte, the swiftest runner of the Fiann. Whenever he passed a house, or people tending their fields and cattle, he would shout, "Stir yourselves, grab your weapons. The Lewismen are coming!" Through field and bog he did not stop for breath till he reached the tacksman's house at Achnahaird.

John McEan knew at once what to do. He sent boys out to all the crofts and settlements and instructed the men to gather, well armed, on the beach at Reiff. He also sent a boat from Badentarbat to warn Torquil in Ullapool of the approaching menace.

By the time the warships were close to the coast, a huge band of men – and some formidable women, I may add – had gathered on the beach. Torquil Dubh, as craven a coward as ever lived, thought it wise to sail on round the headland and find a landing in a less protected spot. But all the way, the men of Coigach followed on the shore, brandishing their weapons and shouting insults. Torquil hoped that his swift ships would outdistance the opposition and he might effect an attack at Achnahaird.

John McEan had roused all the men from his village and round about, and set them along the shoreline and inside the ancient fort which still guarded the entrance to the bay. He had even installed a small cannon there, and fired off cannonballs whose effectiveness was probably more in the clouds of billowing smoke than in any lethal nature. Very few of his men had muskets or pistols but they were enough to frighten the Lewismen away. The fleet continued east, hoping to exhaust the strength and spirit of the defenders, but again Torquil Dubh had underestimated the strategy of the wily tacksman.

Leaving a few to guard the fort, John McEan, with some men on horses and others running as fast as they could, shadowed the ships. He knew there was only one more place along the coast where the galleys could make a safe landing – Garvie Bay. His force was mightily outnumbered but he reckoned the Lewismen would prefer a tactical retreat to assured death for some of their warriors. He drew his men up on the beach and waited to see what the enemy would do.

Torquil Dubh was not about to give up his reckless plan. His mind was full of revenge and fury and not a little greed for spoils of war, such as they were in these poor places. He knew that his men would be attacked as they attempted to draw their galleys up onto the beach, and so sent six of them to land whilst the others held back to maintain covering fire. Perhaps this was his gravest mistake, as the gallant Coigach men could hew down their enemies as they emerged from the boats.

This is where our brave hero, Donnie Ghobha, enters the story. I should tell you a little about him. He was not taller than the tallest man there, nor did he appear particularly muscular, but his work forging and manufacturing tools and weapons had endowed him with superhuman strength combined with subtlety and skill in battle. He watched as a boat drew in and set upon the first man to alight, and dispatched him with but one blow of his axe and a cut from his claymore. Such a reception hindered the next men to land, so that they could be picked off by the Coigach defenders. By this time, Donnie had moved on to another boat and dealt with its leaders in the same fashion. I have no doubt that if Torquil Dubh had had the courage to land with the first wave, he would have been cut down at once and perhaps the invasion would have been turned back at the very beginning. So many good lives could have been saved. As it was, the Lewismen were much dispirited by the appearance of such a formidable, unbeatable foe, and even the men in the boats pointed out with awe the speed at which this single man could obstruct so many attackers.

Torquil Dubh was angry but he was not about to give up. Enough of his men had landed to be able to engage the Coigach men and the fighting was spread out along the beach. Few of his men had firearms and, in any case, they were of little use in hand-to-hand battle. He signalled the rest of his army to join in the attack.

Now you have not forgotten our wily tacksman, John McEan, have you? When he saw what was about to happen, he called his men, few that they were, to form a line standing on the firm turf at the back of the beach. They had time to load and fire off some rounds from their pistols and muskets, holding back the opposition for a moment. Then he unfolded his strategy.

Holding aloft a white cloth on a stick, he marched down onto the sands, stopping but a few paces away from Torquil Dubh in the middle of the pack.

"Welcome to the land of Coigach. It is unfortunate that we have mistaken your appearance as an act of aggression. You must forgive my eager men for their diligent protection of their property. I am sure that you will be willing to settle whatever is in dispute in a manner which is agreeable to all and will cause the least bloodshed."

Torquil was a hot-headed young man, but not without common sense. "I will listen to what you propose and, if my Lewismen concur, we may come to some agreement."

"Very well," went on McEan. "I propose that we each choose a champion to fight for us all. If your champion wins, we will concede defeat, but if ours does, you will embark on your galleys and sail homewards. What say you?"

Torquil's leaders were far less interested in a battle with many who were their own kin – some had been reluctant to come on this expedition at all. They pressed Torquil to accept the terms and settle the matter by single combat. They chose from their midst the biggest, strongest warrior. McEan chose Donnie Ghobha, of course.

To all who saw the unmatched nature of the champions, the contest was as good as won already. The two men circled each other, axe in one hand, claymore in the other, the Lewisman towering over his opponent. It was he who made the first move, slashing with his sword and swiftly following with a swing of his axe. Donnie dodged easily but made no move to counter-attack. This continued, with Donnie merely parrying the assaults. The Lewismen began to hurl derision and hoot with glee, sensing that their champion was demoralising his enemy, but Donnie was biding his time, testing his foe's strength and assessing his possible weaknesses. It was soon obvious to him that this was a man of muscle, but no brain and little agility.

If you had been there, what a sight you'd have seen! Like a cat toying with a mouse, Donnie led his man on, feigning indifference, casually stepping to one side and then the other, seeming not to defend himself but blocking the blows casually. The Lewisman was tiring and growing increasingly frustrated. That was exactly what Donnie wanted. A tired and angry man makes dangerous mistakes.

At length he observed that his adversary's right arm was becoming weaker: a claymore is no light weapon to wield one-handed. He waited till the claymore came down in a furious slice, and chopped into the Lewisman's forearm with his axe. His enemy was mortally wounded and sank to his knees, blood pumping from his veins. Donnie Ghobha had won and the contest was over.

You can be sure that Torquil Dubh was none too pleased with the outcome. He might have reneged on his agreement, but by this time his brother had landed his own fleet of galleys at Badentarbat and galloped over the peninsula to join the battle. The two armies were not equal in size but it was enough to prevent Torquil Dubh from continuing the fight.

Perhaps the two brothers would have challenged each other, but John McEan stepped between them, urging conciliation. Cononach was not easily persuaded but agreed to make a pact of peace with his brother. The continued feuding was weakening both of their peoples. To symbolise the agreement, both brothers threw their claymores into the loch behind the bay. It was known as Loch nan Claidheichean from that day forth.

Cononach shook hands with his brother with all the appearance of amity, but he had seriously misjudged the level of his brother's perfidy. No doubt Torquil's mind seethed with rage at the outcome of events and with no little resentment at the easy defeat of his champion. He had sailed out with hopes of victory and plunder, yet all he had to show for it was many of his good men slaughtered on the beach. As the galleys launched and set their sails, he instructed his finest marksman to fire on Donnie Ghobha. He was killed instantly.

Cononach and the Coigach men were incensed. But what could they do? The enemy fleet was fast disappearing over the sea and their own galleys were at the other side of the peninsula. Revenge would have to wait for another time. They buried their dead behind the bay and, with great ceremony, dug a grave for their gallant smith. The enemy dead they left to be picked by seagulls and mauled by foxes.

Torquil Dubh was not finished with his villainy. No sooner had he rounded the headland at Reiff than he turned his boats inland and sailed into Annat Bay and up Loch Broom. As most of the fighting men had followed Cononach, Ullapool was left unprotected and he proceeded to ravage the lands, set fire to the steadings and murder the remaining people. Not content with that, he continued to the strath of Lochbroom, the domain of Kenneth Mackenzie, Lord of Kintail, hoping to satisfy his men with plunder. Then he hightailed it as fast as he could back to Lewis.

You may imagine the horror which Cononach felt when he finally returned to his home and lands – that his own brother could have carried out such treacherous carnage. He would have been well within his rights to retaliate and attack his kinsmen in Lewis, but he was persuaded by Lord Kintail himself to bide his time and seek redress through the laws of the land.

Kintail immediately wrote a letter to the King complaining of the outrageous behaviour of Torquil Dubh. The Privy Council declared Dubh to be an outlaw, but he had taken refuge with his father-in-law in Harris. It would not have been wise to attempt an attack there, but there are more cunning ways to catch a rat.

Lord Kintail, Torquil Cononach, and his faithful brother Murdo MacLeod arranged a secret meeting with the Brieve of Lewis and hatched a plan to murder Torquil Dubh. The Brieve, returning to Lewis, captured a Dutch ship and invited Torquil and a few of his men to a feast on board. Instead of enjoying fine food, wine and merrymaking, they were seized, bound and delivered into the hands of Cononach.

The men were brought to Coigach and there met their just deserts on the hill of hanging, Cnoc na Croiche.

And so ends my story of the brave heroes and cowardly villains of our time. Our laird Torquil Cononach rules here with justice and benevolence. He has brought peace and prosperity to the people and the land, and we pray he enjoys many more years of life to do so.

Chapter Ten

The Croft

troubles for the crofters

The eighteenth and nineteenth centuries were times of affliction and change throughout the Highlands, and no less in Lochbroom. Private landowners, intent on improvement, cleared crofters from the land where their families had lived for generations, crop failure caused widespread famine, and the Church went through a period of upheaval which split families and alienated friends. Leckmelm, a township halfway along the north side of the loch, experienced all of these misfortunes.

I

Murdo Mackenzie, of the township of Leckmelm in the parish of Lochbroom, did not court his wife. When he came to call, he sat quietly in the corner, and only expressed an opinion in a quiet, measured way when the subjects of animal rearing or religion were introduced. Mary supposed he had not spoken more than three or four words to her: "*Ciamar a tha thu?*" She loved to hear him singing in church, when he intoned the words of the psalms with clarity and perfect pitch, but he never joined in the general singing when an impromptu ceilidh was initiated at her house, and he certainly never danced. Such entertainment was not allowed in his own home. His father read from the Bible or spiritual tracts morning and evening and held weekly prayer meetings.

They had played together as children, of course, and he had been open and friendly then, though never as wild and boisterous as the other boys. Although a year younger than her, at school in Ullapool he had shown his intelligence and diligence early, quickly moving several grades above the other boys of his age group and going on to learn Latin. Girls attended a different school in the village where they were taught spinning, sewing and other branches of female industry. Mary had finished her education and settled into the chores of household life long before Murdo completed his studies.

Despite the apparent aloofness of their relationship, it was generally accepted amongst the neighbours that Murdo and Mary were courting. In a society in which late marriage was encouraged they were not expected to marry for many years, and certainly not until he was in a better position to provide for her and a large family. As the eldest of a family of six sons and two daughters, Murdo could expect to carry on the croft after his father's death, but there were too many mouths to feed at present. Mary resigned herself to a decade or more of spinsterhood. It came as a surprise when her father announced that Murdo had officially asked for her. He was barely eighteen years of age, and she nineteen. They were married quietly in the old church at Clachan and Mary moved into her father-in-law's house in the spring.

It soon became apparent why the marriage had been arranged so soon. Murdo's mother, although only forty years old, was ailing after the birth of her latest child and unable to carry out her duties. The elder daughter, Margaret, at thirteen, was really too young to take on the full burden of responsibility but Mary found her a willing helper and a considerate friend. And she needed one, being suddenly in charge of a sickly mother-in-law and a house full of strong-minded men and a newborn baby.

Mary was surprised to find that, when the father of the house was absent, there was cheerful banter and laughter among the family and Margaret might hum a rhythmic melody while performing tedious tasks such as churning the milk. On the whole they were a happy, healthy and relatively well-off family, and Mary thought herself very fortunate to be settled so well.

Her husband was still taciturn in her presence but over time he became more relaxed. He would talk about the management of the croft and sometimes asked her advice on specific subjects, but he did not talk to her about matters of general interest; he reserved those conversations for his friends, or the minister when he came to visit. It was as if he did not expect women to have any deep ideas, and perhaps he did not want them to.

Mary had not expected any form of romance in her marriage but she found the coldness of their intimate relationship dispiriting. Murdo would perform his husbandly duties regularly but he neither talked to her then nor showed affection. In all their life together Mary could remember no more passionate kiss than a genteel touch on the cheek. As a young virgin she had had very little idea of what went on in the marriage bed but sometimes, when she observed the knowing looks and furtive touches of other young couples, she felt there must be something she was missing. She would put these guilty thoughts behind her and immerse herself in work – there was much of that to keep her occupied.

Her mother-in-law's health deteriorated swiftly after Mary moved to the house. She had never been a strong or strong-willed woman and the trials of eight difficult labours had robbed her of what colour and youth she had. She lay in her bed and endured what was left of life with silent resignation. Mary could feel her great, brown eyes follow her as she went about her work. When Mary brushed and tidied her hair she would acknowledge the attention with a faint smile, but she hardly spoke to her. She was as uncommunicative as her son.

By the time the autumn storms had given way to the winter snows, it was clear that she was dying. The doctor summoned from Ullapool could offer neither physic nor hope, so it was left to the minister, Dr Thomas Ross, to provide spiritual consolation. A learned and much-respected cleric, he had ministered to the local people for thirty-three years but was now feeling the weight of age. He came as often as he could in his pony and trap from the manse at Clachan and sat with the family, leading them in prayers and promising salvation in Heaven for the dying woman.

One evening towards the end of December, Mary had banished the winter gloom by stoking the fire to a cheerful blaze and lighting a single candle by the failing woman's bed. The youngest children were already asleep and the rest of the family were out tending to the last tasks of the day. Her mother-in-law beckoned her over to the bedside. She had little strength left to speak, so Mary had to lean over to hear the strained words.

"It's Murdo, my dear. You must learn to understand him. He is close with himself and shy to say what he feels."

She halted to draw some breath and strength into her body. "Don't think him cold and cruel; he's a good man and will always do his best, in the way he sees it, for you and the family. Try to forgive him for his manner and you may come to love him as I have." She sank back on the pillows, wasted by the effort of speech, but she did not seem to require a response. Mary took her hand and held it till she fell into a quiet sleep. She did not awaken to life again.

The funeral was held three days later. Although she had been an unassuming member of the community, it seemed that every man from the shores of Loch Broom had come to accompany Mrs Duncan Mackenzie to her final resting place, as a mark of respect and consideration for her husband. As was traditional, the coffin was carried by relays of close-related men and neighbours for the four miles from Leckmelm to the church at Clachan. Women did not attend. In other funerals, when the coffin was laid down to rest at a changeover, a fortifying sip of *uisge-beatha* provided strength and sometimes an unexpected degree of informality to the whole proceedings. It was rumoured that some long-distance funeral processions arrived at their destination without the coffin. But, on this occasion, the elder Mackenzie's strict abstemiousness ensured a proper solemnity. If anyone had secreted a small dram in a back pocket, no one cared to comment.

The Reverend Doctor Ross conducted a long but personal service praising the dead woman's industry, dutifulness and humility. She had laboured throughout her life for the sake of others and would now receive her just reward in Heaven. She was a perfect example to all those who spurned the teachings of the Bible and indulged in wicked pursuits such as dancing and other temptations of the flesh. After the coffin was committed to the earth, most of the mourners departed to their homes, but some of the family's closest neighbours returned to the house where prayers were offered for the soul of the departed.

It might have been expected that life would have been easier for Mary after the death of her mother-in-law, but she was by now pregnant and found everything much more strenuous. By the early spring, her first child, Ian, had battled his way into the world and added yet more to her labours. Despite this, she could do nothing but adore the tiny face which looked up at her, so trustingly and demandingly, from the cradle. When the rest of the family were out, she would take him up in her arms and croon him an old lullaby:

Hó! mìn thu,
Ho! soft art thou,
Màn thu, màg thu!
Smooth thou, soft thou!
'S toigh liom fhìn thu,
Well I love thee,
Màn thu, màg thu!
Smooth thou, soft thou!

'S toigh liom agam,
Well I love thee,
Màn thu, màg thu!
Smooth thou, soft thou!

Fo'n a' phlaide,
Under the plaid,
Màn thu, màg thu!
Smooth thou, soft thou!

'S toigh liom agam,
Well I love thee,
Màn thu, màg thu!
Smooth thou, soft thou!
Anns a' mhadainn
In the morning
Mhìnghil, chràghil.
Soft white, red-bright.

'S toigh liom agam,
Well I love thee,
Màn thu, màg thu!
Smooth thou, soft thou!
Mi dha d' chaidriu,
I to companion thee,
Mi dha d' thàlu.
I to lull thee.

Mi dha d' lìonu
I to fill thee
Leis na bàidhean,
With the fondnesses,
Mi dha d' lion o
I to fill thee
Chìoch do mhàthar.
From the breast of thy mother.

Mìn thu! Mìn thu!
Soft thou! soft thou!
Mìn mo ghràidhean!
Soft, my little love!
Min mar shìod dhut
Soft as silk to thee
Crìdh do mhàthar!
The heart of thy mother!

One morning when Ian had been particularly fractious, she at last sang him off to sleep, unaware that Murdo was watching from the doorway. She started a little when she heard a soft cough behind her. Quietly, he took the child out of her arms and placed him in the cradle, then turned to her. In as matter-of-fact a way as he would ask her to stoke the fire, he said, "You shall not sing such songs, such heathen songs, to a son of mine." He said no more, nor alluded to the occurrence ever again, but Mary felt chastened. It did not stop her cuddling her baby or humming little songs to him, but she tried very hard to remember the words of her mother-in-law and forgive her husband's harshness.

A time of great tribulation was coming to the people of Leckmelm. Davidson of Tulloch was by no means the worst of the Highland landowners but, ten years previously, he had cleared the township of Incroash to make way for an innkeeper, and given him some of the crofters' common hill pasture. The ousted tenants had been resettled in the remaining townships of Leckmelm. Eighteen families were expected to subsist on land which had previously supported twelve. As was their way, the people tolerated these conditions and set about building houses and improving the land as best they could by clearing stones. Worse was yet to come.

Davidson had already decided that three more townships nearby should be cleared. Whilst travelling on the Continent, he left the arrangements to his tacksman, Kenneth Mackenzie, who set about moving some of the cleared families to Leckmelm. Mackenzie, son of the innkeeper at Incroash, was a confident, ambitious man who intended to further his status with his employer and carry out extensive improvements on his land. He was of the opinion that the local crofters were unnecessary impediments to new ideas of farm management. Their crofts were too small to support them and got in the way of the larger fields needed for sheep. The sooner the pack of them shifted off to America the better. He was not a particularly cruel man but had no patience with those who obstructed or criticised his methods. Even he could see that there was not enough room for the evicted families in Leckmelm.

The solution to his problem was to get rid of it. He looked through the Leckmelm people and sorted out those who were supernumerary – either too old or infirm, or who had shown a tendency to opposition in the past – and served them with eviction notices.

In the event only three families were concerned: one widow with her five children, an aged, widowed crofter, and a family with three children. Duncan Mackenzie and his extended family were unaffected, being full lot holders and able both to support themselves and provide labour on the estate. They were not, however, untroubled by events. The first Mary knew of the eviction notices was when Roderick, Murdo's sixteen-year-old brother, burst into the house with the news.

"Widow Campbell, Red Jock and Wee Donnie are to leave their houses by Martinmas, and if they're not out by then, they'll be thrown out. It's a disgrace! They have nowhere to go and no one to turn to." Roddy's face was pink with dismay and anger.

"Wheesht now, Roderick," said his father sternly. "It'll maybe not happen, and anyway, if it does Mistress Campbell has a daughter in Ullapool, Jock Macdonald has aye had plenty of friends who can take him in, and the Macleods are young and strong enough to find somewhere else. We must accept the wishes of the laird as we accept the edicts of the Lord."

Roderick said nothing more in his father's presence, but later he continued the subject with Murdo. "Don't you think it's terrible that folks should be turned out of their own houses, that they've worked on and lived in all their lives? And all for the sake of some new notions of improvement that'll benefit no one but the landowners. Can we not do something about it?"

Mary paused in her work to listen to what her husband had to say.

Murdo seldom spoke hastily, but this time he took even longer than usual to consider his reply. "Aye, it seems a cruel kind of benevolence, forcing people out of their homes. And I doubt that the improvements will make it better for everybody. It's not easy making a living off the land now, with too many people trying to coax some nourishment out of a poor, wee bit of soil. I hear there's good land to be got in America for folk who have the will and courage to work hard."

"Pfff!" Roddy exploded in disgust. "If you're so keen on America, why aren't you off there yourself? And you can hardly expect Red Jock and Christie Campbell to be breaking in new ground, chopping down trees and building houses and all that. And that's not the point, anyway. Don't you see how unjust it is to be clearing people off the land they've worked for generations?"

"Well, Roddy, it seems hard, I grant you, but what can we do about it? Mr Mackenzie is the appointed representative of our landowner and he must carry out his wishes, as we must."

It transpired, however, that Davidson did not know what was happening and, on his return to Leckmelm, he was none too happy with the high-handed behaviour of his tacksman. Nevertheless, the evictions had taken place, the new families moved in, and no more changes were made. But Mary could not forget the look on the old folks' faces and the wailing children as they left their beloved homes and set out for an uncertain future.

In the next year, 1843, more troubles were to come to the folk of Lochbroom.

The Church had always been more than a focal point for the religious life of the people. It was an institution which supported their beliefs and culture and provided for temporal as well as spiritual needs. For many, Sunday was the high spot of the week. No work at all was carried out, and preparations were made on the Saturday night to ensure that only minimal, necessary activities took place. The whole day was devoted to prayer, Bible reading or spiritual reflection, and families dressed in their best clothes (shoes were kept for the occasion) and trooped off to the church at Clachan morning and often evening, no matter what the weather or season. The four-mile walk through the woods at the head of the loch was glorious on a fine spring morning. They strolled under golden-green arches echoing with the fluting of blackbirds, scented with the sweetness of gorse and the sharp tang of bluebells, primroses nestling shyly by the track, urgent shoots pushing through the loamy soil. Mary sometimes fancied it was like a grand natural cathedral where all the little creatures gathered to give thanks and praise to the Lord. She did not tell her fancies to her husband.

It was a different matter in winter, when heavy drifts of snow filled the ditches and blizzards raged. Only the severest weather prevented the adults from attending. They toiled through rain, sleet or gale to reach the relative warmth of the well-packed church. Sometimes the minister could see clouds of steam rising from his damp but devoted congregation.

The Reverend Doctor Ross was an erudite scholar and a fine Gaelic preacher. His sermons, though long and severe, were thought-provoking and challenging. Many hearts quaked lest he had observed their licentious behaviour on the Saturday night and chose to pillory them in church. It seemed he had an uncanny knowledge of everything that went on, but he was particularly critical of dancing, playing cards and drunkenness. This was what was expected of a Scottish minister and, despite it, most folks respected and cared for their religious leader.

The visits to church were a social occasion as well. In a community in which hard work was the order for all, there was little opportunity for intellectual stimulus and conversation. The sermons furnished that, and often provoked heated debate amongst the men about finer points of religious doctrine. For younger members of the congregation, it provided a chance to shyly observe the opposite sex, and often a rapt expression of devotion on a young man's face had very little to do with pious contemplation. For the women, it might be the only time in the week when they could gossip quietly with their neighbours and exchange recipes and remedies.

For the last ten years the Church had experienced a period of conflict with the State authority. Ever since the Reformation, Scottish Presbyterianism had jealously guarded its right to independence within the country's governmental and legal system. However, the landowners, who, as patrons of the Church, subsidised the stipends of the ministers and maintained the churches, sometimes forced their choices of ministers on unwilling congregations. Several cases had gone to court, and matters came to a head in 1842 in the House of Lords when Lord Campbell ruled that, while ministers were members of the Established Church and paid by the State, they were public functionaries and must comply with the laws of the land.

Seriously disturbed by what they saw as a threat to the supremacy and authority of Christ, the Church Assembly passed a Claim of Right appealing to the Queen and government to acknowledge the independence of the Church in spiritual matters. At a Convocation later that year, 480 ministers signed a resolution that, if the Claim of

Right was not affirmed, they would leave the Established Church and give up their livings. This was not merely a matter of importance for Church leaders and ministers but concerned all ordinary members of the presbyteries. During the very snowy winter of 1842 and '43, speakers toured the country preaching and explaining the dire threat to the religious freedom of the people. One such came to Lochbroom parish and spoke in the church at Clachan. The debate found its way into every household on the loch.

The family at Leckmelm was divided in their opinions about the controversy. Roddy expressed his views strongly. "Separation has to come. And perhaps the Secessionists are right: State and Church should be totally separate. How can rulers or landowners dictate our consciences?"

Duncan answered severely. "No, Roderick; this is a Christian country and it is right that the State should support the Church and the people should obey their rulers. We must remember that God has set up kings and principalities over us so that we may live our lives in justice and right behaviour. What will prevent us descending into total depravity otherwise?"

"Yes, Father," Roddy conceded, "but it is wrong that ministers are forced on unwilling parishioners. Every man has the right to choose his religious leader. The court judgements have been in error. Aye, we must obey our rulers, but what if they are upholding an injustice?"

As she bent over her sewing in the background, Mary listened but contributed nothing to the argument.

It was Murdo who answered. "Calvin himself said that we must respect our government and obey our betters even if they are tyrannous or unjust; even if they are the declared enemies of God. It is God's wrath for our iniquities to send us rulers who subvert all that is right and good. We must recognise this and submit to His will."

"But don't you see that what's happening endangers the Church itself and the very fabric of our belief?" Roddy countered. "It questions the supremacy of Christ. The courts are made to judge the law but they have no jurisdiction in religious matters."

Duncan silenced the discussion. "Let's hope the government supports the Church's claim and we don't have to consider leaving."

Such conflicting feelings were prevalent in most houses on the loch, but Reverend Ross, who approved the sentiments of the Convocation, urged his parishioners to sign the resolution in support. The minister often chose the Mackenzie household to air his apprehensions and communicate the difficulties of the Church. He respected Duncan and knew his influence was strong in the township. Whatever Duncan decided, others would follow. When he came to visit, the whole family sat in on the discussion, mostly to listen but also for the older men to contribute their opinions.

When the minister had explained the series of events which led up to the Convocation, he paused for effect and then went on. "So you see, it is not only the question of who should choose your ministers; it's now an assault on the very foundation of our Church, with Christ as its sole authority and head. It is not for lords or nobles to set themselves over God. Kings and queens are appointed by

God and must bow to His will, not exert their own over the spiritual freedom of the people," he thundered. Reverend Ross often forgot that he was not speaking from a pulpit. "If you are strong in your faith and wish to uphold your rights, it behoves you to sign this resolution in support of your ministers. Duncan, I ask you to set an example to the community and put your name to this."

Duncan Mackenzie was indeed strong in his faith, but his misgivings were genuine. "I cannot believe that we should go against the law of the land and those with authority over us. Perhaps there will be a compromise and the Lords will accept our arguments. Surely we don't need to be so provocative?"

"Provocative?!" Reverend Ross's side-whiskers bristled with ire. "It is not we who have been provocative but the judges themselves. Do you not see, man, this is a direct attack on the basis of our country's religion? Since the Reformation we have fought for the independence of our Church, for the right of every man to worship as he chooses without interference or repression. Aye, we've had martyrs aplenty who gave their lives but brought kings low. Andrew Melville, who declared King James was a mere member of the kingdom of Christ. The Covenanters – will we forget their sufferings and sacrifice?"

Duncan persisted. "But, Reverend, I don't know that this is right. Surely as God has appointed rulers to govern us, we must obey them? It is not for us to question their decisions. And if our ministers leave the Established Church, we will be cast into the wilderness with no one to guide us. We will lose our church and you will lose your good manse. How will you live without a stipend?"

Roddy burst into the argument. "And we may all lose our homes too. It is well known the factor is not in favour of this undertaking. We could all be evicted."

"No, no, no, it'll never come to that," pronounced the minister. "And have no fear; I shall be your spiritual guide as ever, and our congregation will survive even if we have to worship on the moors and hillsides. We have done so before and can again. It will make us stronger in our faith."

Roddy was sure of his opinion. "I think our worthy minister is right and we should stand up to such threats and hold to our convictions. I, for one, will sign the resolution gladly."

"Aye," continued the minister. "When did we Scots ever bow to evil rule and repression? Even if we lose our income and our homes, even our lives, we must support our Church when it is in danger. It is the very blood and nurture of our life. What would we be without it? Mere slavering curs. No, I will not force you to sign this, but your own consciences must lead you."

Although elderly, Reverend Ross had lost none of his zeal and powers of persuasion. Duncan and his two eldest sons signed the resolution.

Matters came to a head early in 1843 when the Crown threw out the Claim of Right and the House of Commons voted 211 to seventy-six against it. On the 18th May, the Church Assembly in Edinburgh was disrupted when Dr Chalmers led a solemn file of 386 ministers out of the meeting. The procession to a new assembly hall was followed by cheering crowds. By the 23rd May more ministers had signed a Deed of Demission signing away their Establishment stipends. They expected to lose their churches and manses as well.

When the news of the Disruption reached Lochbroom, Reverend Ross was overjoyed. He was now too infirm to preach himself, but attended the last service taken in the old church in Clachan. After the sermon was finished, he rose with tears in his eyes and led most of the congregation out of the church. Thereafter his health was so poor that he was unable to leave the manse, and remained there till his death on the 21st July.

Not everybody was pleased with the events. Many employees and lackeys of the landed gentry remained in the Established Church. Rumours circulated that Kenneth Mackenzie, alleging orders of the proprietor, threatened the tenants with eviction if they left the Church. As usual it was Roddy who brought the news to the family at Leckmelm. "Do you know what is about?" he announced theatrically. "Our lords and masters threw out the rights of our Church and now they will throw us out as well."

Duncan broke into the general consternation with a firm reprimand. "Now, Roddy, what nonsense is this? Have you been listening to the ravings of young Munro – common rights of man and such? I don't like you associating with him and those others. They'll be in trouble before long, mark my words."

But when Roddy explained the nature of Kenneth Mackenzie's warning, Duncan was incredulous and then angry.

"Well," he declared, "I'll not heed idle gossip and I'll not be dictated to in matters of conscience by any pumped-up hireling. I've no doubt Davidson himself has no hand in this."

Other crofters were not so confident, and a few stayed with the Established Church. Resentment burned below the surface of the community and a few hotheads decided to stage a protest. When the elders came to open the church at Clachan, they found the building nailed up, the bell rope cut and a dog in a state of putrefaction occupying the pulpit. During the service to declare the church vacant, stones were thrown at the window. Duncan Mackenzie questioned his second son severely about his participation in these activities but Roddy protested his innocence: he had been out on the hills all day looking for lost sheep and knew nothing about it. Mary kept quiet, but she had seen him sneaking about with young Murdo Munro and had her own opinion on the matter. Nothing more was said in the household, but Duncan could be heard murmuring about 'disgraceful acts' and 'unchristian violence'. Murdo kept his thoughts to himself, but kept a suspicious eye on Roddy for some time afterwards.

As Duncan had predicted, the tackman's threats came to nothing, but he nurtured his grievances and soon after the rents were raised by thirty per cent.

Despite this opposition and being without a church or minister, the congregation of the new Free Church threw themselves into the effort of establishing a ministry. Services were held wherever they could find a place, or in the open air if necessary. The men debated endlessly about what to do but they agreed that the first priority was to find a new spiritual leader.

Reverend George Macleod was the much-loved minister in Maryborough and, before the Disruption, had toured the country preaching and explaining the need for change. He had made considerable impression on the Lochbroom elders who urged his appointment.

On a dark, wet night in September he set out on his pony over the Dithreabh Mor to Lochbroom. The wind howled around him and the rain lashed in horizontal sheets from the west. The road, which was barely a track, was indistinguishable from the surrounding moor and peat bogs, and all he could do was hunker down on his pony's back and leave it to its natural devices. Thankfully the pony had travelled the route many times before and safely delivered its charge to the old manse where the widow of Ross still lived.

Over the next four days Reverend Macleod preached in the open air in Ullapool to crowds of two to three thousand people, many of whom had travelled a long distance from outlying districts to hear him. Mary attended all of these sermons with her husband and family and she was struck by the effect Reverend Macleod had on his audience. He began his preaching to the solemn, fixed attention of all but, as he warmed to his theme, censuring the sins of his listeners and exhorting repentance, she saw the people bowing their heads and some weeping openly. With a shock she realised that her husband, head high and back straight, had tears pouring down his cheeks. Mary looked with renewed respect at the minister and tried hard to listen to his words but, for her, there seemed nothing inspirational about them. He talked very well and performed dramatically, rather like, she supposed, actors on the stage must do. But he failed to arouse either her fear or her faith. Perhaps she was too ingrained in sinfulness to understand.

However, the effect on Murdo was pronounced. As soon as it was decided that Reverend Macleod would be appointed as the new minister for Lochbroom, Murdo offered his help to set up the church.

Mary had never seen him so animated. Every day when he had finished his tasks on the croft, he set out for Ullapool, where the minister and other young men like himself met to discuss the immediate needs of the congregation. The most pressing of these was a new church building.

Lochbroom Parish was by no means a rich community, but the Free Church had made provision for the equal distribution of general funds to pay ministers' stipends and build new churches. In addition, Murdo and his friends sought donations from everyone; a widow might give a penny, a tradesman a shilling, and in a remarkably short time there was enough money to build a fine new church on Mill Street in Ullapool. Murdo gave his labour in the building and local craftsmen gave their expertise. By 1844 the church was completed, but the congregation was so large that communion services had to be held outside whatever the weather.

Fundraising efforts did not stop there. The Free Church leaders determined that education should be available to as many as possible, principally so that people were able to read the Bible themselves. Murdo was seldom at home these days: as soon as work was finished he was visiting neighbours trying to raise money for a new school. Mary was pleased that he had found such a worthwhile interest in life but sometimes she wished he would pay more attention to his family and home.

By now Mary had given birth to their second son, John. The Mackenzie house was large by normal standards but not enough to contain five adults and seven children. Mary sometimes felt that she could not move for people, farm implements, slouching sheepdogs and flapping nappies. Her work was interminable, from dawn to dusk without a break between. Murdo, on the other hand, seemed oblivious to the chaos. Mary struggled on without a complaint and it fell to Roddy to point out her difficulties to her husband. He tackled him one day as he was setting out on his fundraising rounds.

"Murdo, when are you going to build a house for your own family? You've built a house for the Church and a manse for the minister but your own children are squashed in a bed with three others. And your wife has to clean and cook and wash for all of us. Is it not about time you thought about her for a change?"

Murdo was about to protest but, at that moment, he saw Mary lugging a large basket of laundry out to the line, a fractious baby balanced under her arm and trailed by a wailing infant.

Roddy pressed his case. "Margaret is old enough to take over the chores and Duncan and I can help you build a house. I've no doubt the younger boys will want to help too. Come on, Murdo; best do it now before any more children come along."

Murdo was convinced but, true to habit, never mentioned the matter to his wife. The first she knew was when the men began to lay out the foundations and gather stones for the walls.

Landowners and their factors did not encourage the building of more houses on their estates. Indeed, they blamed the subdivision of crofts among younger sons for the shortage of land and the consequent precarious subsistence levels of the people. The Improvers sought to lease out larger portions of land for sheep farming, and thought that crofters would make a better living employed as workers on the estate. Some, like Sir George Stewart Mackenzie, a propagandist for agricultural development, openly stated that improvement should take place at the price of clearance of the 'constitutionally indolent and ignorant' Highlanders.

However, Murdo's house was tolerated as he was proving himself of some value to the factor. It was becoming known that he had a way with animals. He cared for the few cattle and sheep on the croft so that they were in better condition and generally made higher prices in the sales. Neighbours consulted him about sick animals and, even if he couldn't provide medicine for them, he could diagnose the problem and often exerted a calming influence on a distressed creature. The landowners usually brought in shepherds from the south as they considered that Highlanders had no skill with sheep, but the factor recognised Murdo's talent and often employed him on the big farm. So Murdo was allowed his house on the tacit agreement that he would be available to work whenever necessary.

The building went very quickly. Although Murdo's brothers were still young, they were keen to help, but the bulk of the hard work, shifting and shaping heavy stones, was accomplished by Duncan, Murdo and Roddy. The family were able to move in before the winter snows had arrived.

Mary was delighted with her new house. It was not substantially different from any other crofting house but there were improvements: the stone walls were mortared and there were fireplaces in each gable end. Mary loved being able to sit cosy in the dark winter nights, watching the shadows flickering on the wood-panelled walls and listening to the rain pattering on the glass windows. It was so different from the crammed conditions of the old house.

The winter came very late that year but it came with a vengeance. At first it had been unseasonably warm, and into January buds were beginning to peep through the ground. Then came the frosts, spreading a crackly peace over the hard earth. Rime coated tree branches with frozen needles three inches long, and the air sparkled with icy diamonds. The calm did not last long. Blizzards came driving in from the west.

Mary thought little of it. As the winds howled in the chimney and the sleet slashed the windows, she drew her chair closer to the fire and cuddled the baby. But, as the storms raged on into the second day, she could see that Murdo was becoming agitated. He would pace the room and peer out the window regularly to gauge the direction of the wind. At last, when she could stand it no longer, she gently chided him. "The snow will not stop for you watching it, nor the wind cease blowing. Come and sit quiet by the fire and read me a bit from the Bible; Ruth, or the Song of Solomon." She loved to hear his strong voice reading the sweet words of love and liked to imagine they were for her. But he was not to be placated.

"Our animals are all safe inside the byre but, at the big house, the sheep – they are all out in the fields where there's no protection from the wind and snow. They'll seek what shelter they can find and, if it's behind a big wall, they'll be caught in the drifts. We have to dig them out before they suffocate."

"But surely the shepherds and servants there will attend to that? It's not for you to be concerned," Mary urged.

"I've no great faith in these folk from the south," said Murdo. "They have fine notions of cattle- and sheep rearing but no common sense. They'll not think of the animals until it is too late. I've got to go and do something." He followed his words by pulling on his big coat and getting into his heavy boots. He had to dig his way out of the drift at the front door.

He did not return until late that evening, soaked and exhausted, and, as usual, had little to say about what had happened. Mary had to wait till several days later when Roddy recounted the events.

"Murdo came round to our house first to make sure all was well, and then the two of us went over to the big house to see what we could do. You know he was right. The people there were not too concerned about the weather; they thought the sheep could take care of themselves. But Murdo chivvied them out with spades and prods. And it was just as well.

"When we got to the fields, there was not a sheep to be seen. The snow was not too thick in the middle but the drifts behind the walls were many feet deep. Why anyone built big walls like that across the force of the westerly wind is beyond reason. Well, Murdo set us to probe along the drifts from each end wherever they had gathered deepest, and hard work it was. We were floundering up to our chests in the stuff and the blizzard was still blowing hard. I doubt anyone was feeling the cold, though. You had to put the prod in every few feet; one foot wrong and you'd miss a sheep easy. So we went on like that until we found the first ones. Luckily they were all couried together in a big heap, and then we had to dig them out. These ones were fine. It was like they had made themselves an Eskimo igloo and were quite comfy inside. But that was less than half of all the animals – we had to go on searching for the others. They were not so lucky, or maybe not so clever. We'd just go on probing until we found another and then dig it out. Most were alive but some were down deep in the drifts and had no air to breathe. It was an awful shame but you should have seen Murdo; he'd not give up. He'd breathe into the nose of an animal, and sometimes it would start to bleat again. He made us herd all the sheep back to the byres to dry them off and keep them warm. He said some might die yet from the damp and cold. But he went on all day, searching through the drifts until it was getting dark. He wouldn't give up until all the sheep were accounted for. And, you know, all the thanks we got was a wee dram of whisky. I don't doubt the laird would have shown more gratitude for saving most of his animals."

Murdo's reputation grew after this exploit. His neighbours called on him to help with their animals and he could always expect employment from the local farm managers. But life was not easy for the young family, which had now been increased by a daughter, Isabella.

Crofting life was hard at the best of times. The normal diet consisted of oatmeal and potatoes, some fish and milk. Butter and cheese were a luxury as the old habit of taking the cattle to the summer shielings had long died out. A few black cattle were kept as a source of cash which might pay the rent, but prices for them had fallen. Crops failed regularly, the herring were fickle, and often people had to survive on shellfish from the beach or nuts from the hazel woods. Famine stalked the land at regular intervals.

Eighteen forty-six was such a year. The potato had proved a mixed blessing for the west of Scotland. Although it provided the main staple food, it could be attacked by blight, and this year the entire crop was lost. The Mackenzie family subsisted on what fish the boys could catch from the beach. Soon Mary was sick to death of the smell and oily taste of herring.

News of the starvation conditions had spread to the towns in the south and Relief Boards were set up to provide aid. Murdo became active in the Free Church Destitution Committee in Lochbroom, doing what he could to help the poorest members of society – the widows, the elderly and infirm. There was always a substratum of cottars who had no access to land, no animals, and whose only income came from trades or casual labour. These people suffered most in times of famine, when there was no food to spare and no money for extras. Murdo often thought they would be better off emigrating to America or Australia but none of them could afford the fare.

When Roddy came to visit, he expressed different views on the matter. "We'll not solve these problems for good until we have a new way of organising the land in this country. Too much of it is bundled up in big estates producing nothing but sheep and deer, while ordinary people don't even own the land they live on. There's no way to improve your lot and, when the crops fail, you starve. I blame all this on the landowners with their ideas of improvement and clearances."

Murdo did not agree. "You can't blame the famine on landowners, Roddy. The potato failure is an act of God; nothing to do with them. And I believe it's God's punishment for our sins. There's too much godlessness – fornication and drunkenness. We must kneel at God's feet and repent our evildoing."

Roddy's anger was rising. "And just what evil have the poor people been up to, the folks you've been visiting? They haven't the money for drink, or, for that matter, the strength for fornication. You may be God-fearing by choice but they have no choice and no hope. What kind of God is it, who punishes the innocent along with the guilty? He's a bloody-minded God of injustice, I'd say. Either that or it's nothing to do with him either, and that makes him guilty of negligence. You'd be better off praying for him to stamp on the greed of the wealthy than visit his wrath upon the poor folk."

Murdo stood up and, for a moment, Mary feared that he was about to strike his brother, but he seemed to collect himself before speaking. "There shall be no language like that in this house. Your opinions are your own, Roddy, but you can keep them to yourself. I pray God will forgive you for words spoken in the heat of the moment." Murdo sat down again, but Mary could see that he was shaking.

Roddy could see it too, and perhaps regretted his angry words. "I did not mean disrespect to you or your God, Murdo, but I cannot help but question the injustice of man or God when I see it."

When Roddy had left, Murdo urged his wife to kneel with him in prayer. "I fear our brother is losing his faith. We must pray for his eternal soul."

Mary was not so sure – she felt great sympathy with Roddy's feelings – but she knelt with her husband and offered her own prayer for the good of both men. From this time, although there was no overt evidence of disagreement, there was a distance between the two brothers. Mary missed Roddy's visits and hoped there would be a reconciliation soon.

There were many men who shared Roddy's opinions. In England, Charles Dickens was publishing books which highlighted poverty in the towns and dreadful conditions for women and children employed in the factories. Dissatisfaction and unrest amongst the lower classes were growing throughout the country. The wealthy were not immune to compassion, but they had their own way of managing affairs to their advantage.

Relief from money collected in the south came at first in the provision of meal, but it was soon decided that aid would be better distributed in return for labour. The West Highlands had no proper roads and the Relief Board agreed to use some of its funds to construct roads connecting Garve to Ullapool with links into Coigach and Knockan – the so-called

'Destitution Roads'. Big landowners were responsible for organising the road-building and other work on the estate, but conditions were harsh. Managers like Andrew Scott, factor of the Cromartie estate, thought that indiscriminate provision of aid would make the people dependent and lacking in self-reliance. It was also considered economically important not to undercut the meal prices of the local traders. Aid measures relieved the worst of the famine but crop failure continued sporadically throughout the nineteenth century.

The Mackenzie family had fared better than most. Murdo's brothers had been able to supplement the income by working on the roads. It was a precarious existence, and Roddy came up with a plan which might ease their difficulties. He discussed it with Murdo before bringing it up with Duncan and the younger brothers.

"We need some dependable source of income so that we don't have to worry about the vagaries of the potato and the price of cattle. Why not buy a fishing boat? We can get a loan for it and to buy the tackle and nets and we'd pay it off in a few years. We've got four strong men in the family, and the younger boys will be grown soon and able to join us. There's little other hope for employment or a future round here. What do you think, Murdo?"

Murdo was cautious but he could see the logic behind Roddy's proposition. His own family was growing and he could not depend on the casual labour he got shepherding. "I think you have an idea there, Roddy, but do you think our father would agree, and would we get a loan easily?"

"If the old man agrees there will be no problem about a loan. His word and reputation are good enough security for that."

In fact Duncan approved the scheme. Although he was getting on in years, he could still pull an oar and saw the sense in taking advantage of the herring which often shoaled in great numbers during the hungry winter season. Negotiations were made and a small boat purchased in time for the next year's fishing.

Mary was not happy with the new arrangements. She feared for their lives every time the brothers set out to fish. Even on a fine day within the protection of the loch, the weather could change in minutes: fierce storms channelled through the glens and steep mountainsides. A waterspout, like a miniature tornado, would skite across the water and upturn any boats whose sailors were less than vigilant. Most fishing took place at night, so there was always the danger of grounding on low-lying skerries. At least Murdo and his brothers could swim, unlike most of the fishermen on these coasts, but Mary knew that they would not survive for long in the cold northern waters. Fortunately no accidents occurred, but the shifting nature of the herring shoals made it an unpredictable occupation. The extra income was important for both families and now Mary had another mouth to feed: James, born in the depths of winter.

Looking back on these times, Mary reflected that James had been at once the most intense and ephemeral of her children. It was as if he knew he did not have long to spend in this world and wanted to make the most of what time he had. He was walking and talking before he was a year old. He was blithe and bonny, thin and golden blond, and Mary loved him as life itself.

Cholera struck in the winter of 1848.

It was generally believed that cholera was spread by miasma; foul vapours in the air. As soon as Mary heard of the outbreak in Ullapool, she cautioned her husband against visiting the town, but Murdo was adamant.

"I must go about my parish duties. The poor are always with us and, no doubt, there will be more needing my help than before. This disease will pass and it will be God's will if He spares me or strikes me."

"I'm not thinking of you so much as our children, Murdo. You are strong and healthy but they are very young and weak. What if you brought the sickness back to our house?" Mary curbed a flash of anger. "What if our children become ill?"

Murdo pondered before replying. "I don't believe that will happen. We breathe the clean air of the mountains, not the squalid air of the town. And God will protect them."

Mary bit back her words of remonstrance. There was nothing she could do or say when he had made up his mind, particularly when he invoked his faith. He continued his visits to needy neighbours and did not avoid the infected houses in Ullapool. There were many who appreciated his quiet words of consolation and practical gifts of food or old clothes.

It would be a year later before a London doctor, John Snow, established beyond doubt that cholera was borne in contaminated water. By that time it was too late for the people of Leckmelm, who drew their water from communal wells behind their houses. Nearly everybody was infected but, for many, the symptoms were hardly noticeable; maybe stomach cramps and diarrhoea, which passed in a few hours. Some felt nothing at all. Murdo was unaffected but Mary and all the children fell sick.

She refused to take to her bed, struggling to cope, cleaning vomit and diarrhoea, and soothing children screaming in pain. At last she could go on no longer, nearly passing out with her own pain and exhaustion. Murdo took over the nursing and his sister Margaret came to help.

The three elder children improved quickly. They were toddling about while their mother lay almost unconscious, her heart racing, her skin clammy and pale. Margaret tended her, feeding her sips of water and soothing her brow. Murdo cared for James but there was little he could do. Although the baby had fought the disease in its initial stages, he now lay quiet; it seemed as if he might be better but, in reality, dehydration had produced organ failure and he was now slipping away. He died in a matter of hours.

Mary recovered but was left very weak. She could not bear to look on the body of her beloved child unless she was overcome with tears. She lay on her bed with her face turned to the wall. Baby James was laid to rest in the Clachan graveyard under an unmarked stone.

Murdo was solicitous with his wife during her recovery but he did not cry over the death of his son. Mary could not understand how he could lavish more tenderness on his animals than he gave to his family. When the lambing season arrived, he came home with an apparently lifeless lamb cradled in his arms. He rubbed it dry and placed it close by the kitchen stove, crooning soft words to it. "There then, there then. Warm and safe, safe and warm. Breathe your life. Come on, come on." The lamb revived and soon was sucking eagerly on a bottle of milk. Mary watched his dark head bent over the lamb in his arms and was provoked to rebuke.

"How can you care so much for that wee animal when our baby lies cold in the grave? Don't our children deserve more consideration?"

Murdo looked astonished by her outburst. "I give everything I can to my children. I work to provide for all their needs and more. My family comes first and then I give what I can to help my neighbours. What else do you expect me to do?"

"I know you work hard for us all, Murdo, but here you are cuddling a dumb animal when you would hardly give a word of affection to your own ones. Did James ever feel the warmth of your love to carry him peacefully to his grave? Was he less important to you than your sheep?"

"Mary, Mary, you are tired from your illness and talking nonsense. Our Lord Himself has told us to look after His lambs. And don't you understand why there is a difference? We have immortal souls. James, if he is chosen, will dwell in eternal bliss with Jesus. These little creatures have no soul. For them death is the end of everything. We are asked to save them when they are sick and ease their pains when they are dying. That is how the Good Shepherd would have it."

"But don't you miss James? He was with us so short a time; don't you question why he had to die yet I lived? Didn't he deserve a full and happy life?" Mary spoke through her tears.

Murdo touched her hand briefly. "Of course I loved James and miss him deeply. God has chosen to take our child from us but He has spared you for me. I give thanks to Him every day for that. God willing we will have more children to replace the one we have lost."

Mary turned away to hide her angry tears. She did not mention James to anyone ever again.

After the cholera epidemic had passed, it looked as if life in the community and for the family at Leckmelm was improving. The fishing was going well, there was enough money to pay the rents and there was time for a little entertainment. Worldwide events seldom had great impact on the local people but lesser celebrations were often organised at the behest of the landowners.

Although Davidson owned the lands of Leckmelm, most of Coigach and Lochbroom belonged to the Cromartie estate, whose family, after years of financial mismanagement, was in severe debt. Unexpectedly, the daughter, Anne Hay-Mackenzie, married the Marquis of Stafford, heir to the vast, rich Sutherland estate. It was hoped that the marriage would bring some prosperity to the lands of Coigach. To mark Anne's coming of age in April 1950, Andrew Scott, the Cromartie factor, encouraged 'spontaneous celebration' – bonfires, dinner for tenants and drink for the people. Half-crowns were distributed to eighty-three paupers in Coigach.

Scott wrote to Kenneth Mackenzie at Leckmelm: ... *above all there should be no brawling or fighting among the common people on your grand festival day. Let them make merry to the top of their bent and welcome... Wishing you all a pleasant and joyous meeting on the day of your rejoicing.* It is unknown whether the festivities were genuinely spontaneous or had more to do with the promise that all summonses to rent defaulters would be suspended for one year. Certainly the Leckmelm folk enjoyed the chance for a cheerful break in their labours, but Roddy was heard to remark clearly in the presence of his betters, "It will be a grand day for celebration indeed when the Lady Anne pays some heed to the poverty and privations that afflict her tenants for all the rest of the year."

Roddy's words were to be prophetic, for Anne, now Lady Stafford, chose to take a high-handed attitude to rent defaulters on her Coigach estates.

In some ways life for the local people had become easier. A good herring season in 1851 staved off starvation and should have provided money from the sales of fish to pay overdue rents. But there were no long-distance ships in the area to transport the fish to the southern markets. More and more crofters were taking the option of emigration to Australia or Canada. Those who could not afford the fare found themselves unable to pay their rents. The Cromartie factors threatened the defaulters with eviction.

Things came to a head in 1852 when Badenscallie in Coigach was to be cleared for a sheep farm. Most of the crofters signed an agreement to evict to Badentarbat, but eighteen refused. In March the Coigach manager and a sheriff's officer party, carrying summonses for eviction, were met by the local women, who searched the party and burnt the summonses. A second boat was attacked at Achnahaird and the summonses prevented, and a third attempt met with a similar fate. These incidents were reported with glee in the Inverness newspapers and became known as the Coigach Riots. The crofters sent a petition to Lady Stafford asking for clemency, but she was adamant and refused to give way. During the winter of 1852 to '53, scouts kept a lookout for the appearance of officers, and in February the sheriff's boat was attacked again by women at Culnacraig. The officer was stripped of his clothes and the summonses burnt.

Duncan Mackenzie viewed the events in Coigach with disapproval. How disgraceful to be resisting the law of the land and the will of the landowner! But his sons, meeting in Murdo's house, shared differing opinions. Roddy found the spirited actions of the women, and the rumour that some had been men dressed up as women, extremely amusing.

"I wish I'd been there to see it. The sheriff bare to his breeks and the 'ladies' all cheering and dancing round the bonfire of summonses."

Murdo saw the serious side of the protests. "Aye, but it will do no good to carry on like that. They would be better to call for help from the law and appeal to Lady Stafford again. No right-minded person can fail to see the justness of their cause. It's not their fault they can't afford their rents, and she should have some compassion for their situation."

Roddy was not so sure. "All she cares about is making something from the bigger sheep farmers; she would be happier if all the crofters were off her land and away abroad. She'll not be satisfied until all the fields are made over to sheep or deer instead of people."

For once Murdo was correct. A last attempt to serve summonses was thwarted and the Staffords, fearing public disapproval, gave in.

Spring was always a busy time for crofters: sheep had to be brought into the enclosed fields and watched over continuously in case of difficult lambings. For some perverse reason most lambs were born in the early morning, but crofters were used to early risings anyway. Anyone who had enough land for crops had to plough and sow their seed. Even the little kale yards behind the croft houses had to be planted up, usually by the women, with peas and salad vegetables to supplement the often-insipid diet. Murdo was up before dawn every day and often not back until dark.

Mary did not expect to see much of him at this time of year, but one night in May she began to become seriously worried when he did not come back at all. The nights were not dark so close to midsummer, but Mary lit a lamp and put it in the window and waited up for him. He was not the kind of man who would indulge in drink and end up sleeping the night away in a ditch – Mary knew of a few of her neighbours who were not so abstemious. She felt that something had happened.

Despite her fears, she must have fallen asleep in her chair and woke up at around four o'clock when the greyness of the dark was just beginning to lighten. Murdo had still not returned. Mary rushed round to her father-in-law's house to alert the family.

Roddy and the younger brothers set out to search the hills but it was nightfall before they returned, carrying the unconscious Murdo on a makeshift stretcher of branches pushed through the sleeves of their jackets. Mary laid him out on the bed and washed his wounds while a younger brother was sent off in haste to Ullapool to fetch the doctor.

Roddy recounted the story later. "We searched all over the in-bye fields and up onto the common grazing but there was no sign of him anywhere. We thought he must have decided to go further into the hills to look for stray sheep. But we couldn't find him there either. It was coming back that we heard a dog barking in the big ravine that brings the burn down from the mountain. And sure enough, there he was at the bottom. I thought he was dead when I first saw him, lying down there. He was half in the water – a wee bit more and he'd have drowned. But he was breathing, just. We got down to him but it was no easy job getting him out of the chasm. The sides were steep and slippery and we were scared that moving him would hurt him more. He had a great gash on the side of his head but the blood was crusty and dried. But there was something wrong with his legs as well." Roddy paused to wipe a thick strand of his hair out of his eyes. "There was a lamb in the water further down. I think he must have gone into the ravine to rescue it and fallen. The lamb was drowned, anyway," he added wryly.

Mary tended gently to her husband, washing the blood out of his hair and trying to keep him warm. He had begun to shiver at least, and by the time the doctor arrived, his eyes were open, but Mary thought they looked very odd and he was clearly not conscious.

The doctor confirmed that Murdo's thigh bone was broken near the hip. He bound it up with a splint as well as he could. "You'll have to keep him still for a long while to let the bone set itself and he may be left with a limp, but I reckon he'll mend well enough," he counselled. Privately, he was more worried about the blow to the head. It could be simple concussion or there could be more serious damage to the brain. Only time would tell.

Murdo lay unconscious for several days, sometimes waking to a kind of delirium, raving about lost sheep, good shepherds and other images from the Bible. He seemed to be constantly reliving a dream in which he was burying a dead lamb. Mary soaked a cloth in cool water to cool his brow and tried to stop him tossing about in the grip of his dream. One evening, at the height of his fever, he woke briefly and caught her wrist in his hand. Mary winced with the strength of his grip, but even more with the intensity of his gaze.

"You'll not leave me, Mary," was all he said, and then sank back into oblivion without hearing her response. She sat by his bedside all that night, holding his hand and waiting to reassure him if he woke. By morning his fever was abated and he slept peacefully. After a few days, he was beginning to ask after the health of his animals.

Their older sons, Ian and John, were by now old enough to carry out the work of the croft, and even Isabella, at fourteen, was able to take work as a kitchen maid in the big house. Murdo's brothers rallied round during that year, catching as much fish as they could to supplement the family's income and diet. The Reverend George Macleod did not forget his willing helper, and came round to sit with Murdo and discuss weighty matters in the wider world.

"Now, Murdo," he began on one such occasion. "Have you heard what new nonsense the men of science have come up with?"

Murdo shook his head.

"Not only are they telling us that the world is older than the generations of Adam, but they now dispute the story of the Creation. There is this fellow Darwin has a theory that we're all descended from apes – apes, I tell you! Is that not a fantastical – oh, and aye, a heretical – theory?"

Reverend Macleod explained as much as he knew of the theory of evolution, although he had not read the book *Origin of Species*, which had been published, to much controversy, that year.

Murdo listened carefully, as was his habit, before responding. "Well, perhaps I will need to read the book myself. There are those who wish to wipe away all that the Bible teaches us. I do not understand how or why they question the word of God as it has been handed down to us. Perhaps it is Satan's attempt to trouble our faith. So we should stand firm and refute these notions. I'm sure there are many arguments and much evidence we can use."

The two men spent the rest of the afternoon with their heads together, formulating arguments against the monstrous theory. Reverend Macleod was able to reiterate these in his sermons in the church on Sundays.

Murdo's recuperation was long and never really complete. By the end of the autumn he was able to hobble about with a crutch, but he walked with a limp forever after and suffered bouts of pain in his hip, particularly when the weather was damp and cold. The wound to his head had healed but his mood had changed. Mary would find him sometimes standing staring into space as if he had forgotten where he was or what he was doing. There were other times when he wore a black look and his temper burst out at very little provocation. He was never violent or swore like other men she knew, but she would try to keep her youngest daughter, Ann, out of his way at these times.

By the end of the winter, Murdo was able to take up some of the lighter work on the croft. He was not strong enough to go out on the fishing boat but his brothers, Roddy, Alex and Donald, could manage it on their own.

Whatever God had decided about the theory of evolution, He visited His wrath on the people of Lochbroom in 1860.

Summer storms were generally reckoned to be the worst. Perhaps this was because they could come in the middle of a period of good weather and catch people unaware. That is certainly what happened this year. A calm day had tempted the brothers out for a night's fishing on the loch. Generally they stayed within the shelter of the two great headlands which bordered Loch Broom, but sometimes they ventured further out, always staying quite close to the coast. That night, being settled, they had made their way down the coast a little way and had had a successful catch. As morning approached, the seas began to rise and they returned home as fast as the freshening westerly could fill the sails. Other fishing boats were racing back to the shelter of the coastal lochs. During the day, the weather deteriorated, and by nightfall, the wind had risen to gale force and the rain was lashing the house.

Although everyone was used to violent wind, nobody slept that night. Sudden gusts shook even the sturdy walls of the house; the lamp flame quivered in the draughts and

Mary feared that the thatch would be stripped off the roof. You could hear trees moaning, and, at one point, a crack like the sound of a gun was followed by a crash as a tree came down. The storm continued all through the night into the next morning but, by first light, Murdo and his brothers had battled their way down to the beach to check that the boat was safe on its mooring.

At first it was impossible to tell. The waves were colossal as they drove with the full force of the wind up the loch. Then Roddy shouted, "She's gone. I can't see the mooring buoy either. She must have filled with water and capsized."

"No, look there, at the edge of the bay," screamed Murdo into the wind. "She's broken her mooring and come ashore. I can just make out her shape on the beach. God, I beseech you, she is not damaged."

But, by full daylight, it was obvious that Murdo's prayer had not been answered. The boat had been overturned, and her hull showed gaps where the planking had been smashed on the rocks. Her mast was gone, torn out of its base and, no doubt, carried miles inland to the head of the loch.

Murdo walked around, surveying the damage. "Oh, it's not too bad. I think she can be repaired. It'll take a bit of money and some hard work but I think we'll get her back before the end of summer."

Roddy, Alex and Donald said nothing. They could only look on in despair. How would they get the money? They hadn't even repaid the loan for her purchase. If only they had had the foresight to bring the boat onto the shore the day before!

The Mackenzie brothers were not the only ones who lost boats that night. Almost all the small fishing fleet was wrecked, many houses had lost their roofs and crops had been ruined. The people faced a stark year. It was no wonder that, after all the other troubles that had afflicted them, many of the younger people chose to emigrate to Canada, America or New Zealand, where they hoped the weather might be kinder and there were no landlords to hassle them.

Murdo worked to repair the boat when he could, but the other boys showed little enthusiasm and, at last, Roddy made a decision. He came to tell Murdo and Mary one evening when the daily work was finished. "I'm going to New Zealand," he announced without preamble. "Alex and Donald will be coming too; maybe Thomas, although there's a girl he's courting. There's nothing for us here. There was never much chance of us making a living from the land or the sea, so what kind of future would we have? The Highlands are dead or dying, killed off by the greed of landowners with their new way of living. In New Zealand we'll be free, and we can make a life for ourselves with hard work and a bit of initiative. I don't suppose you'll be wanting to come with us," he nodded at Murdo, "but that's fine if you do."

"No," said Murdo. "This is my home and my family is here. I can understand you need to go but we have enough to get by and, when I've repaired the boat, my sons can help with the fishing."

The last of the summer months that year were warm and gentle, as if the weather were making recompense for its earlier behaviour. In September, Murdo's brothers set off on the coach for Greenock where they would board the *Lady Egidia* bound for New Zealand. All the family gathered to wave goodbye. It was unlikely they would ever meet again. Mary felt she would miss Roddy most of all, with his forthright opinions and cheery disposition. A little sparkle had gone out of her life.

Mary felt the lack of Roddy's support later that year.

The family were seated at the kitchen table eating their midday meal when Duncan stormed into the room. "I must know the truth, Murdo. If this is a scandalous rumour it must be silenced at once."

Murdo stared at his father. Mary bowed her head; the rest of the family looked furtively at each other. They obviously knew what had happened.

Receiving no reply, Duncan thundered, "Stop looking like a lightning-struck sheep. Is your daughter, Isabella, with child or not? And what are you going to do about it?"

Mary dared not look at her husband's face. She feared to see the dismay and disgust upon it.

But Murdo's face was stony. He said nothing for many moments and then replied, "The matter is not definite. When it is, you can be sure I'll take the appropriate action."

Duncan continued to rebuke Murdo and point out the dreadful consequences to their respective families of association with licentious behaviour. He glared at the children as if they too had been touched by the Devil, and Ann, the youngest, burst into tears. When he finally left, Ian, at nineteen fully aware of his sister's difficulty, bustled his siblings out of the house. He was a little afraid of how his father might react but knew they must leave their parents alone.

He need not have feared his father's violence for Murdo was confused more than angry. "So, Mary," he said at last. "You must know the truth of this; is it certain? How could it happen? We have brought our daughter up in right and proper behaviour. And the man? Can a marriage be arranged quickly?"

Mary did her best to acquaint her husband with the situation. The father had left the area, probably unaware of the results of his dalliance. Isabella would have to face her disgrace herself but, with the support of her family, things might not turn out so badly.

Murdo sat for some time without reply. Mary wondered if he had gone into one of his dwams, but finally, without looking at her, he said, "Our house shall not be polluted by Isabella's sin. She must leave here now and go, I care not where, but I will never see her or acknowledge her again. That is the end of the matter."

"But, Murdo, she's barely sixteen," Mary pleaded. "Who can she turn to but her family?"

"She is no daughter of mine. You knew of this and chose not to tell me. You bear the guilt of this too. I will not forgive you for this." Murdo turned and left the house without another word.

When Ian learned of his father's response, he took it upon himself to relay the news to Isabella. He had some idea of how such matters could be managed, and paid for her coach fare to Glasgow where there were establishments which dealt with 'fallen women'. Murdo never mentioned his daughter again, or asked what had happened to her. He continued to treat Mary as he always had but she felt the coldness more keenly and relied more and more on the comfort of her eldest son.

II

I never really understood my father. He toiled for the Church and was noted for charitable acts for the poor, elderly and sick around the parish. His croft was better kept than most and his animals always fetched the best prices in the sales. Yet, for all this, there was a darkness about him which could never be penetrated. As children, we did not fear him, but we dared not question his instructions or contradict his opinions. I had secretly admired our Uncle Roddy when he argued with our father. Roddy was gone now, so there was no one to stand up to him. Mother always acquiesced and Grandfather Duncan was only concerned about keeping the good name of the family. I suppose I should have said something then but I was only a young lad, not yet sure enough of my convictions; how was I to rebut generations of religious prejudice? I did what I could for Isabella but I resolved to get out of that house as soon as possible. I did not tell my mother my reasons for leaving; it would have made her very unhappy. I told her it would be more convenient for me to live in the servants' quarters at the big house where I had secured a good job as an under-keeper.

Whenever I could I came round to visit Mother and chat to her about my work and discuss events in the rest of the world. There was civil war in America, and Queen Victoria's beloved husband, Prince Albert, died. We were not to know she would outlive her husband by forty years. I know my mother looked forward to these visits, infrequent though they were. She loved her family and her husband but there was little fun and no intellectual stimulation for her. I was often tempted to follow my uncles to New Zealand; occasional letters told us how they were now farming land which was their own, without landowner or factor above them. Life here continued its round of crop and herring failures; famine a constant fear. But I had a mind to marry and settle down myself. Grandfather Duncan had been living alone for some time and, when he died, I was allowed to take over his house and marry my Janey. I was as happy as a young man with a lovely wife and a good job could be.

I was never as strictly religious as my father – I had my own idea of how God wished to be served. But when the Reverend George Macleod died I took some interest in the appointment of the next incumbent, Reverend John Macmillan. My father at first approved of the new minister, whose sermons were laced with fearful denunciations of the sins of his parishioners, but, before very long, his opinion changed. The minister was a champion of the common man and not afraid to declare his opposition to the totalitarian rule of the landowners, their factors and tacksmen. I was present in my father's house one evening when the Reverend Macmillan had called to discuss some important parish business. In 1872 a new Act of Parliament had placed the provision of schools in the control of the State, and now School Boards were to be elected from the local people.

Reverend Macmillan came to his point right away. "This is one of the most important pieces of legislation to come before us but, if the elections are not carried out fairly, it could cause greater harm than good. You'll be aware that Major Davidson has put his name forward, along with some of the factors." He paused to gauge my father's reaction but, getting none, went on. "Our School Boards must be controlled by ordinary local people, people of good standing in the community, ministers and the like: we who live here day to day and have the best interests of our parishioners in mind. We cannot trust the landowners who have shown all too well that they care more for their own property than the poor crofters who live on their estates. I myself am standing for these elections and I hope you'll see your way to giving me your vote."

I could see that my father was nonplussed by this request. I knew that he supported the rights of landowners as the God-given authorities in the land. When faced with the task of casting a vote for his minister or his landed superior, how could he choose? At last he seemed to gather himself together. "I will consider this carefully and make my decision based on what will be for the good of all."

The coldness of his answer was obvious to Reverend Macmillan, and he very soon left the house. I followed him out and, stopping him on the path, assured him of my support even though, as a mere labourer, I could not vote.

The election was fiercely contested and everyone, whether they could vote or not, discussed the relative merits of the candidates. In many ways the debate symbolised the growing dissatisfaction with our political system: the rule of landlords; the disenfranchisement and lack of power of ordinary men. For so many years we had heard of human rights in France and America, and yet we in the Highlands seemed to have no rights at all. During his campaign, I used to visit the minister and listen to some of these great ideas. I said nothing of this to my father.

The result of the vote caused considerable consternation: of the nine elected, three were ministers, three were landowners, factors or farmers, and the other three were a banker, a merchant and an innkeeper. No ordinary crofters or tradesmen were elected, of course. Major Davidson was not elected and, deeply humiliated, took his revenge on his tenants by increasing our rents to over a hundred pounds a year. As an under-keeper, I could no longer afford to pay the rent and, in any case, I was sickened to be the lackey of the landowning classes. I was lucky enough to get a job in the general store in Ullapool, so Janey and I moved to the village.

Although the boom years of the herring fishing had passed by, Ullapool was a better place to live than the country. Big estates and sheep farms were suffering from the collapse in wool prices and small crofters still endured the vagaries of the weather, poor fishing and crop failures, but those who had skills to sell or entrepreneurial initiative could take advantage of changes in society. Public carriages ran from the railhead at Garve to Ullapool and connected with the steamer service to Stornoway. Anyone travelling these routes would spend the night in Ullapool, so accommodation and provision had to be supplied. I worked hard, saved what I could, and Janey and I soon had a family on the way.

I did not see much of my father in those years. He still worked the croft and the fishing boat with my younger brothers John and James, but I tried to visit my mother regularly. However, soon events in Leckmelm would light a spark which ignited a general conflagration in the Highlands.

Perhaps embittered by his defeat in the School Board elections, Major Davidson sold the estate to Alexander George Pirie, a rich paper manufacturer from Aberdeen. Now that these events are long past, I still cannot conceive of the arrogance or sheer stupidity of Mr Pirie's first action on taking over the estate.

I called at the family home early one evening and found my mother in a state of extreme agitation, and my father only a little less so. "Oh, Ian, I am so glad you have come," she said. "You will not believe the letter we've received from the new proprietor, Mr Pirie. He is going to take all our land and turn us out of our home. Isn't that so, Murdo? Show Ian the letter."

My father was reluctant to suppose such intentions but, when I read it myself, I was at first aghast and then furious.

"This is iniquitous, Father. He is going to take all your lands into his own keeping. And this… I cannot believe it: …*unless you and the other tenants at once prevent your sheep and other stock from grazing or trespassing upon the enclosures and hill and other lands now in the possession of the said Mr Pirie, he will not, upon any condition, permit you to remain in the cottage you now occupy*, da-di-da, *he will clear all off the estate and take down the cottages.*" I read from the letter.

My father could only shake his head and mutter, "Oh, I'm sure this is a mistake; he cannot mean that we give up

283

our crops and few sheep and cows. We have nothing else to live on. The fishing is poor now and we can't all work for him at the big house. Perhaps when he understands the way of life here, he will change his mind."

"No, Father; you may believe in the man's benevolent intentions but I've no doubt that he made his fortune oppressing the workers in his mills in Aberdeen; he'll have no compunction in bullying ignorant peasants in the Highlands."

"But what can we do about it, Ian? The man is rightful owner of the land and can do anything he likes with it and dispose of his tenants in any way he chooses. It is the law of the land."

"Well, the law is unjust and every good man should be made to understand that. You mustn't let this pass without question. At least seek some advice from more educated people. Why don't you gather the tenants together and consult Reverend Macmillan? He'll know the best course of action."

My father reluctantly agreed to my suggestion and set out to talk to his neighbours. Meanwhile, I took the letter to show to the minister.

To say that he was incensed is to put it mildly; he paced up and down the room, waving his fists in the air and calling down the wrath of God on tyrannous rulers. When at last his anger settled, he sat down and looked at me.

"Well, Ian, there is no point in raging and fuming. We must set to work with a counteroffensive. Now, you are well educated and have a way with words. I suggest you use your talents and write some letters to the newspapers

– stir up support in the wider world. I shall do so as well. It is no longer possible for rich landowners to hide behind their mountains in the Highlands. What happens here today will be known in London tomorrow."

So began the campaign which was in no small way to change the outcome of events in the township, and perhaps even affect history itself.

Whether or not it was his intention to further intimidate his tenants by decisive action, Pirie set about clearing his land of unproductive people and cottages. One was a deaf pauper who had lived in what was no more than a bothy for more than twenty years. The bothy was torn down and replaced with a kennel for the gamekeeper's dogs. It seemed that she had left willingly, although I doubted that, but the other eviction was certainly not voluntary. An elderly widow had returned to her father's empty cottage with her two children when she was no longer able to work in service. She paid no rent and Pirie felt legally entitled to turn her out and demolish the house. She had moved to Glasgow and, I heard subsequently, emigrated to America. I reported these events in letters to the newspapers and soon a fine brew of indignation was boiling up amongst the ordinary local people and more influential supporters in Inverness and Glasgow. Pirie's responses played into our hands as he continued to protest his legal rights and good intentions in the most high-handed manner. The matter was escalating into a full-scale battle.

The tenants of Leckmelm, their sentiments ranging from anger to disbelief, had decided to enlist the aid of their worthy minister. Reverend Macmillan agreed to write a petition to Pirie on their behalf, but my father insisted that he include a statement dissociating the signatories from the sentiments expressed in the correspondence in the newspapers. I don't know if this was a specific jibe at me or a reflection of his own fears of retaliation. I know that my mother had been in a state of extreme anxiety after the delivery of Pirie's first letter.

The petition evoked no response from Mr Pirie, but his factor proceeded to implement his intentions by arranging for the sale of all the crofters' sheep. On the day of the sale, the valuator chosen by the crofters could not attend and the factor brought in a substitute. Most of the men agreed to this except one: Murdo Munro. Munro was one of our Uncle Roddy's old cronies and had been something of a hothead in his youth. He was not afraid of landowners or factors and spoke his mind, sometimes with recourse to bad language. He was eventually placated and the sale went ahead but I've no doubt that his behaviour on this occasion made him a marked man for Pirie and his servants.

Throughout the summer and into the autumn, the agitation had escalated to such an extent that the MP Fraser-Mackintosh raised the issue in the House of Commons. Volleys from either side of the battle lines were published in the *Inverness Courier* and the *Scotsman*. Reverend Macmillan spoke at meetings in Ullapool and Inverness and lectured about landownership issues around the Highlands. He was becoming notorious amongst the landed gentry and factors, and I was proud to associate myself with his campaign. I attended most of his meetings and continued writing letters but I refused to get involved in some of the more unsavoury activities of local agitators.

I knew my father disapproved of my involvement but I did not understand the degree of his opposition until he attended one of our meetings in Ullapool. Reverend Macmillan was lecturing on the need to reform the system of landholding in the Highlands, and set up 'club farms' in which the crofters would have a shared security of tenure. The minister berated the actions of landowners, calling down the wrath of God on the perpetrators and advocating lawful resistance. My father sat silently throughout the lecture, but his eyebrows grew increasingly low and his fists were clenched on his knees.

My mother had come to the meeting too, and, being concerned at how frail she looked, I accompanied them home, holding her arm while Father marched ahead.

After some lengths in silence, my father suddenly stopped and turned to me. "This is enough. That man is a troublemaker and an ingrate and you must cease association with him at once. You may not live here any more and you may think you are beyond the reach of the law, but your actions could bring down the anger of our superiors on this family. We have done everything that was expected – sold our sheep and cattle and given over our arable – but that may not be enough to distance ourselves from you and your militant friends. We may be the next to be turned out."

I could see that his words were worrying my mother, so I answered as calmly as I could. "As you point out, I no longer live here and no one will associate my actions with you. But I will carry on what I consider to be a just battle against oppressive forces. This is not a matter of youthful disobedience, as you seem to think. It is a matter of my God-given conscience."

"God-given?! This is *against* the teaching of God. And that man, Macmillan, is no minister of God – he is an advocate of the Devil. He rouses up the common man against his superiors; indeed, he questions the very words of the Bible. And who are you to decide for yourself what is right and wrong? We must do what we are told in the words of Christ."

"And did not Jesus turn out the moneylenders from the temple? Did he not question unjust laws which would stone a woman to death, and the Pharisees' strict interpretation of the Sabbath? I do not believe that Christ would support unjust rulers as oppressors of the poor and weak."

By now my father and I were stopped in the middle of the road. I don't know what would have happened if my mother hadn't intervened. She was shaking and very pale. I turned my back on my father and, taking her arm again, led her on to the house and saw her tucked into her bed with a warm cup of tea. I spoke no more to my father and set off for home at once.

The year 1881 was a particularly bleak one in the West Highlands. The fishing was poor, stock prices were low, the potatoes failed again and there was threat of foot-and-mouth disease. As if this was not enough, in December a dreadful gale combined with the highest tide in memory wrecked most of the local fishing boats. Luckily my family's boat had been taken out of the water, so escaped destruction. My mother took these afflictions greatly to heart, and even my father was heard to question why God was punishing us so severely. I never called at the house now while he was in; I was afraid that our arguments would upset my mother.

In January, Pirie performed what he must have considered his final assault in the battle. It was, however, the action which tipped the force of public opinion throughout the country in our favour and put us on the way to winning the war.

He and his minions had already marked out the unfortunate Murdo Munro as a troublemaker. Munro, his wife, three young children and a six-week-old baby were turned out into the snow, their furniture scattered and the house destroyed. Their neighbours were too frightened to take them in but, when Reverend Macmillan heard of their plight, he arranged for them to be brought to my house in Ullapool. We had not much room but it had to do until more permanent arrangements could be made.

I am convinced this terrible affair literally frightened my mother to death. Shortly after the incident, in the late afternoon I received an urgent message that I was needed at Leckmelm. I closed up the shop as quickly as I could and set out for the township.

The doctor was making ready to leave when I arrived. As he passed he shook his head. "Her heart... I've given her something to help her sleep. She may recover... or not." He hesitated. "Look after your father. He has not taken this well."

Mother was lying, peacefully asleep, on her bed. Father acknowledged my arrival with a nod of the head. We sat together all through that long night without exchanging a word. From time to time Mother's breathing seemed to stop. We would sit tensely waiting and then, suddenly, it would start again. Her pulse was very weak and she looked so frail and insubstantial, like a white moth withering. As the sun began to rise on the next morning, she drew one long breath and then no more. It was the most peaceful, gentle passing I had ever seen.

Despite what the doctor had said I could see little sign that my father was affected. He was a man who had showed no emotion all his life long. Why should he be different now? He sat staring into the fire without speaking, and only gave a cursory greeting to my sister Ann and her husband when they arrived. He seemed unable to do anything, so Ann and I made all the arrangements for the funeral.

Ann drew me aside before she left for her own home. "He looks all right, but I think there is something wrong. He's all alone here now. Would you be able to stay with him through this? My children are too young to be left."

It seemed strange that the duty should be left to me, who had little love for my father, but my employer was a compassionate man and would let me have leave for a few days at least. Gradually my father began to get around to the farm chores but his face was bleak – white and wan-looking. We took Mother to the grave in Clachan and laid her beside the little son she had lost so long ago.

After the last of our guests had left the wake in our house, I was ready to set off for my own home. My family would be missing me. But Father held my arm. His face was blotched with red now, as if he had been sitting too close to the fire.

"Stay a while, Ian. I… need to speak to you."

After all this time of estrangement I felt there was little we had to say to each other, but I sat down and waited. I owed him that at least.

"Oh, I know we've had our disagreements, Ian, and I am sorry for that," he began. "I do not understand, that is all. I do not understand how the world works and I do not understand how God could take away my beloved wife. Why am I being punished, and she… what did she ever do to merit God's wrath?"

Taken aback as I was to hear what was for him as close to an expression of love as he could likely manage, I could not thole the single-minded selfishness of his appeal. "Did you ever stop to consider that maybe it has nothing to do with punishment at all? Maybe it was her time to go. Perhaps she will get some peace now, away from your hard-hearted idea of love. You have shown neither compassion for her nor forgiveness for what you saw as the sins of your children. Who are you to talk of unjust punishment?"

He stepped back as if I had struck him in the face. His colour was now livid. Then, suddenly, he wilted and buried his face in his hands. "So that is what you think of me," he said at last.

We sat for a long time in silence and then, just as I was thinking it was time to leave, he whispered, "Isabella. Isabella and her baby. I didn't mean… I suppose I should have forgiven her. Whatever happened to them?"

If I hadn't been so angry with his self-righteous attitude, I might have answered him in a gentler manner. "Your daughter Isabella is dead these long years, and the child, well, the child is lost; dead or alive I know not." I did not want to spare him any of the details. "I went to Glasgow to look for them. I traced her to a poorhouse but, by the time I got there, she was dead. Died of consumption brought on, no doubt, by the harsh life she had to lead. The people knew nothing of her baby; she didn't have one when she came to them. Perhaps given away, perhaps left to die in a ditch."

If I'd known how my words would affect my father, I would have been kinder. He seemed to collapse in on himself, but it was not in me then to offer any comfort. I blamed him for my mother's death as well as his daughter's. I left him to his memories and, I hoped, his guilt.

I saw very little of my father in the following years. There was nothing to take me to Leckmelm and I had too much to do with my work and family. There was great activity, too, in the Church and with local members of the Land League. Reverend Macmillan's tireless battle for the rights of the crofters had at last paid off and a government commission was set up to take evidence from around the Highlands.

The arrival of the commission, headed by Lord Napier, was a notable event in Ullapool. The hearing was held in the packed church in Mill Street. Crofters from all around Coigach and Lochbroom gave evidence, along with some of the landowners' factors. Reverend Macmillan was one of the leading speakers and gave one of his usual rousing performances. He complained of the tyrannical power of the factors and lairds, and spoke of the need for crofters to have a secure hold of their land. Perhaps his harangue was too radical for the eminent gentlemen of the commission but it was clear that their sympathy favoured him.

Not so when Alexander Pirie was called. His demeanour and dismissive attitude regarding the abilities and industry of the native Highlanders did nothing to support his cause. When it came down to it, the exchange between him and one of the commissioners, Fraser-Mackintosh MP, summed up the crux of the whole crofting issue.

Fraser-Mackintosh MP: "Do you think reducing of the crofters from the status of crofters to labourers dependent upon you is for their benefit?"

Pirie: "Certainly, because I think a man who is able to work and make his own livelihood is in a far nobler position than a crofter who every five or six years has to go and cry out, 'I am destitute and want help.'"

Another commissioner, Sheriff Nicolson, took up the argument. "Do you really think a man is in a nobler position who is working for day's wages to another, than a man who has a bit of land on which, if he is industrious, he feels that he occupies a position of some little importance in the country, and holds up his head with a little more dignity?"

By this time we in the audience were aware that the commissioners were on our side and Pirie's evidence would only serve to drop him deeper into the mire. After a few more heated exchanges, he was dismissed. I could not help a triumphant smile as he left the stand, but I had no doubt that he would continue to fight against the cause of land reform and weaken the conclusion of the commission, whatever that might be.

I was not a little surprised when my father was called to give evidence. He and a cousin, John Mackenzie, had been elected to speak for the crofters of Leckmelm. I had not seen him for more than a year and was shocked by the deterioration in his appearance. He had never been a big man but he had always appeared fit and wiry. Now he seemed shrunken and turned in on himself. He spoke so quietly that the interpreters had to ask him several times to speak up. Perhaps he would have been better to speak in Gaelic, but he would have considered that beneath his dignity.

He did, however, acquit himself well enough, relating the circumstances in Leckmelm now and in the past. But, although full of complaints, he was unable to make a direct criticism of his landowner. He appeared as an indecisive, whining menial. I was glad when his evidence was concluded.

Subsequent to the Napier Commission, the Crofters' Act of 1886 was hailed by some as a victory for land reform but, although it went some way towards addressing the grievances of the crofters, it was not enough to quell further dissatisfaction and agitation. In my opinion, there could be no justice in the Highlands until those who lived on and worked the land owned it themselves and had full common control of it. Without that, the crofting life continued to decline and many more people opted for immigration instead. Even the big farms withered as sheep rearing became unprofitable. The big estates were reduced to hunting reserves for wealthy businessmen.

I was living comfortably enough on my wages but we only had money for essentials. With another child on the way, Janey and I decided to move to Glasgow. There were more opportunities there for a young man with skills and some ambition. I had not visited my father in the years since the Napier Commission but I owed it to him to say goodbye.

My father had deteriorated even more by the time I went to see him. It seemed that my mother's death had taken all of the life out of him. He was not at all surprised to hear of my decision to move to Glasgow.

"Aye, there'll be more opportunity for a young man in the city. There's little enough here anyway. But what will you do? I've heard it's not so easy to get work there unless you're wanting to work as a labourer in the dockyards or such."

"I'm very lucky, Father. A friend of mine has put me in touch with a small printing-and-publishing firm. They're willing to take me on at the bottom rung, so to speak. But it's still more salary than I get at the moment and there's a chance to rise in the firm. I might go further with my writing, too."

"Hmm." My father seemed unimpressed. "Well, I wish you the best of luck. All my children are leaving – it's a wonder there'll be anyone left here soon." He sank into a gloomy reflection, but then he looked up at me with a sad kind of appeal in his eyes. "Would you be able... do you think you might look out for the bairn when you're in Glasgow? Isabella's child, you know. You said you couldn't find her but maybe there's a chance she's still alive. I can't bide the thought that there's a grandchild of mine living in poverty and not knowing anything about her family. It would gladden my heart, Ian, if you could find out. The child will be grown up by now... a girl, or maybe a big strapping boy. Someone must have records."

I shook my head. "There's not much chance of finding out now. It's too long ago."

I saw the light in his eyes die.

"But I'll try, Father; there may be some lead I can follow from where Isabella first arrived in Glasgow. But I've not much hope." It was on my mind to tell him that he should have thought of all this when he turned Isabella out of the house, but it was not in my heart to do so. I left soon afterwards.

I never did find Isabella's child. A girl had been born but there were no records of whether she had lived, died or been fostered. I wrote to tell my father the news. He must have taken it badly because the next I heard from Ann (the only one of our family left in Ullapool) was that he had died a few days after receiving my letter. I often wonder if he died of grief or guilt – if, at the end of his life, he regretted the strictness which had denied him human compassion and forgiveness. I shall never know.

Chapter Eleven

The Peat Road

coming home

In a land where few trees grew, peat was the main fuel for the crofters. Tracks led into the valleys, where trenches cut into the peat hags testify to generations of families who carried out this back-breaking task. For the young, it might have been a convivial activity when the whole community shared in the work of cutting the slabs of peat and stacking it to dry. In the spring, with larks trilling in the blue sky, it was pleasant enough. Old folks still remember the taste of the tea brewed on a fire in a hollow in the rocks: "It was the best cup of tea in the world." The labour was more arduous in the summer when the peat had dried and had to be transported back to the townships. People were lucky if there was a horse and cart, but often it was carried in creels on the backs of the women.

No one could pretend that the peat cutting was easy. It was heavy and repetitive and, if the weather was hot and midgy, could be unmitigated torture. But today was perfect. The sun glimpsed through fleeting clouds and gentle breezes lightened the air. Catriona arched her back to straighten out locked muscles, listening to the stillness for a moment. The silence was thick with memories.

At every peat cutting, families toiled – fathers bending to cut and heave the sods; mothers lifting and piling the peat, or suckling babies during a restful minute. The children, too, had their share of work but, in between times, would gather together to chatter and play simple lamb games of chase and rush and leap. Patient horses dozed, one foreleg bent, between the shafts of carts ranged along the peat road. How much fun it would have been then, when a communal necessity like this gathered all the people together!

Now, however, Catriona was quite alone. No one else cut peat these days, what with the electricity and central heating. She was a fool to do it really but her mother loved the warm, acrid smell of peat on the fire, and Catriona had welcomed the excuse to escape into the wildness. The physical exertion calmed her mind. The slow solemnity of the task lifted her depression. When the peat was good and dark, it sliced swift and neat like cheese. You cut a perfect straight row and then changed your movement to stacking, imagining the hours of cosy winter fires in preparation.

Her knife jarred against a thick heather root, sending a shaft of pain through her arms, and she reminded herself that she must not dig too much for too long. It was well past lunchtime anyway. Leaving her knife propped by the cuttings, she followed the tiny burn which led up to the lochan at the peak of the hill. It was not a long climb but it was arduous, picking a way through heather tussocks, and, by the time she had reached the top and dined on her simple sandwiches and sweet tea from a flask, a weariness stole over and whispered in her ear.

She awoke slowly and wondered, only for a moment, why her bed was less than its usual softness. She must have fallen asleep for some time, as the sun, though still hot on her face, had moved over the western islands. A heather bed might not be as gentle as fine linen but she surely could not recall, in the recent past, a sleep so unexpected, so deep and so completely dreamless. Well, the air here was like no other air on Earth, light and effervescent like champagne, seeming to pluck you up and waft you away as if the normal rules of gravity did not apply.

She stood up and turned slowly, surveying the view on all sides. The peatland rose up gently and, where she stood at the very top, seemed to press right up against the sky. To the west, the sea loch led out to distant and yet further islands; to the north, stretches of more moorland led away; to the east and south, jagged mountain peaks only showed precipitous summits against the edge of the humpbacked moor. There was something very gratifying in seeing that, whichever way you looked, there was no sign of man or his creation.

This would be a very good place to die. The thought startled her not because the idea of death was new, but because, for the first time, it suggested feelings of tranquillity and completion. She had seen enough of the worst kind of death: the pointless, the pathetic, the patriotic. It was good to come upon the realisation that, for some lives, death is meaning and complement, rather than escape and antithesis.

If only her life had turned out the way she had hoped. "A gifted and promising pupil," her schoolteacher had said, and she had surely fulfilled that, gaining a place at the university and leaving her slightly bemused, but smugly proud, family for the city. Not many families hereabout could afford to send their daughters to university, and not many thought it was truly fitting.

She laughed a little to herself, remembering how excited but frightened she had been, experiencing the city for the first time. Tram cars, dirty tenements, raucous children in the streets, and people, people everywhere, crowded together, bustling about as if there was no time ever for rest or contemplation. And she had been mortally terrified going up to the university itself. It was an imposing building, with turrets and quadrangles and enormous lecture halls full of earnest, serious young men and women. For weeks she could barely steel herself to walk into the room in front of the tiered rows of faces. Walking down University Avenue was sheer purgatory; so many young men, tall and handsome and intelligent, and, no doubt, looking in disdain at her home-made country fashions. Within a few days, however, she had met another girl from the country like herself, and, within months, they had evolved into serious, earnest students themselves, discussing Descartes in the refectory (philosophy a necessary substitute for solid nourishment for most of them) and debating politics heatedly in the pub in the evenings.

Perhaps if she had not met Brian so early; had waited to marry later after she had established her career? He had been there at her first-ever lecture, sauntering into the lecture hall, dressed flamboyantly in a white jacket and carrying a tightly rolled umbrella. He sat down in the front row, casually confident. She found herself an unobtrusive niche in the very back row. She continued to observe him from her eyrie for several weeks until, one day, he ascended the steps and sat down beside her. She felt gratified as the chosen object of his attention; embarrassed but also slightly angry that he so obviously expected her thankful admiration.

He had swept her off her feet in a very real sense, since, all through their relationship, she had walked in airy heights of metaphysics, Russian poets and socialist ideology. None of it had meant much to her then. He had once berated her for being ignorant of strife and poverty, for living untouched by and oblivious to all the ills and evils of humanity. She accepted his criticism, unquestioning, as she always did, only realising in later life both the truth and the vacuity of his dogma. It had been the image of him in her mind she had admired and loved, not the real man.

But she had work to do. Peat would not cut itself, that was sure, and she was the only able-bodied person in her family left to do it. Before the thought of Angus – teasing, bright, blithe Angus, gone, lost in the war – could surface in her mind, she turned back down towards the peat cuttings.

The little burn that emptied out of the lochan cut a swathe of lush grass through the heather and, here and there, stony mounds testified to long-abandoned summer shielings. She loved to wander through them and speculate on the life these people led – poor and simple, surely, but also peaceful and satisfying; up with the dawn and the lark, breathing the soft breath of the beasts throughout the long day and at last to an untroubled rest through the light summer night. She rounded the corner of a more substantial ruin and, suddenly, came upon the body of a man.

After her first shock had passed, she saw that he was not dead, but sleeping or resting, leaning against the warm stone wall. She stood awkwardly, momentarily undecided whether she should attempt to steal away without wakening him, or cough discreetly. Then she saw that his eyes were open.

"Hello," he said simply.

By her first impression, she had thought him a visitor, but she recognised the warm, quiet lilt in his voice, and now she noticed the thick grey hair and gaunt but structured features of the Highlander. He was not a man she knew, however.

"Hello." She hesitated. "I didn't mean to disturb you. I was just taking a break from the peat cutting."

"Och, no. I'm not doing anything that can't be disturbed, and wouldn't you think an old bodach like me would welcome being disturbed by a young lass like yourself?"

For some reason, Catriona was not offended by his words; indeed, his tone put her at ease. "I'll have you know I'm thirty-five years old, and sometimes I feel like ninety," she countered.

His bright blue eyes regarded her for a moment. "So if you're at the peats, you must be from hereabouts, but I don't know you."

"I've been away in Glasgow for a long time but I was born and lived half my life down there." She pointed towards the lochside, where the little cluster of houses was hidden by the brow of the hill. "My name is Catriona Mackenzie." Her married name would mean nothing to him.

"Ah, so you'll be Hector's daughter. I know him well. There's many a grand entertainment we've had with a story and a song lubricated by a golden bottle at his fireside."

Catriona was struck by his eloquence, but then she caught a memory of a smoother, younger face, nimble fingers on a squeeze box, laughter and deep conversations, absorbing and hypnotic but well above her childish understanding. She would doze until her mother whisked her off to bed, but the noise and male voices often grew louder through her dreams and Angus would whisper some of the more outrageous stories to her in the morning.

"So you've come home then." It was more of a statement than a question, and she found it strangely disconcerting.

"No, I'm just back for the holidays, and my parents need the peat cut." Why did she feel the need to be defensive? She did not need to explain anything to this man.

"Aye, that's the way of it. All the young folk are off to the big city or further afield if they can get the chance: Canada or Australia, following the footsteps of the old Scots emigrants. Well, I've no doubt it's a better way of life they have, and more money. Have you a good job in Glasgow, then?"

It was the first time he had asked a direct question, and she felt the need to elaborate.

"I went to university first, studied English, French and Philosophy, and then I became a teacher." Leaving Brian, and the baby, and all that agony and despair out of the story.

"English will be very useful, I'm sure, but I've always thought that those that can read will learn all they need of English from books. French, now, is a grand thing to know, for we have a lot of tourists coming from Europe for their holidays. But then, I've never had much time for other languages; to my mind it would make the world an easier and a happier place if we all spoke the same tongue. I wouldn't mind if it was some strange foreign language and we all had to learn it, just for the cause of better understanding and communication." He waved an arm at the air as if encompassing all the world in his argument. "They stole the Gaelic away from us a long time ago, after all.

"Philosophy, too," he went on. "Now that's different. Those ancient Greek philosophers knew something about it. Mankind will have no respite from trouble until either philosophers gain political power or politicians become by some miracle true philosophers. That's Plato's idea, and a damn good idea it is too. We need people who can think to guide the reins of State." He looked at her quizzically.

Catriona sat down beside him on a fallen stone. She loved a good argument. "I'm not so sure about that. Philosophers are too impractical and they often seem more interested in ideas than people; don't have much empathy, too absorbed in themselves to be capable of altruism. That may be intelligence but it's not wisdom." She faltered for a minute, shyly looking down. She noticed, amusedly, that he had taken his boots and socks off, and his toes, pale and clearly unused to the light of the sun, wriggled like worms luxuriating in the cool grass.

"You're right there, lass. I've often found the most intelligent people are the stupidest. No common sense and no mettle. I suppose that's what comes of studying one thing in detail all the time; your eyes become focused so much on the one spot that you can't see anything round about." He was getting into the stride of his argument.

"Now, that's not like the old Scots. Oh, aye, some of them were bright, I grant you," he added, when he saw she was about to protest. "But it was a mechanical brilliance;

engineers and builders, innovators and land-makers. They built and moulded the countries where they settled. They made them strong, efficient, self-confident nations." He chuckled. "All the best spirits must have gone out of Scotland, like the export whisky, for those that are left are weak, self-deprecating apologies of men. You must have met the kind: dewy-eyed when they get in drink and so desperate for a word of approval from anyone that they've forgotten that they have the right and the pride of a grand nation. They're all good men at heart, and clever too, but they think, because they didn't run away and make their fortune, that they haven't proved themselves."

Catriona could say very little in opposition. Privately she thought he was probably correct but she suspected that he also wanted to provoke her to argument. She tried a different tack. "I suppose you're a Nationalist then; you'd like to see us separate from England once again?"

"Now what makes you think that? I hope I sound more like an internationalist by what I've said," he protested gently. "Though I don't like the way Scotland has gone; I don't think she's much different from any other country in the modern world. I think we've all lost the place, so to speak. We've all searched and searched the world over for a dream that's been with us all the time. You young folk with your material prosperity, fancy houses and mental breakdowns. Did anyone ever find the fount of wisdom in the city, or Canada or America, unless he carried it in his own heart?

"It's time we stopped searching. It is time now for Scots to return to their homeland. Oh, I don't mean literally, although it would probably do a lot of them good, but to return to some of the old values: the grandeur of labour, the satisfaction of simple pleasures, all this." He nodded his head to the surrounding wilderness. "The land, the land, the good earth itself! There's nothing means more to a Scotsman."

Catriona was suddenly so moved that she had to turn to hide her face. How had this man, this complete stranger, so perfectly caught the mood of her dissatisfaction?

It seemed he too was overcome with the force of his emotion, embarrassed at speaking too vehemently. "But the day's not over yet," he said. "You mustn't let a foolish old man keep you from your work." He dismissed her kindly enough but she knew he did not want to talk any more.

"Bye-bye, then," she said.

"Goodbye. Give my regards to Hector and your mother." He lay back against the wall and closed his eyes.

She was halfway down the hill before she remembered that she had forgotten to ask his name. She thought of climbing up to find him again but an uncouthy feeling stopped her. He had finished his conversation and old folk did not like to be interrupted in a deep cogitation.

Her digging went easily now that the heat had gone out of the day. The varied colours of brilliant moss green, umber heather and green-blue sky were infused with the damask of the declining sun. A solitary skylark, completely lost in the heavens, sent a spiral of notes spilling down upon her and then stopped abruptly. The silence rose from the peatlands again: a breathing, living silence which grew and grew until it engulfed her in a swell of emotion.

She sat down heavily on the peat bank and let the tears flow at last. That it had taken her all this time and all this travelling, and what she had sought was under her nose all the time. It had just been too clear and pure for her to see.

Well, there was no harm after all. She could repair the damage. Brian had long since ceased to care whether she came or went. Her school could find another teacher and, if nothing else, she would have plenty work to do on the croft.

She finished stacking the peat and set off down the peat road as the sun tipped towards the horizon. At home she recounted her meeting with the talkative man on the hill. "He asked to be reminded to you but I forgot to ask his name. You'll know him, though – he used to come to ceilidhs in our house long ago. He was very thin, with thick grey hair and the most piercing blue eyes I've ever seen. Liked to talk philosophy."

She noticed her parents exchanging a glance before her father responded. "Well, your description sounds just like Donnie Beg who used to live in the end house. He was aye keen on a good argument but it'll no be him – he's been dead these twenty years. So I don't know who it could have been. Some tourist, most likely, or an emigrant returned to visit the old country." He turned away as if the subject was closed.

Catriona was disappointed – why hadn't she gone back to ask his name? But the opportunity was gone now; maybe she'd meet him at another time. In any case, their conversation had been important – had given her the insight and incentive to recognise where she belonged.

Here, where she had found everything that she'd really wanted long ago.

Yes, it was time now. It was time now for Catriona to come home.